The Duke of Desire

(THE 1797 CLUB BOOK 9)

By

USA Today Bestseller
Jess Michaels

THE DUKE OF DESIRE
The 1797 Club Book 9
www.1797Club.com

Copyright © Jess Michaels, 2018
ISBN-13: 978-1723147678
ISBN-10: 1723147672

For more information, contact Jess Michaels
www.AuthorJessMichaels.com

To contact the author:
Email: Jess@AuthorJessMichaels.com
Twitter www.twitter.com/JessMichaelsbks
Facebook: www.facebook.com/JessMichaelsBks

Jess Michaels raffles a gift certificate EVERY month to members of her newsletter, so sign up on her website:
http://www.authorjessmichaels.com/

DEDICATION

For Michael. You see all my many moods and still, somehow,
love me.

PROLOGUE

Spring 1809

Miss Katherine Montague pushed out onto the terrace and sucked in a great gulp of brisk spring air. The Rockford ball always launched the Season and was forever too crowded and loud. Tonight was no different, and Katherine rubbed her temples as she crossed the wide terrace, moving away from the estate house and toward a quiet corner where she could just…think for a moment.

There was a great deal to think about, after all. This was her second Season and it was already not going well. She had danced with two gentlemen, both of them very nice, but her father had intervened, whispering loudly for her not to be so whorish in how she leaned into them.

Leaned into them? She had done no such thing! She was too terrified to do so, after all. God forbid her father see sin in anything she did. That always resulted in punishment. From him and from the eyes of Society, which turned toward her when he berated her. She had no doubt they judged her as harshly as he did.

She hated it. Hated hearing her name on the wind. Hated watching certain gentlemen turn slightly away because they were uncertain of her fitness. Tears stung her eyes at just the thought.

"Good evening."

She tensed and turned toward the darkness where the deep, slightly slurred voice had come from. "H-hello?"

He stepped from the shadows in one long, lazy stride and stopped about a foot away from her. Katherine's breath caught for she knew exactly who he was. *Everyone* knew who he was. One couldn't avoid the knowledge, even if one wanted to, say, run away from it.

Robert Smithton, Duke of Roseford, grinned at her and then leaned against the terrace wall with his hip. Great Lord, but he was a handsome devil, even more so up close. He had thick dark hair that was rakishly messed like fingers had been run through it. And his dark eyes, now a bit bleary from drink, were impossible not to stare into. She could feel herself doing it now, connecting with him on an entirely inappropriate level.

"Oh, yes," he drawled. "A *very* good evening now."

She swallowed hard and watched as those same eyes swept over her from head to toe. She felt every moment of that wicked regard.

"We've met before, haven't we?" he asked.

She nodded slowly. Oh yes, they had met before. She'd been introduced to the man by an acquaintance, the Countess of Portsmith, at the end of the last Season. Charlotte's brother had long been a friend to him, but the countess had seemed reluctant to make the introduction.

Roseford had been considerably less drunk that night, but no less focused on her. Katherine had felt a strange ache in her when he looked at her, when he repeated her name slowly.

She felt the same ache now.

And after that brief interaction? Well, her father's rage that she would speak with such an infamous rake had been loud and insistent and cruel. She shivered and took a step away from Roseford out of a sense of self-preservation.

"We have," she said, answering his question at last.

He smiled. "Oh dear, I know that tone. Was I *very* poorly

behaved?"

Katherine worried her lip to smother the smile his teasing question drew from her. He was so very charismatic, it was hard not to be drawn to him. But he was a flame. He destroyed little moths like her without even trying hard.

She couldn't afford that. Not with her father breathing down her neck and offering *pious* marriages to *good, decent* men who made Katherine's skin crawl.

"Not any worse than tonight," she said, teasing back, and then slapped a hand to her mouth. What on earth was she doing?

He tilted his head back and laughed, and Katherine stopped backing up. He was...fun. Everyone knew it. That was his reputation, after all: fun. Katherine had never been allowed to have much fun in her life. Not since her mother's death when she was very young.

Her father didn't like fun.

"What was your name again?" he asked when his laughter had faded.

She pursed her lips. Apparently, she had not made the same impression on him as he had on her. But why would she? She was the drab daughter of a second son. He was...*him*. A god amongst men. A god amongst gods.

"Katherine Montague, Your Grace," she said.

He extended a hand and she stared at it. He wasn't wearing gloves. She had taken hers off after getting hot inside. Skin would touch skin. There was something wicked about that fact. Something naughty. Something that doubled the tingle she felt when she looked at him.

"I don't bite," he said with another smile. "Not unless it's what the lady likes."

Katherine felt heat flooding her cheeks, and somehow she managed to take a step closer and hold out her hand. When he took it, his warm, rough fingers enveloped hers. To her surprise, he did not shake her hand, but lifted it to his mouth. Just before he brushed his lips over her knuckles, he said, "The Duke of Roseford at your service, Miss Montague."

His mouth touched her and she froze. There was nothing simple about the touch. Nothing that she could pretend was innocent or misread. When his hot breath steamed over her flesh and his dark eyes held hers in challenge, she recognized something her innocent brain ought not to have known: this was seduction.

She should have stepped away from it. From him and his dangerous beauty and charm. From his slightly drunken state. It obviously lowered whatever inhibitions a man like this normally held when it came to ladies.

Only she didn't. She stayed where she was, hand in his, staring as he lowered their clasped fingers but did not release her. If anything, he got bigger, stepped closer in the moonlight.

"Your uncle is the Viscount Montague, isn't he?"

She nodded, stricken mute by the odd encounter and all the strange feelings it inspired.

"And this is your second Season," he continued.

"You know a great deal for a man who couldn't recall my name a moment ago," she whispered, her voice shaking.

"I remember information and faces," he said. "Especially when I am being pursued."

She blinked. "I was not pursuing you."

The corner of his lips quirked up, but his eyes grew hard as he said, "Every eligible lady in Society is pursuing me, no matter what I do to discourage their chaperones."

She lifted both her brows. "Is that what all your wild behavior is about, Your Grace? Discouraging the chaperones?"

He gaze held hers evenly for a beat, then another. Something in the air between them shifted, subtle but oh, so powerful, and Katherine forgot to breathe for a moment. Roseford edged forward a tiny bit more and suddenly his body brushed hers. His breath stirred her face as he leaned in. His free hand, the one that wasn't still scandalously holding hers, trailed up to trace the line of her jaw with his fingertips.

"Not all of it," he whispered, and then he was moving closer.

4

Katherine realized, in a second that seemed to take a lifetime, that this man was about to kiss her. She also recognized, without shame or judgment, that she desperately wanted him to. This dangerous, shocking man of ill-repute didn't frighten her. He drew her in, and she wanted whatever he offered with a power that made her shake.

She tilted her face up, offering her mouth, and just before their lips touched, she heard something on the wind. Something horrible.

"Katherine!"

She realized through her fog that it was the sharpness of her father's voice. The shame and judgment she hadn't felt a moment ago rushed to her as his steely hand closed around her upper arm and he ripped her away from Roseford.

"You're coming with me," her father snapped, glaring at the duke before he hauled Katherine off the terrace, through the ball with everyone watching, and to their carriage around front. His fingers dug into her bare skin, he yanked hard enough that it felt like her shoulder was being separated from her body, and when he hurtled her into the vehicle, she staggered and slammed her knee against the seat edge. Tears leapt to her eyes.

As the carriage began to move, she hauled herself into a more dignified place and dared to look at him. She flinched. His round face was almost purple with anger, his arms were folded and his jaw was set.

"Whore!" he shouted, and she turned her face. That was his favorite slur to hurtle. And it would soon be followed by his second favorite. "Whore's daughter."

She bent her head as the tears of physical pain became tears of rage and emotional destruction. "I didn't do anything," she protested softly.

"We both know what you were about to do," he snapped. "And if you were so willing to give such a man as the Duke of Roseford your mouth, what else would have you given him? What else *have* you given? You think I do not know your mind?"

"You don't!" Katherine protested, lifting her hands in

pleading. "You *don't* know. I did not go out onto the terrace to find the duke. I didn't even know he was there. We were only talking. Perhaps things escalated, but it was *innocent*, Papa, I swear to you. I would not have gone so far."

Except that didn't feel true as she said those words. Not when she thought of the fuzzy image of Roseford's handsome face swinging in toward hers. His mouth tantalizingly close.

That darkness he was bringing with him, it was exactly the kind her father feared, and she had been willing to walk right into it.

Montague stared at her and his eyes glazed. "You truly are just like your mother," he murmured.

Katherine flinched. She hardly remembered her mother, though the fleeting images she had were nothing but kind and soft. Yet her father railed against the dead woman near daily. To be compared to her was the lowest of insults, at least in his mind.

"I'm not," Katherine whispered. "I'm not like what you say she was."

His gaze held on her, and then he nodded. "Perhaps it isn't too late. What you need is a stabilizing influence. What you *need* is a firm hand that can guide you or punish you as needed."

Katherine shook her head swiftly. This was, yet again, another conversation she'd had with her father a dozen times or more. Since her coming out the year before, it had been a topic he had worn into the ground.

"Please don't say marriage," she said. "You told me I could have another Season to find a match on my own."

"That was before I found you spread out in front of the Duke of Roseford, ready to become another of his whores," her father snapped, and his hand lifted as if to strike.

Katherine flinched from the violence. She'd felt it enough. Today, though, he didn't swing but lowered his hand slowly. "I've been speaking lately with the Earl of Gainsworth. Your uncle's friend."

Katherine's mouth dropped open. "He is twenty-five years my senior, Papa! Older than you."

"And that is what you need. A man that will give you no quarter, will grant you no room for your wicked desires. A pious man like me."

Katherine shook her head. She'd seen the Earl of Gainsworth at parties. Despite his advanced years, he wasn't exactly unattractive, and the way he looked at women her age could scarcely be seen as pious, no matter how much he gave to the church or spoke to her father like he was an acolyte.

"Please don't," she whispered. "Give me a little more time, Papa."

He pursed his lips. "No. The time is up, my dear. I need to arrange this before your worst impulses are known to the world. Before they are out of hand and I lose all control over you. I will go to the man tomorrow and sign the betrothal. I will see you married to him before another fortnight has passed."

She flew to the opposite side of the carriage, catching both Montague's hands in her own as she cried out, "Please, Papa, no!"

He shook her away and looked at her with pure disgust and distain. Then he folded his arms. "It will be done, Katherine. There is nothing that could be said that could change my mind. You will be brought to heel and this marriage will do it. One way or another."

CHAPTER ONE

Fall 1812

Robert Smithton, Duke of Roseford, looked out over the ballroom floor with disinterest. He'd never enjoyed this exercise in exhibition, but as of late it had become almost unbearable. He felt his mouth turn down even lower as he looked at the couples bobbing about the floor. Friends of his, many of them with happy brides in their arms.

Once upon a time, he would have said those men had thrown away their freedom. But it was hard to feel that way now when their joy was so clear. So sharp. Like a knife to the gut.

"What are you brooding about?"

Robert jumped and turned to find three of those very friends standing at his elbow. The Dukes of Abernathe, Crestwood and Northfield. James, Simon and Graham respectively, because the titles were so damned tedious.

It was Graham who had spoken, and he handed over a drink for Robert with a grin. Robert refused to return the expression. "Who says I'm brooding?"

He took a slug of the drink and found it watered down, indeed. God, he would be happy when the Season was over. When his friends would retreat back to their estates and their frustrating contentment and he would be left to prowl and dive into all the darkness that kept the pain away.

"I'm an expert," Graham retorted, but then another grin brightened his face. Robert was warmed by it. Just two short years ago, his friend would not have smiled so easily. Love did that, it seemed. "Or I used to be."

"Ha," Robert grumbled, winking at the men so his ill humor would not be perceived as a slight. "As if any of you are experts in anything anymore. I am the last bachelor."

Simon let out a long laugh that turned more than one interested female head. Not that he noticed. He only had eyes for his wife, just as all the others did. "You are not the last bachelor."

"There's Kit," James said with a shake of his head. While he smiled, Robert felt his concern just below the surface. James had always been the King of the Dukes. Robert had always been his most troublesome subject.

"Kit?" he repeated with a snort of derision. "He is a saint— he hardly counts. No, it is left to me to sow all the wild oats for all of you *old* married men."

Now all three men looked concerned and Robert began to calculate how quickly he could make a run for it.

"Aren't you *tired* of it all?" James asked, his tone soft, all teasing departed.

Robert tensed and looked out at the glittering ball without answering. He couldn't answer, at least not without gathering himself first. He didn't want them to see, he didn't want them to know, to hear it in his voice that James was right. He *was* tired of all of it.

Once upon a time he used to take such pleasure in…well…*pleasure*. All the parts of it, anticipation to orgasm. But now, now he went through the motions. It was rote. Expected. He was never fully satisfied, even when the experiences were passionate. And if he stopped, he feared the reasons why would catch up to him, overtake him.

He certainly didn't want to face them. What his friends had found was not for him. It didn't exist and he didn't want it. That kind of intimacy was not something he wished to share with any other human being.

"You believe everyone's path must take them to where you are," he said at last, because it was clear they were waiting for some kind of answer. "Just because mine hasn't and won't doesn't mean I am tired of it."

James caught a breath like he was ready to argue that point, but before he could, another man approached. The Marquess of Berronburg was not a member of their duke club, and judging from the way James, Simon and Graham all recoiled slightly as he stepped into their midst, he was not about to be invited into the periphery. Robert couldn't blame them for it. Berronburg was often rude, he imbibed too much and his lechery for women was nearly as legendary as Robert's.

Of course, Berronburg was far less subtle in his advances. He was a lout. But he was Robert's lout. They often prowled together since he had no old friends to do that with anymore.

"Ah, look, four dukes, all in a row," Berronburg crowed loudly. "Do I get some kind of special prize if I find them all?"

James shook his head slightly. "I have no idea, Berronburg." He glanced at Robert. "Perhaps we can continue this conversation later. For now, I will find my wife."

He turned, and Simon and Graham excused themselves as well. Robert stared as they walked away. As the other men met and married the great loves of their lives, he had often wondered if he might one day be pushed from their ranks because of his refusal to do the same. If at some point his old friends would look at him and see someone no better than the marquess who was prattling at his side.

That would break his heart.

"I say, are you listening at all?"

Berronburg shook his arm and Robert blinked, coming back to the present and turning toward the man with a scowl. "Who would not hear you when you're practically shouting the ballroom down? A bit of discretion, if you please, my lord."

Berronburg pursed his lips. "Those dukes are a bad influence on you, Roseford, I swear to Christ. I was asking you if you'd heard the news."

Robert stifled a sigh and settled himself back into the role of rake, rogue, scoundrel. It settled onto his shoulders, but less readily than it once might have. "News?"

Berronburg was practically bouncing. "Yes, yes, yes."

"Well, you always do have the best gossip. What is it then?"

"The Countess of Gainsworth is returning to Society."

All of Robert's maudlin thoughts vanished in an instant at that unexpected information. He tilted his head. "*The* Countess of Gainsworth?"

Berronburg grinned. "The very one. The infamous lady whose sexual prowess was so great that she struck her husband dead while in flagrante delicto!" The marquess rubbed his hands together and his eyes lit up lewdly. "Can you imagine?"

Robert shook his head. Everyone knew the story. It had circulated through Society like wildfire about a year ago. The whispers had died down, of course, after the man was buried, but now that his wife was coming out of mourning, there was no doubt the world would go abuzz again.

He almost felt sorry for the lady.

"Can you?" Berronburg insisted, elbowing him.

Robert smiled. "I can, indeed. Who could not? She'll have her pick of lovers, of course."

Berronburg laughed. "I agree. There will be dozens who would be willing to risk the cost."

Robert snorted in derision. "Please. Her husband was an old bastard. Put her with a younger man of…talent? No one will suffer but the bed sheets. Are they taking wagers yet on who will win her to his bed?"

"Of course," Berronburg chuckled. "I assume you will be putting yourself into the mix."

Robert jolted at the suggestion. *Had* he been considering it? In truth, he could scarcely picture the countess. He rarely pursued married women. Too much complication. But certainly the rumors of her prowess interested him. As did the feather that winning her would put in his cap.

He glanced over to find Berronburg watching him closely. Intently, even. "Why are you waiting for my answer with such focus, my friend?"

Berronburg shook his head. "Half the men with interest will drop out if you enter the fray, Your Grace. Including me. That is too much rich competition for my blood."

Robert shrugged. "I have not yet decided what I will—"

He stopped midsentence because something had caught his eye. Someone, to be more specific. Two ladies had entered the ballroom. The one was slightly older, with dark hair and a kind expression. But it wasn't the elder who caught Robert's eye. No, it was the younger. She was stunning, truly beautiful, with thick brown hair and a face that could stop any man in his tracks. She shifted as she said something to the footman at the door and seemed to take a deep breath before she was announced.

"The Countess of Gainsworth," the footman said. "And Mrs. Sambrook."

The reaction of the crowd was immediate. There was a stunned silence that rippled through the entire room and then a low rumble as talk began. The countess stood, almost frozen, for a moment. Her companion said something to her, and Lady Gainsworth set her shoulders back and stepped into the ballroom. The women were greeted by the hostess of the ball, Lady Vinesmith, who looked around the crowd as if she regretted asking the countess here now that the room was reacting so strongly.

Robert watched it all unfold, this little drama, and couldn't take his eyes away. Couldn't shake a tiny niggle of...*memory* that itched in the back of his mind as he watched the exquisite countess edge to the wall and stand there, a blank expression on her face.

"Better tell the others to put their blunt away," he murmured.

"Why?" Berronburg asked, his own gaze fixated on the countess, just as Robert's was.

"Because the lady is mine. I guarantee it," Robert said with a grin.

Katherine could hardly breathe as she and her aunt stepped away from their hostess. The hostess who had almost sneered at her the moment the crowd turned. And here Katherine had been friends with Lady Vinesmith since they were girls, when Francine had been far less exalted than she was now. And yet *she* sneered.

But then, so did the rest of the room, so there it was. Her ruin, begun years ago by a foolish mistake—*two* foolish mistakes—was now complete. Her life was over.

"You're doing fine."

She jolted, for she'd all but forgotten the presence of her aunt. She reached back and found Aunt Bethany's hand, and squeezed for comfort. That was one of the few things she could praise had come from her marriage. Once free of her father's influence, she had been able to reconnect with her mother's family. She and Bethany had become close, and now she could scarce recall not having her aunt in her life.

"I don't feel fine," she whispered as they took their place along the wall. "They are whispering and staring, and *that* was the cut direct, right there."

"Be strong," her aunt assured her.

Katherine would have laughed if she didn't want to cry. "I do not feel strong."

"Then pretend," Bethany said softly, gently.

Now Katherine did dip her head and laugh a little, though she felt no humor in the circumstances. Pretend. Yes, she was good at that. Her whole life was a farce, after all. A play. *Pretend* to be satisfied as a countess. *Pretend* to mourn his death. *Pretend* to be unmoved as they looked at her, sniffed at her.

She pushed the thoughts away and lifted her chin. Pride. She had to have some pride or they would tread all over her and there would be nothing left.

She scanned the crowd. There were a few of her old friends here and there. Ladies who had not come to call since her husband's death, but still. They had been close once. She stepped forward, and there was a tiny hiss from one corner of the room that sent her back to the wall in one long step.

Her aunt's hand tightened on her arm, a motion of solidarity, but not one that would fix this untenable situation she found herself in. She was about to suggest they run together, run away from this horrible night, when a lady stepped from the crowd toward her. She did not know the woman, though she certainly knew of her. It was the Duchess of Northfield, one of the most powerful women in Society.

She was very pretty, with honey hair spun up elaborately on the crown of her head and bright, friendly eyes. Katherine knew that meant nothing. Vipers often disguised themselves as sweet little bunnies. She stiffened her spine, waiting for whatever attack was to come.

"Mrs. Sambrook," the duchess said, extending an elegant hand. "How lovely to see you."

Some of Katherine's starch softened as she watched her aunt's face light up. Bethany was a good judge of character, and it was clear she liked this woman.

"Your Grace," Aunt Bethany said. "You look beautiful, as always."

"Adelaide," the duchess said with a laugh. "There are too many duchesses in my circle to have such formality with friends."

"Have you met my companion?" Aunt Bethany said, turning the focus toward Katherine.

"I think, perhaps, long ago," Adelaide said. "Before I married Northfield."

"Katherine, the Countess of Gainsworth," Aunt Bethany said. "Her Grace, the Duchess of Northfield."

"Adelaide," the duchess said again, and extended the same hand she had with Bethany.

Katherine couldn't help but hesitate still, and yet the duchess took her hand without reluctance. Her blue eyes were bright, unclouded by ulterior motives, at least none she showed outwardly.

"I was hoping you two would come join our group," she said, motioning over to the small circle of women beside the dancefloor.

Katherine caught her breath. These were the famous Duchesses of the 1797 Club. Wives of the dukes who were one particular man's friends. A man she did not want to see or interact with.

But she was given no chance to refuse, for her aunt nodded enthusiastically and practically dragged Katherine across the room, with all its eyes focused on her, to the ladies who stood there.

"The Duchesses of Tyndale, Abernathe and Willowby," Adelaide said, motioning to the ladies. "Isabel, Emma and Diana. There are a few others floating about, but they all seem to be dancing with their husbands at present."

Katherine nodded, though she had no intention of calling any of these ladies by their given names. She had enough impropriety haunting her. There was no need to create more scandal.

They began to talk, just about silly things, conversation that was of no import. To her surprise, Katherine felt at ease with the ladies. And when she looked around the crowd, she no longer felt the heavy, accusatory gaze of others on her. She glanced back and found the Duchess of Northfield smiling at her.

"Perhaps you'd come get a punch with me?" she said. "I'm parched."

Katherine squeezed her aunt's arm before she stepped out with the duchess toward the refreshment table across the room. They walked in silence for a moment, comfortable until Katherine heard her name whispered on the wind. A snap of the syllables, an accusation with just the word.

To her surprise, Adelaide huffed out her breath and took her arm, squeezing it gently before they continued their way across the room. "You are holding up beautifully, my dear," she said as they reached the table at last.

Katherine glanced at her from the corner of her eye, uncertain again as to the woman's motives. "Is that why you approached us? To see firsthand how a woman of my...*situation*...was faring?"

Adelaide faced her, and her expression was one of horror. "Oh no, of course not. I was asked to look out for you by a friend."

"A friend?" she repeated.

Adelaide nodded. "Yes. Charlotte could not be here tonight, but she knew of your intention to return to Society and asked that I offer you a bit of friendship."

Katherine's lips parted. She and Charlotte were friends of a passing nature, but she'd always liked the other woman. She was a duchess, too, now. She'd almost forgotten that. Married to the famous Silent Duke of Donburrow a year and a half before.

She worried her lip. "I suppose Charlotte and her husband would know a great deal about whispers."

Adelaide's blue gaze snapped with protectiveness. "Indeed. And even if I wasn't sent by one of my closest friends, I would still have approached you. I like your aunt—she gives generously to a charitable society I dabble in. And I abhor bullies. There are those aplenty in this little room."

Katherine looked at her more closely. She wanted so much to like the duchess, to believe that she was a champion. Certainly, Katherine needed one of those now. Becoming friends with a powerful group of duchesses would help her.

And having friends of any kind sounded wonderful after the past few years of pain, isolation and confusion.

She shrugged. "They see blood in the water, I'm afraid. At least the Season will be over soon and I can have a few additional months for them to forget my..." She blushed, as she always did when this topic came up. "...to forget my particular scandal."

The moment she said the words, Katherine longed to pull

them back. She didn't like letting her guard down. She'd been punished for such foolish action many times in the past. No matter how kind or friendly Adelaide appeared, Katherine didn't fully trust her. And now her face felt hot and her hands shook a little at her sides.

Adelaide looked as though she would say something, and Katherine took a step back and held up a hand. "I find I'm a bit overheated in the crowd. Will you tell my aunt I took a moment of air and to excuse me?"

Adelaide held her stare for a moment and then nodded. "Of course."

Katherine forced a smile and pivoted, abandoning her companion rudely, she knew. The duchess would likely lament her offer of friendship. Katherine regretted that as she burst from the ballroom onto the terrace and raced to the edge of the wall to draw a few long breaths.

It was dark out. The night was cloudy, obscuring the moon and the stars. She flashed briefly to another night on another terrace. When she had sought darkness and found it. A night that had destroyed her life. Brought her to this particularly unpleasant future.

"Lady Gainsworth."

She stiffened. A male voice said her name. Slowly she turned to find one of her husband's acquaintances stepping on to the terrace and shutting the door behind him. Mr. Adam Morley, who was of an age with Gainsworth. Another old man who let his eyes roll over her like she was a prize.

"Mr. Morley," she said, forcing herself to be polite when what she really wanted was to be alone. "How nice to see you."

"And you," he practically purred. "As soon as I saw you enter the ballroom tonight, I knew I would have to find a moment with you."

Katherine set her jaw. He meant a moment alone. Not on the dancefloor where others might see. No, she was too damaged for an open approach.

"Well, here I am." She folded her arms. "Though if this is

about something between you and Gainsworth, I'm afraid I am not the one to speak to. His nephew has taken the title. I would reach out to him or to Gregory's solicitor."

Morley tilted his head. "It isn't about my dear old friend, rest his soul. I wanted to speak to you, *Katherine*."

She caught her breath. The way he said her given name, emphasized it, there was no denying his interest. It lit up in his cloudy green eyes. It hung on the air between them. And to pursue that kind of interest here, on the terrace, hidden in the dark, that meant it wasn't a genuine one. It was about desire.

"I would prefer to be called by my title, sir. And now I have left my aunt for too long. It was a pleasure to see you. Good night."

She strode past him, feeling his gaze on her with every step. Feeling stripped and vulnerable from it. Disgusted. As she reached the door, he said, "I will call on you again, my lady."

Her hand shook as she ignored the parting words, pretended she didn't hear them as she re-entered the ballroom. She had scarcely a second to gather herself when she caught two gentlemen watching her. One leaned into the other, whispering something that made them both laugh. Then the first tilted his drink to her, as if in salute.

She spun away, staggering across the room. It was one thing to hear the hisses and the judgment. This was something else. Everywhere she turned she caught another man looking at her. Smiling in that lewd, suggestive way. She knew want. She had been taught that concept, if nothing else, in her marriage. It was on all their faces. Stark and lecherous.

She lifted up on her tiptoes, desperate to find her aunt so she could cry off this awful night at last. Bethany was nowhere to be found in the crush. Panic clawed up in Katherine's chest as she scanned the crowd and found only cruel faces and faces that were lined with desire. She pivoted and froze.

There, standing across the room, was the Duke of Roseford. The world came to a screeching halt as she stared at him. He was just as handsome as he had been three years ago. Even more handsome, if that were possible. With his thick, dark hair, sharp, brown eyes and impeccable dress, there was no way one couldn't look at him. He was staring back, just as so many other men in the room had been. And yet his expression was different. The duke was not a panting dog. He was a wolf. Leader of the pack. Bored and indifferent.

She remembered that moment on the terrace years ago. A stolen moment that had changed her life. She'd come to hate him for that moment and for the moments that had come after. But now, in this blink of an eye when she was caught in the snare of his gaze, she could recall how very much she had wanted him to kiss her.

"Damn him," she muttered, pushing the memory away. Letting her anger return. *He* was the one who had ruined her life. She couldn't be so foolish as to forget that.

A slight smile turned up Roseford's lips, and then he took a step toward her. *Toward* her! One after another, right in her direction as he held her stare with that smirk on his face.

She turned on her heel and stalked away from him. She wanted nothing to do with that man and his handsome face and his knowing grins and his devil-may-care attitude. She had already suffered greatly for it once. She had no intention of ever putting herself in the position where he could make her suffer again.

CHAPTER TWO

Robert settled into a comfortable leather chair before the roaring fire and accepted the cup of tea Matthew, Duke of Tyndale, handed over. He wanted something stronger, but, given the time of day, did not ask for it. Matthew would push and he wasn't in the mood.

He hadn't been for three days. Not since the ball where he'd seen the Countess of Gainsworth and determined that he would take her as a lover. Of course, now that was up in the air. The woman had given him such a look, like he was a viper. And then she'd just...disappeared.

"...the Vinesmith Ball," Matthew said, finishing a sentence that Robert had not been attending to in the least. But it was about the very ball he had been brooding about, so Robert set his cup down and straightened up.

"I'm sorry?"

Matthew arched a brow. "I was just saying it was a crush and asking if you had a good time. What in the world is wrong with you? You've been out of sorts since you arrived."

"You were out of sorts for years and you didn't see me troubling you about it," Robert said with a shrug.

He immediately wished he could take the words back. Matthew had been grieving the loss of his former fiancée for years. Only his bride, Isabel, to whom he had been married for only a few months, had brought him from the depths of his despair.

Matthew tilted his head, but there was no anger in his voice as he said, "That was a tiny bit different. And you are full of horseshit. You troubled me about my melancholy at least once a week for three years."

Robert smiled. "I did do that. Dragged you off to places you didn't want to be. I'm the reason you met Isabel, after all. You owe me."

"You are," Matthew said softly. "I owe you my life."

"God's teeth," Robert said, pushing to his feet and pacing away. "I was in jest. Let's not get into an emotional upheaval over my role in dragging you against your will to the Donville Masquerade."

"Very well, then answer my question. Did you have a good time at the Vinesmith ball?"

Robert turned to him. "You talked to James, Graham or Simon."

"They might have mentioned you seemed out of sorts," Matthew said. "Do you wish to talk about it?"

"The ball was boring as hell. Those proper gatherings always are," Robert snapped, perhaps more sharply than he had meant to. He didn't like that his friends were all putting their heads together about him. "The only positive development was the return of Lady Gainsworth to Society."

Matthew wrinkled his brow. "Ah yes, that was the talk of the night. Poor woman. It seems she will suffer the consequences of her husband's...er...death."

Robert hesitated. Isabel and Matthew had suffered some gossip themselves after their marriage. He had to tread carefully. "Lady Gainsworth did fuck her husband to death. That is bound to cause a stir in both your Society and mine."

"Are we in two separate societies now?" Matthew asked with an arched brow.

"Of course we are. You and the rest of the married couples are in good Society. Good Society looks at poor Lady Gainsworth and sees scandal. They wish to shun her for something out of her control."

Matthew's lips had thinned. "And *your* Society?"

"*My* Society looks at her and wonders what a woman like that could do with a man more suited to all that…passion."

His friend's eyes went wide. "Wait, are you saying you are hoping to take her as a lover?"

"Everyone wants to take her as a lover," Robert corrected him. "They're betting on it right now. I'm just the one who is going to win."

"Robert!" Matthew said, his face twisting with shock.

Robert chuckled at the reaction, but it was forced. Seeing his friend's repulsion created a shame in his chest that he normally did not allow himself to feel. Now it burned there and it took all his energy to tamp it down.

"Isn't it better with me than with those other idiots who are going to chase the woman across ballrooms for the rest of the Season?"

The door behind them suddenly slammed and both men turned to find Matthew's wife Isabel standing there. Although she was petite and her tummy was slightly rounded from the baby growing inside of her, she looked a formidable foe at present. Her dark eyes flashed with outrage and her mouth was set in a deep frown.

"How could you?" she snapped.

Robert looked at Matthew to intervene, but his friend shook his head slightly and backed away, leaving Robert to the lioness who had suddenly appeared. "Isabel, you look lovely, as always," he said.

She folded her arms. "Don't try to distract me. I overheard what you said. Robert, you must know that Katherine is facing a fire. No, not just a fire—an inferno. And you want to fan the flames?"

Robert held up his hands as that kernel of shame Matthew had created began to grow. "You know me, don't you? I'm not going to hurt the woman."

Isabel blinked and her disbelief was clear. "How can you

say that with a straight face? A woman's life is difficult enough."

"You are quite the protector for a lady you do not know," he said.

"I know enough. I know she is Charlotte's acquaintance. I know she had to endure slurs and whispers at that ball. I saw her face. I know that when I spoke to her she was interesting and kind. The sort of person the duchesses would like to be friends with. I know she doesn't deserve *you* taking advantage of her situation. Of *her*."

"No," Robert said immediately. "I would never do a thing unless she was as interested as I was. I will just be irresistible."

Isabel stared at him for a beat. Two. Then she shook her head slowly. "Great God, Robert. How can you surrender to your worst nature at every turn? How can you not see how it does you as much a disservice as it does to everyone you damage? You are better than your impulses. I wish you would see that."

She turned and left the room without another word. Leaving Robert to stare after her. To feel that shame grow even larger.

He forced a smile as he glanced at Matthew. "Emotional in her pregnancy, I see."

To his surprise, Matthew didn't return the expression. "She isn't. She's emotional at seeing a friend do the wrong thing. I am, too."

"Would you like to lecture me next?"

Matthew let out his breath in a frustrated rush. "You have seen with your own eyes what a fall from grace can do to a lady. Adelaide? Helena? Even Meg suffered after the situation with Graham and Simon. To pretend as if you don't understand that is, as my wife says, beneath you."

Once again Robert felt the distance between them. The chasm that had been created by his impulses, by the strength of his friends' bonds of marriage. And once again, he realized that someday soon he would lose them all.

"You think so ill of me."

Matthew reached out and squeezed his arm. "Not so ill. But

I would reconsider involving yourself in something so low as a wager of seduction."

The shame and the pain this entire exchange had brought pushed wide in his chest, and Robert scrambled for anything in the world to make it stop. To make it less. And he found it in anger.

"Says the man who had an affair with his wife at an infamous sex club," he said softly.

The color drained from Matthew's face slowly, but he never removed his gaze from Robert's. "Don't be the worst of yourself, Roseford. Good day."

He said nothing else, but strode from the room, leaving Robert alone in the silence of the parlor. Leaving him feeling far worse than he had when he entered it.

Katherine settled into a chair before her fire and took a sip of her tea with a contented sigh that made her aunt smile.

"You are happy here?" Bethany asked.

Katherine looked around her at the cozy room. It was a little parlor, in a tiny townhouse, but unlike in her home with Gainsworth, she had put her own personality into it during the time when the world thought she was mourning. When they were waiting for her to return so they could gawk at the woman whose husband had died in such an unseemly way.

"I am," she said softly. "I suppose it would be seen as far beneath the palace I inhabited with Gregory during our marriage. But I'm not sorry for the change of circumstances. Thanks to my inheritance, it is *mine*. No one can take it away. Even if they take everything else."

Bethany frowned at the passion with which the last was said. "You lived a long time worrying about having things taken."

"How could I not, living with my father as he was? My

husband? They both took to punish. Gracious, I didn't even get to meet you until after my marriage. My father kept you from me."

Bethany reached out and took her hand, and for a moment the two women sat together in teary silence. Then her aunt said, "It was a devilish thing, to lose my sister and then have you torn away from our family. But we are together now. Reunited."

"And my father, no matter how he judges and rails, cannot do anything about it."

Her aunt shifted. "Does he know that you see me now?"

"I suppose he must. Since I…" Katherine blushed and ducked her head. "Now, how did he put it? Since I *murdered my husband with my whore's ways*, he has scarcely spoken to me. It has been a blissful time, in truth. Though I'm sure he will reinsert himself in my life now that I'm back in Society."

Bethany's face paled. "I worry about you. He can be cruel, I know."

"He has far less power now that I am independent," Katherine said with a shrug. "He can rail away all he likes, but I am a widow and that has given me…I suppose one might call it power."

Bethany seemed to be about to reply when Katherine's butler, Wilkes, stepped into the doorway. "I'm sorry to disturb you, my lady, but you have a guest."

Katherine got up as he crossed the room to deliver it. It was gilded and on heavy paper, and as she looked at it, her eyes went wide. "The Duchess of Tyndale?"

He nodded. "Yes, my lady. Shall I inform her that you are in residence?"

"Certainly," she said, though she cast a quick glance at Bethany. Her aunt had also gotten to her feet. As Wilkes departed to bring their unexpected companion, Katherine pursed her lips. "This group of duchesses is very persistent."

Bethany tilted her head. "Does that mean you doubt their true desire to be a friend to you?"

"How could I not considering my stained reputation? It's

difficult to assume anyone would want to be near me except for some ulterior motive." Katherine sighed and felt the sound down to her very soul.

Her aunt crossed to her and took her hand. "I know the Duchess of Northfield, at least a little, and you said you were once friendly with the Duchess of Donburrow. Can we agree they are both kind women?"

"Yes."

Bethany smiled gently. "Then perhaps we should not judge their choice of friends so harshly. Assume the best."

Katherine bristled at that idea, of letting her guard down only to perhaps be hurt. But before she could address it, Wilkes returned with the Duchess of Tyndale, introducing her briefly before he excused himself.

"Your Grace," Katherine said, coming across the chamber to take her hand. "What a lovely surprise. Do you remember my aunt, Mrs. Sambrook?"

The duchess's gaze flitted to her aunt, and Katherine thought she saw a bit of disappointment in her stare. But it was erased in a moment as she smiled kindly. "Of course. From the party a few days ago. Lovely to see you again. I am so sorry to call on you without an invitation."

Katherine shook her head. "There's no need. We were just having tea. Would you like to join us?"

Again, the duchess's gaze flitted to Bethany, and then she nodded. "Of course. That would be wonderful."

Bethany stepped forward. "You know, dearest Katherine, I was actually thinking that I ought to depart. I have a matter of some urgency that I've been putting off. Would it be very rude of me to cry off?"

"I—no—I—what matter?"

Bethany wrinkled her brow. "Nothing to concern yourself about."

"I hope you aren't leaving because of me," the duchess said, but there was no mistaking the expression of relief on her face.

"Of course not," Bethany said with a kind smile.

"Very well," Katherine said. "Let me show you to the foyer. Your Grace, I will be right back. Please make yourself comfortable."

The duchess smiled as she walked to the window to look out on Katherine's little garden. Katherine linked arms with her aunt and together they walked toward the foyer.

"What are you doing?" Katherine asked through clenched teeth as she glanced over her shoulder to ensure the duchess could not hear them.

"The woman clearly wishes to speak to you alone," Bethany whispered. "I realize you are reticent to make friends under your current circumstances, but these duchesses could be very helpful in your return to Society. You ought to at least hear her out. Call on me later and tell me how it went."

Katherine pursed her lips. Her aunt was not wrong. That didn't alleviate the tension in her chest, of course.

"Fine," she managed before she kissed Bethany's cheek. "I will come with a full report as soon as I am able."

Her aunt said her farewells and headed toward her carriage, leaving Katherine to take a deep breath and return to the parlor. She forced a smile to her face before she entered. "My aunt gives her most sincere apologies for the haste of her departure."

The duchess was standing at the window still and turned with a bright smile. "I was sorry to see her go, but I do admit I am happy to be alone with you, my lady."

Katherine worried her lip. "For any particular reason, Your Grace?"

For a moment the duchess hesitated, but then she shook her head. "I simply wish to know you better."

"Well, tea is the way to do that, isn't it?" Katherine asked, motioning to the settee. As the duchess took her place, Katherine noticed something she hadn't at the party a few nights before. There was a little swell to the duchess's belly. One she placed her hand upon as she settled in. "I did not say it before—many felicitations on your impending motherhood, Your Grace."

"Oh, Isabel, please," the duchess said with a wide smile.

"We are going to be friends. I feel that in my bones. None of us in our little group stand much on circumstance when we aren't in public."

"Isabel," Katherine said, handing over her cup. "Then I am Katherine."

"And thank you for the congratulations. The duke and I are very happy. We are married so recently, you know. I could not have asked for a happier start to our union. I always longed to be a mother, and seeing all my friends begin to have children has made the anticipation all the sweeter."

There was no mistaking Isabel's true pleasure and Katherine found herself smiling, though the topic was not a particularly happy one for herself. "I can imagine."

"You and the earl never had children, did you?" Isabel asked.

Katherine flinched as her mind filled with images that were only painful. Images of denial and recrimination. She shook them away. "We were not so blessed," she said softly.

Isabel tilted her head, and for a moment Katherine thought the duchess could see through her a little. An uncomfortable thing, for someone of such a brief acquaintance to penetrate the shell she put up to protect herself. Especially since she still had no idea as to this woman's motives when it came to her.

"May I be honest with you?" Katherine asked.

Isabel nodded. "I would ask nothing less. Please."

"I am a little confused as to why you and your friends have taken such an interest in me," she said, trying not to fold her arms like a shield in front of herself. "My reputation as I return to Society is sullied to say the least. I would think such exalted women would want nothing to do with me."

Isabel was quiet for a moment. "You worry that perhaps our motives are not...true?"

Katherine's lips parted in surprise. "Well, *that* is direct."

"We are being so, yes?" Isabel shifted. "My dear, if you give our little band of friends a chance, I think you'll determine this for yourself, but there is not a one of us who would ever cruelly enter a friendship. And any one of my dear duchesses would gladly explain their own relationship with scandal."

Katherine blinked. She had almost forgotten that several of the duchesses had been whispered about over the years. It was difficult to hold that in mind when they seemed so certain, so happy, when the group of them was so powerful.

Isabel continued, "Charlotte spoke highly of you and that is a recommendation, indeed. If we have a motive, it is only to use whatever status we've obtained to help make your return to Society a little easier if we can."

Katherine sat for a moment, cheeks burning. She could not look at this woman, not in the eye, after such a direct addressment of the matter. Nor could she parse out exactly how she felt about it. There was embarrassment that these ladies felt she had to be saved, but also an intense feeling of gratitude that they would offer that salvation without any apparent desire for something in return.

"If you did, I could not say I wasn't grateful," she finally managed.

Isabel reached out and caught one of her hands, squeezing gently before she said, "I've been putting off a duty I do not relish, but I think considering this subject, I cannot do so any longer. I was actually happy your aunt left us, for I came here on a mission."

Katherine glanced up at her at last and saw her companion's face tense with grim determination. "Oh dear. This does not sound good."

"It isn't. And it must be said privately."

"I am afraid I have no idea what you could be referring to," Katherine said. "We've only just met—I don't know what you could be so serious about."

"Yes, our friendship is young and now I must risk that in order to be frank. As I would hope a friend, old or new, would be toward me under the same circumstances."

Katherine swallowed hard. "I suppose it is best if you just say it and have it done with."

Isabel seemed as uncomfortable with this topic as she was, but she let out her breath in a long sigh and stammered, "I-I have found out that you are the subject of some very ungentlemanly…er…wagers."

CHAPTER THREE

Katherine's ears began to ring as she stared into Isabel's gentle face and those horrible words she'd said sank into the very heart of her.

"Wagers?" Katherine repeated. Her voice sounded like it was coming from under water. "Whatever do you mean?"

Isabel shifted with great discomfort, and that revealed the kind of wager even before she explained further. "The circumstances of the earl's death are obviously under scrutiny— I would be foolish to pretend that you didn't know it."

"I didn't murder him!"

Katherine tried not to recall the earl's face, strained and purple as he gasped out his last breath beneath her. Of the horrified servants as they came to find her naked and screaming for help. The facts of what they had been doing were too obvious not to be spread through her household and beyond. She knew what they said below stairs and above it. *All* the horrible things that the collective *they* said behind her back. She'd known it even before she returned to Society.

"Of course you didn't," Isabel gasped. "I *never* thought you did. That is a cruel whisper that others should be ashamed of. The man had an apoplexy, clearly. It just as easily could have happened when he was out for a walk in the park."

"Only it wasn't. It didn't happen in the park." Katherine folded her arms. "The thing that makes it so enjoyable for all those biddies to cluck about is that it happened in our marital bed."

Isabel ducked her head. "Unfortunately, yes. And that fact seems to have drawn the interest of *some* of the men in Society, as well. They think the circumstances have to do with…with…"

"My prowess?" Katherine whispered. Yes, she'd heard that, too. Quieter, but there in the background.

Isabel nodded, her cheeks suddenly dark with color. "Yes. And now they are clamoring to see who might take you as a lover first."

Katherine jumped to her feet as shock rushed through her. "*What?*" she burst out even though every word Isabel had said rang clear in her ears. She'd known they talked, but not like this.

"I'm sorry to be so blunt," Isabel said. "Or to embarrass you. But I thought you deserved to know what their wager was about."

"About who would take me as a lover?"

Tears of humiliation flooded Katherine's eyes, but beneath that, in some wanton place she tried to push aside, she felt something else, too. Something wickedly drawn to the idea that men were interested in her body, her pleasure.

After all, hadn't it been the pursuit of that same pleasure which had killed Gregory? That need she felt deep within her? The one he'd liked to tease her with. The one he'd never truly fulfilled.

She shook the thoughts away. "How do you know this? Were these men so uncouth as to discuss this in mixed company?"

Isabel ducked her head. "No, of course not. I-I overheard a friend of my husband's discussing it in private. I gave him a dressing down, I assure you."

Katherine stared at her. One of her hesitations about the duchesses as a group had to do with the fact of who their husbands were. Lifelong friends, a club of dukes. Everyone knew the men were as loyal to one another as brothers. And one of them was the man she despised more than all others. The one who had dared to try to approach her at the party a few days before.

Roseford.

That was the only friend of Isabel's husband who might speak of her in such a blatant manner. Only one of that group of dukes who was so cruel and heartless.

"The Duke of Roseford," she whispered. A statement, not a question.

Isabel drew back. "I—yes. How did you know it was him I was talking about?"

Katherine shoved to her feet and strode across the room, hoping to keep Isabel from seeing her face. The strength of her reaction, not just in its anger but in the call of longing that doubled as she recalled Roseford's handsome face swinging in toward hers all those years ago.

"The dukes are spoken of as highly as you duchesses," she managed to say, and hated how her voice trembled. "Save one. The Duke of Roseford. A cold-hearted snake of a man."

Isabel caught her breath and Katherine glanced at her. The duchess's face was pale and she was shaking her head as if to deny the charge.

"Robert is…misguided, but he is no snake," Isabel said.

Katherine managed to bite her tongue. She would not waste breath arguing that point with the woman. She knew Roseford in a way no one else did. After all, that near kiss on the terrace wasn't the only time she'd been alone with the man. There had been one more encounter after that.

And nothing would ever change her mind about his character. Or the fact that she hated him down to the center of her being.

"I have no idea why he would make some wager on me," Katherine muttered, more to herself than to Isabel. "He made it more than clear he wants nothing to do with me."

Isabel stood and tilted her head. "Oh…I thought your comment on Robert's character had more to do with his public reputation. I had no idea you were personally acquainted with him."

"We interacted." Katherine ground out. "But perhaps he does not recall it. I wouldn't doubt that was true, drunk as he was on both occasions. I suppose then it is almost as if it only happened in my mind."

She flinched at the memories that flooded her once more, sharper now as she let herself drown in them. Roseford's breath on her neck. His gaze locked with hers. That flare of desire in her belly that she hadn't understood at the time. Then she'd been an innocent. Now she had known pleasure, been desperate for it.

"Katherine?"

"No," she said, jolting herself from the thoughts that made her body weak. She was better than this. She could overcome it.

Isabel stared at her in confusion. Then her expression softened with empathy. "I'm sorry," she said, her voice barely carrying.

Katherine thrust her shoulders back, forcing strength she didn't feel into her countenance. "Well, just because that pompous man, or any other of his ilk, has decided that he wants me doesn't mean I have to surrender to him. Or stoop to his level."

Isabel took a tentative step closer, worrying her hands against that tiny belly. "I—did I do the wrong thing in telling you, Katherine?"

"No." Katherine reached out and took Isabel's hand, squeezing gently as her rage was tempered. "Truly, you did me a kindness. There are challenges facing me. I knew that would be true before I dared take a step into a ballroom. Now I understand those challenges better than before." She shook her head. "And perhaps that helps me establish what my limits will be."

"Limits?" Isabel asked, drawing Katherine back to the settee. "What do you mean?"

Katherine swallowed hard, trying to bypass the lump that had formed in her throat. "I just…I wanted to return to Society, you see. I have a little of my own money, no longer have my father or my husband to police my actions."

"You feel now that you can't," Isabel said.

Katherine nodded. "I must be practical, mustn't I? The reaction of Society when I walked back into the ballroom was...not good. And now that I know these so-called gentlemen have placed a wager on who will make me spread my legs...it won't help my cause. I must accept that I may never have a true place in good society again."

She said the words and they tasted like sawdust on her suddenly dry tongue. She'd spent a lifetime under one man's thumb or another. She had so looked forward to being free. Now that future seemed dimmer and dimmer.

Thanks to Roseford.

"If I can help..." Isabel began.

Katherine yanked herself back from those dark thoughts and shook her head. "I appreciate it, as I said before. But hearing what you have to say, it makes me question why you would. You and the other duchesses cannot truly wish to involve yourselves with a woman who inspires such urges in the men of Society."

Isabel pursed her lips. "First off, that they would make a wager like this reflects on *them*, not you. And secondly, you didn't know me before."

"Before?"

"Before Matthew," Isabel whispered. "Before I was his wife, at any rate. You don't know how I came to be the duchess that I am now. If you did, you'd realize I know a little of what you must feel. I know a little about scandal and the desperation it hatches in your chest."

That was an apt description. A hatching of fears and pains and longings that then spread. "Do you?"

Isabel took her hand again and nodded. "I do. And I want to be your friend, Katherine. Truly."

Katherine held her stare in disbelief. Until that moment she hadn't truly realized just how much she'd held herself off from others during the past few years. Fearing their judgment. Anticipating their recrimination. Unable to trust that anything another person offered was true or that it would last.

But here, sitting with this woman, she wanted to take that leap. To believe that the friendship Isabel held out to her was something she could truly take without fear.

"Thank you," she said softly.

Isabel leaned forward and bussed her cheek. Despite the forwardness of the action, Katherine couldn't help but smile as her new friend pulled away. "All right, that is done. Now I do not wish to talk about this anymore. We will chat about happier things and truly get to know each other."

The duchess crossed to the sideboard to pour the tea. Katherine allowed it and kept the smile on her face as Isabel watched. But deep in her heart she couldn't stop thinking about what Isabel had told her. About the men in Society. About Roseford.

So even if they didn't discuss it, Katherine knew it would be a topic she would not stop thinking about for a very long time. Nor would she stop searching for an escape from the prison the Duke of Roseford thought to put her in.

CHAPTER FOUR

Robert stood in the middle of Charlotte and Ewan's ballroom with a party in full swing around him. Normally he might have been enjoying himself. Tonight he could not. Tonight he felt restless and unhappy, just as he had during the past few days after his encounter with Matthew and Isabel in their home.

His friends disapproved of him. All of them. Once upon a time, he hadn't let that fact trouble him. He was different than those he spent time with, that was all.

Only right now he couldn't dismiss the way their eyes moved to him, the way they darted away. He was on the precipice of losing them all. And their disapproval made him doubt himself like never before.

He knew the feeling. He could name it. *Shame.* That was not something he often let himself feel. And yet here it was, sitting heavy on his chest, growing heavier each time he caught the stare of a friend from across the room and saw their eyes flit over him like he was a stranger.

There was a ripple through the crowd as he stood brooding, and his gaze followed theirs as the room turned to watch Ewan's footman announce, "The Countess of Gainsworth."

Robert's chest tightened as Katherine stepped into the room. She was, of course, stunning. Her dark hair was expertly styled to frame her beautiful face to its best advantage. Her gown was a cornflower blue silk, elaborately designed with swirls of darker blue stitching. It fit across her breasts perfectly, the swells peeking out the top like gifts waiting to be unwrapped. As she stepped forward, her hips twitched a little and his gaze was drawn to the seductive movement.

"…whose mistress she'll be…" one of the guests behind him murmured, allowing him to catch a fraction of their conversation.

He stiffened and so did she, although she could not have heard what had been said as she was so far away. Perhaps someone else had said something, hissed something, as she passed by. Her cheeks pinkened, and Robert's heart sank a little.

Isabel was right, of course, in what she'd said to him when she was scolding him for ungentlemanly behavior. Katherine had been damaged by the circumstances of her husband's death. Society would never look at her the same again. Oh, they would quiet about it, of course. Some new scandal would come along and Katherine's would fade. But it would never fully disappear. Never fully heal.

He watched as Charlotte and Ewan crossed to her. Katherine smiled, but he saw tension in the expression. Even with a friend, she did not truly relax. Didn't truly trust.

God knew he understood that.

Charlotte embraced her, and he could see the duchess introducing her to Ewan. Katherine smiled as the couple signed back and forth in that private little language of theirs. Katherine looked at Ewan when she spoke to him—she didn't speak around him as some people did. Robert couldn't help but smile at that fact. It infuriated him when people did that.

The couple talked to her for a moment, then she touched Charlotte's arm and the couple walked away. Katherine drew a long breath, then pivoted and started across the room toward the wall.

Robert began to move before he even realized he wanted to, trailing after her as she maneuvered through the crowd. She turned to put her back to the wall, and that was when she saw him. Her breath caught, just as it had a few nights prior when he tried to approach her. Her eyes widened, the dark brown nearly disappearing in smoky black. Her lips parted, inviting as hell, and then tightened as her demeanor shifted. She folded her arms, putting them in front of herself like a shield, even as her gaze flitted toward the door and he could see she would run from him.

This time he was not about to allow that. He stepped up swiftly, cutting off her escape. Her cheeks filled with high color and she glared up at him. He started. She truly despised him. That was clear in every part of her demeanor.

Interesting since he didn't think they'd met more than once, a very long time ago. Who had introduced them? Charlotte, perhaps? Meg? He couldn't recall. It was a flutter of memory.

"My lady," he said, pushing the thoughts from his mind as he gave her his best smile. The one that melted any steely woman.

She did not melt. If anything, her expression went stonier. Colder. "Your Grace," she growled, making the address sound like a curse.

"How nice it is to see you again," he said. "My condolences on your loss."

Her nostrils flared slightly and she drew in a long breath before she said, "Thank you. I did not think you knew the earl well."

"I did not," he said. "But I can imagine his loss is not easy."

She stared at him, silent. It was then he noticed the other ladies along the wall were edging closer, watching and listening. Katherine's gaze slipped toward them and the pink in her cheeks darkened further. He smiled. This could be his way to pierce the veil of her distain.

After all, she would not wish to make a scene.

"I wondered, Lady Gainsworth, if you had space on your dance card for the next with me?" he asked.

She swallowed and the action trembling down her long, slender neck and made him wish to trace the line of it with his fingertips. His lips.

"How dare—" she began, her voice elevating slightly.

He held up a hand and whispered, "People are watching."

She let her gaze slide to the staring women and her lips slammed together, becoming an impossible-to-cross line. She took another deep breath and then said, "I would be pleased to dance with you, Your Grace. Thank you."

He heard sarcasm drip from every word, but he smiled as if she had accepted sweetly and held out an elbow. She hesitated, staring at his outstretched arm like it was a snake that would surely strike. He waited her out, keeping his face impassive as if this long pause was usual.

It was not, of course. He'd spent his life with women tripping over themselves to get to him. This was the first time one acted like he was poison. It was an interesting experience, to say the least.

At last she pressed her fingertips lightly into the crease of his elbow. She barely touched him—she wore gloves and he two layers of fabric between them—but he still jolted at the awareness she created in him. He caught a whiff of her scent as he led her out to the floor. Cinnamon, honey, vanilla. Sweet treats stolen in the night. He wanted to see if she tasted the same.

Soon enough, though. He had no doubt in his own ability to seduce. He just had to get past this shell of hers. Pick the locks. He was good at that.

The music began and her eyes fluttered shut. A tiny moan escaped her lips. He laughed. "Don't like to waltz, my lady?"

To his surprise, she didn't respond, but just stared up at him, unmoving as he placed a hand on her soft hip and lifted her hand with the other. They stepped out in time together, falling into the circle of dancers.

For a while, he allowed her the silence. Being this close to her let him study her a bit and that was paramount to what he was doing. She had a smattering of light freckles across her nose. That was the only imperfection on her skin, and a telling one. The widow, it seemed, had not completely locked herself away in grief over the past year. She had been out in the sun, at least a little. Without a bonnet, perhaps.

Interesting. It indicated a desire to live again, certainly. Something he could…well, *manipulate* seemed a harsh term for it.

She had full lips. Very full, actually. They were a pretty shade of pink, bordering just on red. Her eyes were a chocolate brown, but there were lighter flecks there. Greens and ambers. He wondered briefly if one could count them all, parse them out from one another if he took enough time.

He blinked, drawing his gaze away with a start. Was he waxing poetic? A desire to have this woman was playing tricks on him. Or perhaps his mind was simply creating a narrative where he was not the evil bastard his friends believed him to be.

He glanced back and found Katherine had not removed her gaze from his face. She continued to stare, unwavering as he twirled her 'round and 'round. It was disconcerting, actually. Ladies tittered, they blushed behind fans flirtatiously. They did not simply stare, expressionless, at a man.

"You are quite graceful, my lady," he said, hoping to break the tension with the compliment.

"Ladies are taught to be," she said, tone as flat as her expression. "You would know, wouldn't you? I'm certain you have *danced* with a hundred of us."

"None so light-footed as you," he said with another smile.

He had meant to flatter her, but it clearly did not work. She rolled her eyes. Rolled her eyes at him. Like he was some stupid, uncouth, green boy stammering over his words.

He wrinkled his brow, pushing away the discomfort her reaction caused in him. The song was ending soon, he was running out of time to pursue her, and now he had a question pulsing through his mind. Troublesome. Undeniable.

"Why do you dislike me so much?" he said.

He expected her to blush at the directness. To stammer and deny what was so patently obvious. Perhaps even feign politeness.

She did not. Instead, she kept her gaze firmly on his and

said, "Because you are a cad, Your Grace. Someone who cruelly uses others for his own purposes and doesn't care a whit about the consequences because he is too spoilt and cruel to ever experience them."

His mouth dropped open and she stepped from his arms, performing a curtsey as the song ended, as if she had said nothing out of the ordinary to him.

"I hope that settles this, Roseford," she said. "And we do not have to have this conversation again. Good evening."

She pivoted then, walking away to leave him on the dancefloor, staring after her in shock. At least for a moment.

And then...he followed her.

Katherine's hands would not stop shaking as she burst onto the terrace behind the ballroom and fled to the wall. She rested her palms there, pressing hard so that the rough surface would dig into her flesh and remind her to be grounded. She had not been grounded with Roseford.

She had been emotional. She had lashed out. How he would laugh at that, she knew. And how he could turn it against her if that became his whim. He was good at that: twisting circumstances. Just look at the waltz they'd shared. His fingers had pressed so warm into her skin, his gaze had held hers with such intensity. That was seduction and she had been forced to fight not to be wrapped up in it like a little fool.

She would have to be a fool to believe in his attentions when she knew the purpose behind them. That bargain he'd made with his friends, the one that said he would win her...as if she were a twisted prize!

"Arrogant bastard," she muttered into the wind.

"Why all the vitriol, my lady?"

She froze. She'd been so focused on her tangled emotions, she hadn't heard Roseford come out onto the terrace behind her.

Now she pivoted and found him a few steps away. They were alone. Just as they had been all those years ago.

Her heart stuttered at the moonlight slashed across his face. At the longing his expression created in her lonely body. She despised this man for what he had done and not done. She couldn't forget that. Ever.

"Must you stalk me across terraces all over London?" she snapped.

One brow arched as he took a step toward her. He looked confused and the irritation she felt toward him ratcheted up another notch. That long ago night on another terrace had been a pivotal part in her life, as had the one after. He didn't even remember it or her. She was just another in a long line of ladies he'd discarded.

"Please, just go away," she said, her voice sounding as heavy as it felt, as everything felt in that moment.

He shook his head. "No. I want to know why you are so against me when I have done nothing to you."

She pursed her lips. *Done nothing to you.* That was an apt way of putting it. *Done nothing* for *you* would have also been accurate.

"Why am I not allowed to simply think ill of you? Are you so concerned with having the love of every single person that you cannot allow someone the space to disagree?"

A flicker of something crossed his face. Something dark and painful. She caught her breath at the sight of it, for it was entirely unexpected. Had she hit a nerve?

But then the reaction was gone. His smirk was back. Perhaps she had imagined his pain, wanted to see it there so badly that she'd placed it where it didn't belong.

"I'm sure plenty of people think ill of me," he said with a shrug as he moved closer again. He stepped around her and set his hands on the terrace wall next to where hers had been before she turned. She edged away slightly, not wanting to be too close. Just in case.

Why did he have to smell so good? Something leathery and

male.

"Do you pursue all of them across ballrooms, then?" she asked. "Demanding to know why they don't count you as a friend? You must spend a lot of time shouting at the wind."

He laughed. "First you accuse me of believing everyone must and does love me, then you say I must spend my time trying to convince the naysayers. It is very confusing, trying to parse out exactly what it is that offends you so about me."

She folded her arms and glared at him.

If anything, his smile widened. "Did I tread on your feet while we were dancing?"

She refused to respond.

It did not deter him. "I forgot an appointment we once had?"

Her lips tightened. He was teasing her, and the worst part was that some piece of her liked it. His charisma was a weapon of the worst kind.

"You hate my eyes?" he asked.

She darted her gaze to those eyes. Dark brown, sharp and intelligent. She swallowed hard as she gazed into them, lost in their depths for a moment. Then she caught her breath and backed up another step.

"It is your attitude, Your Grace. Your history. Your reputation. Must I go on?"

"I would think you, of all people, would not judge someone so harshly based on gossip," he said, this time his voice was soft and there was no longer teasing in it.

Her lips parted and she felt the color draining from her cheeks. "How dare you say such a thing to me?" she choked.

"At least I am doing it to your face and not behind your back," he said. There was no cruelty to his voice, but she felt every word as if they were daggers stabbed to her heart.

She dropped her head. She had been trying to be strong so that no one would see how much she was broken by their judgment. By their unkindness. But in that moment, she couldn't be. And she hated herself for losing her mask in front of this man, of all men in the world.

"So you wish to laugh in my face then. Am I supposed to thank you for being bold about it rather than surreptitious? Is that meant to reduce my humiliation?"

"Why should you be humiliated?" he asked, and she jerked her head up. He was closer somehow. Bigger. "You did nothing wrong."

She caught her breath. A few years ago when they'd stood together on a terrace like this one, she had not understood the flutter low in her belly. She hadn't recognized what the dilation of his pupils meant. Now she did.

Yet one thing was similar to that night long ago. As he eased in a tiny bit closer, she recognized that he was going to kiss her. And just like that other night, she wanted him to. Even though she knew his ulterior motives, even though she'd already experienced how he would do as he pleased and not give a damn about how she was left in shambles, she wanted his mouth on hers.

So she did the only thing she could. For the sake of self-preservation, she turned on her heel and walked away. Her hands shook as she waited for him to follow once more. To demand. To touch her and shatter any hopes she had to keeping these desires at bay.

"Katherine," he said as she reached the terrace door.

She froze there, refusing to look at him. Refusing to let him see how just saying her name made her knees shake.

When she didn't respond, he continued, "You should not be so afraid of your nature."

She tensed. Her nature. Yes, that was the trouble in all this. It always had been. But she refused to say anything in reply. She just entered the ballroom and left him without daring to look back.

As she stepped into her foyer, Katherine was still shaking from her encounter with Roseford, even though it had been over an hour ago. That damnable man was a menace. She had to stay far, far away from him or risk destroying herself even more than she already had been. She certainly needed to stop obsessing over his wager that he would win her body. She didn't want that. Not in the slightest.

"Wilkes, you do not know how happy I am to be home," she said with a forced smile as her butler took her wrap and gloves. "I'm going to have a drink and turn straight in. Will you ask Evelyn to meet me upstairs in a moment to help me ready myself?"

Her butler nodded slightly. "I will do that, my lady, but I must tell you that you have a visitor."

Katherine froze and stared at him. "A visitor," she repeated in confusion. "At midnight? Who in the world could be here at this hour?"

"Mr. Montague, my lady," he said.

Any happy feelings she'd had at being safe and sound at home now fled. "My father," she said softly.

Wilkes pursed his lips. "I did try to dissuade him from waiting, as we did not expect you home from the ball until much later, but he was insistent. I hope I did the right thing in surrendering the parlor to him."

Katherine bent her head. "Yes, of course. He would not have been moved from his stubbornness no matter what you said, Wilkes. I'll go see him. And I'll ring for Evelyn myself when I'm ready—no need to find her for me now."

The butler nodded and she walked away, legs shaking just as they had been after her encounter with Roseford. But for very different reasons.

She hesitated at her parlor door. It had never seemed so big and daunting before. She'd never dreaded opening it so much. And yet she did so because there was no other choice.

Her father was standing at her fire, staring at the flames. He had never been to this house. She'd liked that about this place. It was hers, not Gregory's or her father's or anyone else's.

And now he stood in the middle of the room and somehow

it was spoiled by his presence. At least for the moment.

"Father," she said softly.

He pivoted and speared her with an immediate glare. "You look like a whore in that gown."

She lifted a hand to her chest at the slur, spreading her fingers as if to cover the skin that her dress revealed. It was current fashion, of course, nothing the world would judge her on. Her father was another story.

"I'm surprised you are here," she said, ignoring his glare and his heated, cruel words. "You don't call on me, and certainly not at this hour."

"I had to come when I heard you have made a return to Society," he said. "You are a little fool."

She set her jaw and crossed to the sideboard where she stared at the bottles lined up there. She had intended just a sip of sherry to calm herself before she went to bed. Now she grabbed for a bottle of scotch, Gregory's best, one of the few things she'd brought with her when she departed his home months ago.

She poured half a tumbler full and took a long sip. "I'm tired," she said. "And in no mood to hear you go on about my many sins. Perhaps you could write them in one of your many warm and wonderful letters. Isn't that how we communicate? Why change things?"

His face twisted in anger at her impertinence and he took three long steps toward her. She braced herself, though she wasn't certain for what. He had struck her before, of course, but not for a long time. He had very little power over her now, not when she had her own money and title and home.

Over her heart...well, that was another story. His ugliness had always moved her, cut her, made her long for acceptance.

"How can you go back after what you've done? You are a marked woman—they will never accept you. You will be seen as what you are and always have been. A wanton."

She bent her head for the second time that night and blinked against tears. The worst part was that her father wasn't wrong. There seemed to be no going back to Society, just as he claimed.

She was seen as dirty or broken or damaged because of how Gregory had died.

"Please stop," she whispered, willing herself not to break down in front of him. That would give him too much pleasure.

"I know you've been seeing your aunt," he snapped.

She jerked her head up and saw that her father's round face had gone purple in his anger. "Are you spying on me?"

"Reports come back to me," he growled. "Do not question me when you are the problem."

She almost laughed at that. The problem. Oh yes, she had always been that to him. Just as her mother had been. So many problems for a man with such piety.

"Then wash your hands of me," she said on a heavy sigh. "This is the perfect time to do it, isn't it? You can tell everyone that you will not support your whore daughter who killed her husband in the most shocking way. That should keep your godly friends praying for you for years."

He moved up again and caught her arm, his fingers digging into her flesh as he shook her. "This impertinence is entirely because of Bethany's influence. You three are all alike. You, her, your mother…loose women who will not come to heel. It is in your nature to be lost. It is in your nature to be rotted to your very core."

Katherine tore her arm from his grip and fled across the room from him. "Go home, Father," she said. "We have nothing more to say to each other."

"We do not," he agreed. "This is the time for me to sever my ties to you. It's the only way to my own salvation. You are no longer my daughter, Katherine. Goodbye."

She stared at his departing back, tears stinging her eyes. She wasn't certain how much of them were tears of relief and how much were tears of heartbreak. Her father had declared her a lost cause many a time in her life, but this time there had been a finality to it. A clear break that she knew she would not make any attempts to repair. What was between them had never been whole and she had no intention of trying to make it so now.

Still, though, his words rang in her ears even long after he was gone.

He'd spoken of her nature. It was funny that he had used that phrase to describe what he saw as wanton depravity. Roseford had used the same words on the terrace not so long ago. And to describe what she supposed was much the same part of her. The part these men saw as...loose. Wild.

Her father had hated that part of her. When she was a girl, he had railed on her for having too much fun or learning too much or wanting too much.

Judging from the bet Roseford had made about her, *he* didn't hate her for it. He wanted to use her for it. Harvest the desires she'd been harboring for so long. Cultivate them for his own pleasure and then crow that he had won her.

The duke had said her nature wasn't wrong. That she ought not deny those things that woke her hot and needy in the night. That they weren't wrong as her father had said or her husband had said.

But was he right? She didn't even know anymore. Not when her mind was swimming and her heart was breaking. At any rate, she'd probably lost his interest when she walked away from him. Perhaps that was for the best.

CHAPTER FIVE

Robert watched as James leaned over the billiard table and took a careful shot. He had lined it up perfectly, as he always did, and the balls snapped together before one glided into the pocket. James stood and smiled at him.

"I see it, I see it," Robert grumbled. "You've always been better at this than I am."

"It is perhaps the only activity where I am superior," James said with a chuckle.

"Emma would likely disagree," Robert said, looking over the table for a shot. To his frustration, he had few options. Sort of like his life at present.

"Emma would argue that I am perfect in every way. Don't you dare tell her the truth, for I'm certain she would run away."

Robert leaned his cue against the side of the table and faced his friend. "No, she wouldn't. She adores you, flaws and all."

James's expression softened. "She does at that. We are…she is with child again. She is due around the same time as Isabel, actually."

Robert's eyes went wide. James and Emma already had a little girl, Beatrice, born just over eighteen months before. He had watched, rather shocked, as his dear friend had surrendered himself to the two women in his life. Emma and Bibi had James wrapped around their fingers like no one else could ever do to the powerful duke.

"Congratulations," he said.

"Do you mean that?" James asked as they shook hands. "You aren't going to rail at me about how I'm becoming old and boring?"

"Not tonight," Robert said with a sigh. "Though I do wonder when *you* are going to start lecturing *me*. I know you know. I know Matthew told you."

James's smile faded a little. "He told me you two quarreled," he said. "And yes, he said why. Even if he hadn't, Isabel told Emma everything."

"And all you couples are like units. If one knows, the other does," Robert said. "I wrote Matthew a letter of apology and he wrote back with forgiveness. But I wonder if he told you something different. We'll see each other before all of you leave for your country party and I'd like to know what I'll face. I know I crossed a line."

He felt his face heat with that last admission, just as it did every time he considered what he'd said to Matthew. How he'd brought up the circumstances of his meeting Isabel, yes. But also what he'd said about Katherine and his plans for her. Matthew's eyes had been so filled with...disgust.

"Tyndale doesn't hold a grudge," James said softly. "You know him. At this point, I think he's merely worried about you. As am I."

"And that is why you invited me here," Robert said with a shake of his head. "All right, my friend, tell me what an ass I am. How ungentlemanly. How beneath me my plans for Lady Gainsworth are."

James blinked and held his gaze. "You have already decided what I would say. I wonder if it's because those are the feelings in your own heart."

Robert pursed his lips. "You assume I am far better than I am. You'd think you'd know me after all this time."

"I do know you." James moved toward him a step. "And I know about her. Gainsworth was...I didn't know him well. He was far older than us, far older than her. What I did know was a rather cold, seemingly pious man, though there were rumors to the contrary. I have no idea if his wife loved him, but he has not left her in the best position."

"She has money," Robert said. Oh yes, he'd had his man look into her since their last encounter. Isabel's words had tweaked him. James's were starting to do the same.

"Yes, Emma said something about her having her own little home here in London. Charlotte thought she had a small inheritance to live on. But you cannot believe that is all a woman needs in life. To return to Society after such a scandal, to come into those rooms with one's head held high." James let out his breath. "That takes a strength of character I wouldn't guess half of us have."

Robert thought of Katherine's expression when he'd asked her to dance. How her gaze had darted to the women watching, flickered with humiliation. And then she'd been all strength. Confidence. That was part of what drew him to her, not just her beauty.

"I'm certain it isn't easy," he agreed.

"And then there is her father," James said. "I remember Mr. Montague from when she was out three years ago. It was the Season before I met Emma, and there were whispers about the man. He was obsessed with morality. I think I might have considered asking his daughter to dance and was put off by another gentleman who said I was inviting a scene. For her. For me."

Robert tensed and stared at his very rich, very handsome friend. "You had an interest in Katherine?"

James blinked as he stared at him. "*That* is what you brought out of that story? That I considered asking the lady to dance with me once three years ago?"

Robert shifted. "No, of course not. I was simply having a hard time imagining you with a tendre for anyone but Emma."

"I didn't have designs on Lady Gainsworth, or is she *Katherine* to you?" James rolled his eyes. "I was eligible and she was available and I danced with a great many ladies in those days. Christ, man, the point was that her father's behavior had already ostracized her on some level. So she has a bad start with him, and now this nonsense with how her husband died. Her prospects are not the best."

"But she doesn't have to get married," Robert repeated, circling around to the beginning of their argument. "So what do prospects matter?"

"I realize this is a foreign concept to you, but perhaps she *wants* to get married. Not for money or standing, but on her own terms. For love, even. I can imagine she might have been starved of it these last few years if her late husband's public coldness stretched to their home."

Robert shifted. "None of those things are my fault."

James smiled, almost a pitying expression and Robert's heart began to pound. "Of course not. But if you are bent on this idea of wagering to seduce her, you'll make her life all the harder. Those friends of yours, the ones who don't belong to our group, they will crow of any conquest that is completed. Society will judge her even further. She could be ostracized and isolated completely. I know you are not so cruel as to want that. To be blind to how you would make another person's life so much harder."

Robert squeezed his eyes shut and ground out, "Please don't be my conscience, old friend."

That inspired another laugh from James, this one warmer. Like he'd said his piece and he could just be Robert's friend again. When Robert looked at him, James chucked him in the shoulder gently. "You have one of your own. I just need to pluck it from time to time to keep it awake."

"Alive," Robert corrected.

James laughed again and slung his arm around Robert. "Come on, don't be so glum. I know what you'll do. Come to Abernathe with the party. Join us there for ten days and be with your friends who love you and see the man you truly are beneath that swagger and nonsense you show to the world."

Robert pulled away and walked to the other side of the

room. "Come, James, I appreciate the invitation, just as I did the first time you made it three weeks ago. But you know I'm busy here."

"Busy," James repeated. "Carousing keeps your schedule full, does it? At least give me the real reason for your reticence."

Robert ran a hand through his hair as he considered that request. Order? It felt like an order. One he wanted to deny because the answer felt very...vulnerable. Only James was staring at him and he knew he couldn't avoid speaking forever. Nor could he think of what to say that wouldn't reveal the whole truth.

"Kit is busy with running the estate and making final arrangements as his father's illness progresses," Robert said. "And the rest of our friends who are making the trip to your estate are married. I will be the sole bachelor amongst the blissfully happy couples and families."

James cocked his head. "Is that the lilt of regret I hear in your voice?"

"No," Robert said firmly. "Love is fine for you lot. I admire that you have found it. But I am not seeking it, I assure you."

"Please come," James said. "Don't think of it as being amongst couples, think of it as being amongst friends. Hugh and Amelia are still locked away at his estate celebrating their marriage, so they will not attend. Lucas and Diana will also be away. Do you ever get the feeling he and Diana aren't as separate from his old work at the War Department as they claim?"

"Every time I talk to them," Robert chuckled.

James grinned. "And Kit won't be there, of course, as you mentioned. But the rest of us will be, and we want to have you."

Robert drew a deep breath. "You only want me there in the hopes I'll forget my bargain regarding Katherine."

"That's not true. But if it gives you time to reconsider your decision, I won't lie and say that wouldn't please me. Come and remember who you really are, Robert. Please."

Robert's foot tapped nervously and he pulled away from James to lean on the billiard table as he considered the invitation.

James's words, Matthew's words, Isabel's words…they all rang in his ears. As did Katherine's spectacular set down at the party a few nights before.

Perhaps going away was the best thing. It wasn't as if the Season had much left in it. In fact, London Society in winter would be an easier place to find Katherine. With his friends all ensconced on their estates, making more babies with their wives, no one would be around to cluck at whatever he decided to do about the comely countess.

"Very well," he said. He straightened and nudged James with his shoulder. "I hate you, you know."

James burst out in laughter and nudged him back. "I know. Now, let's finish the game."

Robert grabbed for his cue and leaned back in for a shot. Yes. He would finish this game, one way or another. And he didn't mean the one he was playing with James.

Katherine smiled as she freshened Bethany's tea and then took a place beside her aunt on the settee.

"So you never told me, how was the Donburrow ball? I'm sorry I had to cry off. My head feels much better."

Katherine's face fell. She had been feeling so happy. It had been three days since her encounter with Roseford on the terrace at Charlotte's ball. She'd been working hard to forget it, forget him, and declare to herself that her set down would put him off his pursuit for good.

And now one word from her aunt and her mind spun right back to the man. To the fact that he'd wanted to kiss her. The fact that she'd wanted it right back. And to his declaration that her nature was not wrong.

"It was fine," she lied, forcing a false smile for her aunt. "I must say though, I'm glad to see the Season winding down as autumn chills the air. London will be easier in the winter.

Perhaps I can regather myself before next year."

Bethany's brow wrinkled in worry, but then she reached out to pat Katherine's hand. "Well, I'm glad it was uneventful."

Katherine worried her lip. She might not tell her aunt about her unexpected exchange with Roseford, but there was something else she had to share. Something that would go over just as well.

"My father was here waiting for me that night when I returned," she said.

The fear that lit up on her aunt's face was immediate and powerful. Katherine physically recoiled from it, even as Bethany's hand clutched hers tighter.

"Was he?" she asked, breathless. "Is that the first time he has pursued you here?"

Katherine nodded. "Yes. Since Gainsworth's death, he has avoided me. He writes, occasionally, to remind me to repent all my wickedness before it's too late. But it seems my return to Society drove him to come tell me in person." She drew a short breath. "That and...Bethany, he knows that you and I have been reunited. That we are seeing each other now."

Her aunt got up and walked away. Her back was to Katherine for a long time as she stared out the window to the street below. Finally, she turned and she was pale as paper.

"I suppose I should have known that would happen. When you were married and did not go out much, our occasional meetings could go unnoticed. But now that we have gone out to parties and balls, of course he would hear that we found each other." She shivered.

"You're afraid of him," Katherine said softly.

Bethany nodded. "I am, I admit. He is...dangerous."

"Why?" Katherine asked. "We have been reunited for two years now, but I've never had the nerve to inquire about what separated you from my mother, from me, in the first place."

Bethany frowned. "I suppose now is as good a time as any to explain. Your father wasn't always as he is now. When he married Jane, I actually thought they'd be good for each other.

She was such a bright light and he so serious. But instead of being warmed by that light, he snuffed it out. He isolated her, just as he did to you. Just as *your* husband did. Even when you came, it wasn't enough for your father."

Katherine squeezed her eyes shut. She had few memories of her mother, but the ones she did were difficult. "She was lovely, but so sad," she whispered. "And he got so cold and so hurtful. She was alone, I could see that even as a child. And look at me. I am the same."

"No," Bethany said, catching her hand. "It doesn't have to be that way."

"Of course it does," Katherine said, trying to laugh when what she wanted to do was scream. "What happened with Gregory, the scandal it has created...that has damaged my chances to have any kind of life that I once imagined."

Bethany squeezed her fingers. "Unless you find powerful friends who can sweep away that scandal with their influence." She smiled. "I have an invitation for us to join the duchesses for tea today. In half an hour, actually, so we should go now if we're to make it on time."

"The duchesses—you mean, *the duchesses*?" Katherine blinked. The women had all been very kind to her thus far. Isabel had even been the one to warn her about Roseford, but to invite her into their circle for tea? Could they really be so determined to help her?

"Yes, *the* duchesses," Bethany laughed.

"I don't know," Katherine sighed. "I appreciate their attention, but—"

"If you are not certain, let me be for both of us," Bethany said, all but dragging her to the foyer. "This is your chance to still have those dreams you buried. The ones my sister never got to live. Now come, we'll dry our tears in the carriage."

Katherine blushed as Isabel stepped into the foyer and smiled at her and Bethany from across the room. She hadn't realized that this invitation had been to the house of the very woman who knew Roseford's plans for her. Now she felt exposed as the duchess came toward them.

"Oh, I am so pleased to see you," she said, squeezing Bethany's hand and then quickly embracing Katherine. "Are you well?" she whispered.

Katherine nodded as she sent a quick side glance to her aunt.

"Come, the others are waiting," Isabel said, and took them down the hall to a large, beautiful parlor.

Katherine forced a smile as the other ladies in the group turned. Margaret, Duchess of Crestwood, and Adelaide, Duchess of Northfield, were Isabel's other companions. To Katherine's surprise, the ladies each held a child in their arms. Meg's child was older, a boy with a bright smile who giggled incessantly at Adelaide's little girl, dressed in a pretty gown with a pink ribbon in her blonde hair.

Katherine's stomach clenched and she pushed away all the natural reactions to seeing the children except for surprise. Most Society women she knew, women of wealth and title, hardly interacted with their children. But here Adelaide and Meg were, smiling and cuddling their babies joyfully.

"And here she is!" Isabel said, drawing Katherine in.

The other two women looked up and their smiles were just as welcoming as Isabel's had been earlier. She was promptly introduced to James, named after his beloved uncle, and Madeline, then governesses were rung for and the children were taken away for their naps.

Soon the ladies were all seated and talking about everything and nothing at once. Katherine was surprised at just how...easy it all was. No one ever looked at her askance. No one used the opportunity to casually ask about her late husband or his death.

The three ladies were simply kind and welcoming, funny and sweet. They were exactly who she would wish to be friends with under any circumstance.

Isabel settled back, her hand coming to rest on her belly beneath her gown. "I must say, I will be glad to depart London next week."

Katherine tilted her head. "Going back to your estate with Tyndale now that the Season is winding down?"

"Oh, we'll retire soon enough to our estate, yes. To winter and welcome the baby." Her cheeks brightened. "But first we will join Emma and James—Abernathe—for a final gathering at their estate."

Meg's eyes lit up and she shot Katherine a quick glance. "Are you going to ask her?"

Katherine exchanged a look of confusion with her aunt, but hadn't the chance to ask anything before Isabel giggled. "I'm *trying* to be subtle."

"Subtly is overrated," Adelaide said over the edge of her teacup. "Be direct."

Isabel shook her head and met Katherine's eyes with a smile. "If you hang about these ladies for more than ten minutes, they will influence you in such wicked ways. Emma couldn't be with us today, as she and James are preparing to depart to ready the estate. But she wished for me to convey an invitation."

Katherine blinked. "An invitation?"

"She would like for you to join our party at Abernathe. Both of you. Imagine it, Katherine! Ten days away from London, amongst friends."

Bethany leaned forward, her face lit up. "That sounds wonderful."

Katherine smiled but didn't respond to the offer as she got up and went to the window to look out at the garden. Once again, she was torn. Were the duchesses being kind, offering her help? Or was there something more sinister afoot in their kindness?

Isabel was at her elbow in a moment, and both women glanced back to where Bethany was still chatting with Meg and Adelaide. "Are you well?"

Katherine worried her lip. "I'm sorry to be rude. It is a

wonderful invitation. I know your group is quite exclusive and others would fall all over themselves to be involved in this gathering."

"But you're nervous about why?" Isabel pressed.

Katherine nodded. "I am, a little."

"The best practice is honesty, I think. After our talk last week, *I* suggested inviting you," Isabel said, holding Katherine's stare so that she could truly evaluate Isabel's motives. What she saw was pure, genuine warmth.

"Why?" she asked slowly.

Isabel cast another glance back at the others. "I was thinking about you since I visited you and told you of Roseford's pursuit."

Katherine blushed and shifted. "I see."

"Emma told me he will not be there. He prefers to stay in London. That made me think of how nice it could be for you to come with us. You will be with friends, and obviously Society would know you were included…"

"Which would help me," Katherine said softly.

Isabel nodded. "As you said, everyone is clamoring for an invitation to Abernathe's. And the best part of it all is that you won't have to face Robert. He is a creature of whim at times. If he doesn't see you for a couple of weeks, he may decide to entertain himself in some other way."

Katherine tried to fight the little starburst of pain that expanded in her chest at the thought. Of course that was exactly what she wanted. She didn't want that cad pursuing her across terraces and ballrooms, trying to pretend he was truly interested when all he wanted was to win some wager about bedding her. She didn't want to interact with him at all.

And yet the idea that he would forget her now as easily as he had forgotten her all those years ago was…not pleasant.

"Katherine?" Isabel said, touching her hand.

She blinked and came back to the moment with a shake of her head. "I'm sorry, just pondering my options."

"We'd love to have you," Isabel repeated. "Even if this

situation with Robert weren't part of the equation, we would still love to see you. Please?"

Katherine drew a long breath. She lifted the elevation of her voice to tell the room at large, "I would be honored to join your party. Aunt Bethany, will you also accept?"

"I already have," Bethany said with a laugh. "I've heard the Duke of Abernathe has a beautiful estate with a property worthy of my morning walks. And getting out of the city would do us both good."

"Excellent," Adelaide said, clapping her hands together. "That will please Emma greatly. I will tell her tonight when I join them before our departure."

Katherine smiled. "You and the Duke of Northfield are going down to Abernathe with Emma and her husband?"

Adelaide shook her head. "Northfield had to take care of a bit of business on one of his far-flung estates and left two days ago to do so. He will meet me in Abernathe, so James and Emma offered to let Madeline and me ride with them and Bibi."

Katherine nodded. "You and Madeline will miss him, I suppose."

A flicker of sadness passed over Adelaide's face, but she smiled nonetheless. "Although she's young, I know Madeline does seek him out. She is her papa's daughter through and through. As for me, I *always* miss him. Even if he is only gone an hour. Dratted man has bewitched me entirely. Luckily, he claims I have done the same to him."

"And he's already written her three times since he left," Meg teased.

The women all laughed as Adelaide blushed, but there was something hollow Katherine felt at the exchange. She had been married for two years and Gregory had left her at his estate plenty of times to take care of business. She did not think she had three letters from him in that entire time. As for missing him…during her mourning period she had certainly been sorry he was dead. But miss him? No.

And watching Adelaide, seeing how her entire face lit up

when she spoke of her husband, Katherine felt jealousy rise up in her. A feeling she tamped down with all her might as the subject switched to all the activities they would participate in during their time in the country.

But the hollow feeling didn't fade, even as the topic of much-beloved husbands did. And she tried very hard not to think of how it would feel to experience that weight in her chest for the rest of her life.

CHAPTER SIX

Robert drew in a long, cleansing breath of fresh air as he galloped through the gate of James and Emma's country estate in Abernathe. After the past few weeks in London, where he had felt stifled and out of sorts, the days of riding in the brisk autumn air had done him good. He felt a new man, untroubled by thoughts of the future. No longer obsessed with how he would bed Katherine.

Not that he was certain he still wouldn't try. But some time away would give him perspective. He maneuvered up the long drive and grinned as the huge manor house came into view. James had made quite the life for himself here. At first, that hadn't been certain. Abernathe had been so unsure of how to be a duke, it had caused a great many problems for him in the past.

But now that was all over. James was happy and settled with Emma at his side, Bibi in his arms and a new child to come in the spring. Robert was happy for him. Happy, that was all. Nothing else. Nothing sharp and empty that taunted him at night.

No. Just happy.

He rounded the last bend and saw that a carriage was already sitting on the circular drive. Emma and James stood at the top of the stone stair to greet their guests. The carriage must have just arrived, for servants were just getting down from the top of the rig and rushing from elsewhere to help the occupants.

Robert pulled his horse up behind the vehicle and swung

down, stretching his back as he watched for the other guests to come down. He couldn't see the crest on the rig from this angle, so he wasn't certain which duke and duchess would greet him to walk up to their hosts together.

A lady's hand extended from the vehicle and he craned his neck as she stepped down. Suddenly the world shifted, stopped spinning, for as she turned her face toward the house, her identity became clear.

It was Katherine.

Robert took a step toward her with a gasp. She had not yet noticed him as she moved aside to allow her aunt to join her on the drive. The two ladies conferred for a moment. Katherine said something to her driver, then glanced around and her eyes caught him.

They widened, a look of pure shock flowing over her features. Her aunt was talking and Katherine waved at her to go, so the older woman began to make her way up the stairs to their hosts. Meanwhile, Katherine just continued to stare, blinking as if she could make him disappear if she just focused hard enough.

He moved toward her, almost against his own will, for he had no idea what he would say to her, what he would do now that she was standing there, looking fetching in that lovely burnt orange dress that warmed her skin and brought out hidden highlights in her dark hair.

He reached her and she dipped her chin, muttering, "Son of a bitch."

He stopped up short and grinned despite the fact that she wanted him anywhere but near her. God, but she was a spitfire. She never backed down, even though it was clear he made her nervous. He liked that. In some odd way, he liked having to work for even her barest regard.

"My lady," he said, casting a quick glance up the stairs to where James and Emma were greeting Katherine's aunt, though both were staring down at the two of them and neither appeared happy. "What a surprise."

She folded her arms and looked up at him with a nod.

"Indeed, it is that."

He arched a brow at her cool tone. Dismissive, even. He wanted to get under her skin. "I believe I was invited here in order to avoid you."

Her eyes went wide and her arms dropped away from their position as shield. "I—well...yes, I believe that was the same reason I was asked to come here."

He chuckled at her honesty, forced from her by surprise. With her guard down, she was even lovelier. The flush to her cheeks made her look alive, made him wonder how low that blush traveled down her curves. How it would look if it were coaxed by pleasure and not shock.

He nudged his head toward the others. "Do you think they are secretly trying to put us together?"

Her lips parted as if she had not considered this option. Her gaze flew to the top of the stairs, and together they looked at James and Emma again. Now that Katherine's aunt had stepped aside, the couple had their heads together and were talking, apparently at once, and staring down at Katherine and Robert.

"Judging from how all the color is out of Emma's cheeks and the animation of their conversation, I would say no," Katherine said.

"Well, at least we are entertained," he said, looking back at her.

She glanced at their flustered hosts once more and then she smiled. Robert promptly forgot how to breathe as he stared at her. He'd never seen her smile. Not really smile, as opposed to some fake thing she wore as a mask. She was...stunning. All the life of the world was in her bright eyes, and he wanted nothing more than to keep that expression on her face forever. It was as warm as the sun.

He blinked, trying to clear his mind of these errant thoughts. He held out his elbow and winked, hoping she would not see past the cad he played in public. "Shall we make the best of it?"

She made a little sigh. Just the tiniest sound from the back of her throat. His body tensed because it was a sound of…surrender. Then she took his arm and let him lead her up the stairs to their horrified hosts.

Robert smiled. This was going to be a very interesting ten days, to say the least.

It took every fiber in Katherine's being to control herself and not tremble as she held her hand in the crook of Roseford's arm and moved up the stairs at his side. He was very warm and very handsome and very…*hard*. His arm was very *hard*, and it was as distracting as his unexpected appearance was.

But of *course* he was here. She had come to Abernathe to escape him, but her life had never been about escape. She had been forced to face her demons, fight them and never quite win, for as long as she could recall. Why would it be different now? Roseford was here. How, why, she didn't know. But she would have to deal with him and that was that.

They reached the top of the stairs and he released her, his warmth clinging to her body even after she moved away to greet Abernathe, then stepped toward Emma.

Her friend's face was pale as paper as she drew Katherine in for a brief embrace.

"Katherine, I am so sorry," she whispered. "I had no idea James had convinced Robert to join us. And somehow in the excitement of our coming, I hadn't mentioned to him that you would be in attendance."

Katherine drew back and smiled at the pretty duchess, whose brown eyes were now soft with concern and guilt. There seemed to be no treachery there. She looked truly horrified and that somehow comforted Katherine. At least she was only dealing with one enemy.

"You don't owe me an apology, Your Grace, I assure you," she said, and was pleased that none of the conflict she felt was present in her voice. "The Duke of Roseford is a friend of your family—I would never presume to be upset at who is at your estate. I will manage just fine."

Emma did not look certain, but she smiled at any rate. "Well, Adelaide is already inside if you'd like to share tea with her. I see another carriage arriving, so we will have to stay outside a while longer. Otherwise, I hope we can talk in depth later."

Katherine linked arms with her aunt, who was waiting for her a few steps away. Bethany gave her an odd look, which Katherine ignored as she cast one last glance down the line toward Roseford. He was talking to Abernathe, their heads close together in what seemed a very serious exchange. He didn't look at her. Of course he wouldn't.

"Thank you, I look forward to it," she said to Emma, and then she and her aunt entered the house. The butler rushed to take their things.

"May I show you to your chambers?" he asked.

"I would love a lie down," Bethany said even though concern still lined her face. "Are you coming up?"

Katherine paused. She actually wouldn't mind a moment alone in her chamber to re-gather herself. But if the look on Bethany's face were any indication, that would not be what would happen. Her aunt had questions, ones Katherine wasn't ready to answer.

"No, I think I'll stay downstairs," she said, and turned to the butler. "The duchess mentioned something about tea?"

He nodded. "I will call on a servant to take you."

"Oh, just give me the direction," Katherine said. "I know your staff is busy, I can find it."

The man looked relieved at her suggestion and quickly told her how to find the parlor. Then he and her aunt moved up the stairs so he could show her to her chamber.

Katherine took a deep breath. The first since she'd turned on the drive to find Roseford staring at her. She was trying not to panic about that fact, but now her mind was beginning to turn. She was here ten days. He was so intent on following her around, trying to...well, whatever he thought would fulfill that bet he'd made about her.

Trying to bed her.

She shivered and tried to tell herself it was in disgust, but she couldn't help but picture all those moments when he'd nearly kissed her. Old and new, merging together. Imagine those hard arms she'd had around her when they danced or when he escorted her up the stairs, that hard body that *had* to go with them. Imagine a man so well-versed in sin giving her a taste of it.

No matter what his motives were.

"Stop," she growled to herself, shaking away the thoughts.

She headed down a long hall and quickly found the open parlor door the butler had described. She stepped inside to find Adelaide sitting by the fire, a book in one hand, teacup in the other. She lifted her gaze as Katherine entered and smiled.

"You've arrived, wonderful!" she said, setting all her things aside and coming to briefly embrace Katherine. "How was your trip?"

"Uneventful," she sighed as she watched Adelaide go to the tea service to pour her a cup. "Until I arrived here and found Roseford on the drive watching me."

Tea sloshed from the cup Adelaide was preparing and the duchess turned, eyes wide. "What?"

"There was a miscommunication." Katherine said. "Abernathe invited Roseford in order to separate him from me. Somehow he didn't know Emma had done the same with me. And so we are both here. For ten days."

Adelaide set the teapot down, bent and opened a lower cabinet. She set a very expensive looking bottle of scotch on the top, then two glasses. She splashed the alcohol into both and handed one over.

"This calls for something much stronger," she said with a shake of her head. "Oh, Katherine. What do you think?"

Katherine tipped her glass and took a sip of the burning alcohol. "I think *you* know why I was invited here to be away from him. Isabel told you all about his bargain, didn't she?"

Adelaide hesitated a moment and then nodded. "She did. But it is only because we are all so close. Not a one of us would judge you for it. Though we as a whole do judge him. He will not find many friends amongst the duchesses at present."

Katherine smiled at the idea of this wall of women rising up before her in sisterly protection. She had not ever had that kind of support in her entire life. It was nice. Yet she didn't want to depend upon it. She knew from bitter experience that the husbands made the decisions. No matter how loving the dukes seemed to be with their wives, the men would take Roseford's side. They'd been friends with him for so long.

And eventually it would pull the duchesses away from her.

"I don't want anyone's relationships damaged by taking sides over me," she said. "In the end, I must deal with Roseford and his intentions myself. I know his goals, I do not think he would be the kind of man to force his desires on me."

"Never!" Adelaide said with a shake of her head. "I do not believe he would ever do such a thing. My husband would kill him, for one, and Robert is too self-preserving."

Katherine arched a brow at the strength with which Adelaide said the last. She seemed certain, although she couldn't be right. The Duke of Northfield was Roseford's friend. There was no way his reaction would be as strong as Adelaide described.

Katherine shrugged. "Then Roseford is not a danger to me physically."

"No," Adelaide repeated.

Katherine sighed. "The best thing I can do is ignore him. Do my damnedest to avoid him. It will be no different than it was in London."

Adelaide worried her lip. "Except that in London you were not under the same roof with him. And there were far more people to create a buffer between you. There will only be a handful of couples here except for when James and Emma have a ball, like they will tonight. Or a garden party, or something like that."

Katherine wrinkled her brow. "Are you trying to comfort me or make me run screaming from the house?"

Adelaide laughed and stepped closer. "No one wants you to run screaming from the house, I assure you. I was being blunt. Graham will tell you I do it a little too much, I fear. You are right, of course. Ignoring him is best. I doubt he's ever had a woman do that, especially one he is actively pursuing. It will serve him right."

Katherine chuckled as the pleasure lit up in her friend's eyes. "I suppose I hadn't thought of it that way. He has no idea I know of his intentions, his bargain, so his pursuit of me will go on as planned. And if I utterly ignore him, I will wound him, at least a little. That makes the entire endeavor seems a little more..."

"Wicked?" Adelaide supplied.

Katherine jolted at the word choice. Wicked was something else. Something heated. But she nodded. "I suppose there is a wickedness in teasing him so." She thought of the consequences of such a thing and shivered. "So perhaps what would be best is to confront him directly. Not about his wager, which I will never discuss with him. But just to tell him that I am not interested. That I don't want his attentions."

"That would likely send him away. If you were very blunt like that. And the duchesses will do whatever we can to assist you—don't hesitate to ask a one of us to be on your side for rescue or to plot against him," Adelaide said.

"Do you all hate him so much?" Katherine asked.

"No!" Adelaide's eyes went wide. "There is a big difference between being annoyed at him for being so unexpectedly cruel and hating him. In truth, he is a good man. He is very intelligent—he can match wits with anyone. Not just clever, you understand, which he is, but truly intelligent."

Katherine shifted. She had never liked a stupid man. Gregory had been rather...stupid.

"And he can be incredibly kind, supportive, loving. I have

watched him be so gentle with a friend when they are in need. He tries to pretend it away when he is caught, but there is a core of goodness to him. And yet...as the rest of the dukes marry, I think he feels increasingly isolated. He is the wild one of the bunch. The others joined him on his adventures in the past, tempered his worst impulses, perhaps. And now...well, he is in transition and it's obviously not the best for him. But no one in our circle hates him. And I hope you will not either, despite his awful bet."

Katherine had been silent, staring at Adelaide as she recited this warm and loving description of a man Katherine had hated for three long years. To hear him spoken of in such tones softened her a fraction, and she pulled herself up straight as she recalled his cruelty to her, not just in his wager, but in the interactions they'd shared so long ago.

She could not afford to do anything but hate him. And there was no way to say that to Adelaide or anyone else.

So she shrugged. "Well, I will call for help if I need it, thank you. Now, when is your husband expected?"

Just as she'd hoped, the change in subject lit up Adelaide. "Tonight," she said. "Though I'm not certain when. He may be here before the ball, but it might not be until after it begins."

"You must miss him," Katherine said, unable to be anything but happy for her friend at how deeply she loved her spouse.

"I do," Adelaide admitted. "Desperately, deeply. It is the longest we've been apart since our marriage, and I do..." She blushed a little. "Long for him. And the time, it goes so slowly."

"Well, perhaps I can help with that," Katherine suggested. "My aunt told me that Abernathe's property is one of the loveliest in all the country."

Adelaide nodded with enthusiasm. "It is. I see where you are going. Would you like to stretch your legs and have a turn about the garden to pass the time?"

"You read my mind," Katherine said with a smile.

Adelaide grabbed for her hand and squeezed before she rushed off to arrange for their bonnets to be brought. In that

THE DUKE OF DESIRE (1797 CLUB 9)

moment when she was alone, Katherine took a final sip of the scotch that had been meant to bolster her courage. With Roseford swaggering around this place, bent on seduction, she would need it now. More than ever.

CHAPTER SEVEN

Robert had to give Katherine her credit. She was adept at avoiding him. Here they were, eight hours after the full party had arrived at Abernathe, and she had neither spoken to him nor gotten near him. Despite a supper and now a ball, she was separate from him.

Except for looking at him. *That* she did. He'd caught her several times during the night, those dark eyes held on him with an unreadable expression.

It was disconcerting, really. This entire situation was. He'd come here to take a break from the woman. To do as his friends required and avoid her for a while. Avoid his wishes, his desires, which had nothing to do with some wager. In truth, he just wanted the woman. Once he had her, he was certain that desire would fade. It always had with other ladies. In fact, he hadn't been sure that ten days away from her company wouldn't kill the desire all on its own.

But here she was. Temptation in a pink dress that clung to her curves and accentuated her long, slender neck. She was a complication to his plans. He didn't like complications.

He turned away from her, focusing instead on the drink he pulled from a servant's tray as the man walked by. It was not strong enough by half. "Ridiculous."

He faced the dancefloor once more and jumped. Somehow, as his attention was elsewhere, Katherine had crossed the room to him and was now standing at his side, eyes straight ahead and focused anywhere but on him. He caught a whiff of that cinnamon scent of hers and his body reacted of its own accord to her presence.

"Your Grace, we must discuss our situation," she said, her tone very calm and careful.

"Must we?" he asked, unable to keep himself from laughing at this unexpected confrontation.

"Yes." Her tone was sharp and silenced his chuckle as she glared at him from the corner of her eye. "You told me today that you were brought here in order to be separated from me. So please don't sport with my intelligence by pretending that we do not have *something* to discuss."

He inclined his head in an attempt to acknowledge and apologize. She was clearly upset despite her tranquil tone. "I would certainly never sport with your intelligence, my lady," he said, then winked at her. "Other things, perhaps. But not your intelligence."

She faced him full on now and put her hands on her hips. That drew his attention to them, of course. Made him think about replacing her fingers with his, digging those fingers into her skin as he pulled her flush against him.

"You should not say such things to me," she said, her skin suddenly rosy red with emotion. "You forget yourself."

He arched a brow. "Is it I who forgets myself, or you?"

She shook her head. "What does that mean?"

"Of course there is a situation between us, Katherine," he said. "I don't deny it. But it may not be the one you think it is."

She lifted both eyebrows and her lips pursed in displeasure. "Do enlighten me, oh great Duke of Roseford who knows so much."

"I don't know anything," he said. "I see things—there is a difference. And what I *see* is that you have a scandal to overcome. Or at least you *think* you do."

"You think my husband…" Her cheeks darkened further. "…*dying* the way he did is not truly a scandal?"

"I don't think his death is the scandal." He smiled. "You see, my dear, a passionate nature isn't appreciated by Good Society. And yours has been revealed. So *that* is your scandal. The world knows you have wants and needs, things that wake you in the night, trembling and wet and shaking as you try to find release." Her lips parted and she stared up at him, hands trembling, eyes glassy and dilated with desire. He leaned closer, taking another generous whiff of that amazing smell of her hair. Her body. "Or am I wrong? Am I forgetting myself?"

She straightened her back and folded her arms, putting up that useless shield she wanted so badly. "I don't have to tell you anything."

"Of course you don't," he pressed. "Because I can already see it. A tiger knows another tiger if they're in a room of housecats. I see what you are. What I don't see is why you so desperately want to deny it. Deny yourself instead of embrace it."

She tilted her head. "And I suppose the way you define embracing this nature you see is by giving myself to you."

He smiled a little, but didn't respond. It was almost impossible not to. Almost impossible not to touch her and draw her into his embrace to let her feel what it could be like. This wasn't the time. Chasing her wasn't working—he had to make her lean into him now.

But she didn't. She glared at him and hissed, "I will never—"

She didn't finish her sentence. Instead, her gaze flitted past him. He turned. Graham was standing at the door to the ballroom. The footman said, "The Duke of Northfield," as an announcement.

He barely got the words out when there was a little cry from the crowd. As everyone watched, Adelaide rushed across the room. Graham started toward her and they collided midway through the chamber. Apparently oblivious to everyone else, he caught his wife in his arms and placed a kiss right on her mouth. Her arms came around him and they stood like that together for a moment. Far too long for propriety.

When Adelaide stepped away at last with a blush, there was no mistaking the tears on her joyful face.

Robert glanced down at Katherine, expecting that now that the spectacle had passed, she would return to railing at him. She didn't. She stood there, staring at the happy couple as they faded into the crowd of friends. Her face was no longer blank, no longer controlled.

It was twisted in a pain so powerful that it was palpable. Robert felt it in his gut as he watched her.

"Katherine?" he said softly.

She jerked her face toward his for a beat. Two beats. Then she shook her head. "I'm sorry, excuse me."

She said nothing more, nor did she wait for his response before she broke away from him and tore off through the crowd. He watched her exit the room and turned his face.

His purpose with this woman was seduction. That was all. He didn't care about her crumpled expression. He didn't care about the emptiness in her eyes that called to the emptiness in his own broken soul. He *didn't* care.

And yet he felt this foreign desire in his chest. Something unexpected and unwanted and unwarranted given his plans for her. He felt a need to follow her. To comfort her. To somehow soothe the pain in her face and in her heart.

And that had nothing to do with seduction or wagers or need. It had to do with something else.

He tried to fight it. Tried to ignore it and put Katherine out of his mind. But it didn't take sixty seconds before he swore and followed her same path out of the ballroom. He had to find her.

And once he did, perhaps he'd know what to do.

Katherine's hands shook as she staggered down the long hall and into the first parlor she found unlocked. She pushed the door shut behind her and moved across the room. The curtains were shut, so she shoved them aside and revealed a bay window that jutted out from the house. Stepping into the space there, she looked out into the moonlit garden and tried to breathe again.

Her eyes stung with the tears she didn't want to shed, with the feelings she didn't want to feel. She liked the duchesses. She truly did. And despite the fiasco of Roseford being here, she appreciated their attempts to assist her.

And yet, being around them made her so very aware of the emptiness of her life. They all had love, families, futures. The abstract of that was painful. The concrete? The very real exchange she had just witnessed in the reunion of Graham and Adelaide?

That was excruciating, for it highlighted all she had secretly wanted in her life. All she had been denied. All she had pretended didn't truly exist. And yet there it was, played out in color as Adelaide and Northfield rushed to each other in a reunion that didn't care who was watching.

She gripped the edge of the curtain with her fist and bent her head.

"Katherine."

She stiffened. Roseford. Of course he was here. To see her in this most vulnerable of moments.

"Oh, please," she whispered, hating how her voice cracked. "*Please* stop following me."

He was silent for a moment, then she heard him move closer. Felt him move. Felt his presence. "You are not on a terrace," he said, his tone very gentle. "I thought my not following you was limited to terraces."

She spun toward him. "Do you mock me?"

"No," he said, and to her surprise his normally cocky expression softened. With the edge off, he looked a different person, almost. Warmer, younger. "No. You were upset. I wanted...I wanted to know that you were well."

She blinked, for the hesitation in his voice told her he wasn't accustomed to such kindnesses. Which made her wonder why he was extending them now. Part of his never-ending game? Another chapter in his seduction? Pretend to care and make a fool of a lady?

She lifted her chin. "Stop troubling yourself."

He didn't leave, of course. He moved closer. Why did he have to keep doing that? Cutting off half the room, looming up in her line of vision like he was the only thing that mattered?

"Adelaide and Graham's reunion…it bothered you," he said softly.

She fought not to let the truth cascade over her face. She would not be vulnerable with this man. Not now. Now ever. "Of course not," she snapped. "Why would it?"

He arched a brow. "You are a *terrible* liar, Katherine."

"And you are a good one," she said, but some of the heat was gone from her voice. She was simply too exhausted by all of this to stoke it. "What is your point?"

He stopped moving then. It had been all she'd hoped for, and yet now that he stood, more than an arm's length away, she wished he'd edge closer. And she hated herself for that.

"You look and see their connection."

"Everyone sees their connection," she argued. "Everyone with eyes. They do not hide it."

"But it makes you long for something, Katherine," he said, his voice so soft it barely carried. "Something in your blood."

She tried to draw breath but found very little. The room felt off kilter now, hot. He was pressing into her boundaries without even touching her, and she found herself allowing it. Even though she knew how foolish that was.

"Their love," she blurted out, saying the one thing she doubted Roseford wanted anything to do with. "Who wouldn't be envious of that?"

He arched a brow and a shadow of a smile crossed his face. "That isn't what you feel in your stomach. That isn't what makes your hands shake at your sides as they are doing now."

Katherine glanced down and scowled at the betraying shudder of her fingers. She shoved them behind her back and glared at him.

"How long has it been since anyone touched you?"

She caught her breath at the direct, wildly inappropriate question. The one that made her legs shake beneath her gown, her thighs clench together with awareness of the wetness that was already pooling there.

"Y-you h-have no right," she gasped out, hardly able to say the words.

He stared at her a beat, then stepped closer once more, and now he could touch her even though he didn't. Now she could touch him even though she shouldn't. She looked up into his eyes, dark as pitch they were dilated so wide with desire. He was ridiculously handsome and she wanted him. She hated him and wanted him all at once.

"Unless you grant me the right," he said. "How long?"

She was backed into the alcove of the window now, her backside so close to the glass that she could feel the cold of it through her skirt. There was nowhere to run. Oh, perhaps she could push around him. He'd let her flee his presence.

But there was nowhere to run from the question. It would hang between them until she answered. And she did, voice shaking. "Since *his* death."

He nodded. "And how long since you were satisfied by a man?"

Her lips parted and any breath she had left in her lungs dissipated. He edged in closer, his body brushing hers.

"Before his death?" he asked, his fingers reaching up to trace her jawline. "Months? Years?"

She heard a gasp escape her mouth. Felt herself nod. Betray herself, give in to him. And he smiled, softly, gently.

"I can change that, Katherine," he murmured.

He lowered his lips and she tensed. They'd been here before. Twice. But he'd never kissed her. And then he was. His mouth pressed to hers as he caught her waist and gently pulled her against him.

His lips were soft and just as full as they looked from a

distance. He held them firm against hers, allowing a moment to pass between them where he let her become accustomed to his touch. She couldn't help the gasp, the sigh, that escaped her lips. They parted on it and he deepened the kiss.

His tongue breached her and she gripped for his arms to remain steady. He stroked her, tasting her, savoring her, drawing her in, coaxing her pleasure. In that moment, she understood, in a way she never had before, just why he had the reputation for pleasure.

This was pleasure. She'd never experienced anything like it, and it promised, darkly and sweetly, a deeper sensation if she surrendered. Just surrender. Her body screamed it, her mind pulsed at it, and he wrote it on her tongue with his as he cupped the back of her head with one hand and angled her for better access.

She was flush against him, lifting her hips even though she hadn't told herself to do so. She was gripping his sleeves in her fists, trying to mold herself tighter.

And on and on he kissed her, pressing her fully back against the window as he learned her mouth thoroughly.

What would have happened next, she had no idea. Perhaps she would have given herself to him. Perhaps they would have kissed until the world stopped turning. Perhaps she would have found the strength to turn away, to remember herself and their past and why she didn't trust him.

She didn't get a chance to discover what would happen. Behind them, there were voices in the hall. Muffled, but getting louder.

Katherine's eyes went wide and she pulled away from Roseford in an instant. "Someone is coming," she gasped out, hardly able to stand up straight when she was shaking so hard.

He shrugged. "Let them come."

She glared at him. "I have enough troubles," she growled. "Wouldn't *you* like to deepen them by having me found with the biggest cad in London?"

With that, she caught the edge of the curtains and yanked

them shut, closing them in together in the little alcove, blocking their view of the main parlor except for a sliver of space between the curtains.

The door to the parlor opened and Katherine watched as Graham and Adelaide staggered in together. They were kissing, more deeply and passionately than they had been out in the ballroom. Her hands dug into his hair, and long blond locks fell from the queue and around his handsome face as he shoved the door shut and pressed her hard against it.

Roseford leaned down and his hot breath swirled around the shell of her ears as he whispered, "In a moment, it will be too late to reveal yourself."

She glared at him and lifted her finger to her lips to silently hush him. He smiled, wicked, and then pointed to the part in the curtain fabric.

Graham was pressed against Adelaide, dragging her hair down around them. He only pulled away to smile at her. "Thank God," he murmured.

That elicited a giggle from his wife. She caught his lapels and dragged him to the settee.

"Good show leaving a room open for us," Graham panted as he flopped her onto the cushions and went down on his knees before her. They were half-hidden now, for the settee was faced partially away from the window. Katherine could see Graham inching her skirts up, see Adelaide's pretty stockings on long legs as he revealed her.

"As if I could wait once I saw you," she whispered. When Adelaide sat up and dragged him in for another kiss, Katherine caught a glimpse of her face. Pure love, deepest passion. Everything that stung Katherine with regret.

And yet she couldn't turn away. Nor could she ignore that Roseford was standing halfway behind her now, his body touching hers as they watched his friends through that dastardly narrow parting of the curtain.

Graham pushed Adelaide back and leaned in, disappearing from view behind the arm of the settee. But there was no doubt what he was doing as he draped one of his wife's long legs over a shoulder.

Adelaide let out a little cry in the silent room.

Katherine shut her eyes. This was wrong to look at. Wrong to spy. But it didn't matter if her eyes were opened or closed. She could picture Graham's mouth pleasuring Adelaide. Picture how a man's tongue would feel there where everything tingled right now.

Only it wasn't Graham she pictured. Great God, no. It was Roseford. She found herself leaning back, shamefully letting her body press into his. He was still for a moment, then his arms came around her from behind. One pressed into her belly, his fingers splayed. The other cupped her breast through the gown, and she ground back against him with a gasp.

He chuckled softly, then slid his hand up from her breast and covered her mouth with it. Not hard. Just a weight there that reminded her to be quiet. Reminded her that he was in control.

She opened her eyes, watching as Graham's broad shoulders moved, his hair popping in and out from behind the couch. Adelaide's breath was shorter and shorter now, her cries growing in earnest as her hands clawed at his shoulders.

Robert's fingers stroked at her stomach, slow and hypnotic, gliding up and down. And each time he stroked down, he went lower. The back of his hand caressed her hip, around to her thigh, and then he cupped her sex.

She froze and so did he. He was touching her. Through her gown, yes, but touching her nonetheless. She felt the weight of every finger. The warmth of his skin. The anticipation of what he would do with that talented hand.

Adelaide jolted, her toes pointing as she shook and her cries filled the room. Graham was wrestling with the placard of his trousers now, and Katherine turned her face so she wouldn't see his body. Roseford leaned in from behind and his hand moved away, replaced by his mouth. He kissed her, deep and probing as he lifted his hand against her mound. She ground back against him, pleasure arcing immediately. He lifted, fingers curling against her as he let his other hand slip beneath the bodice of her gown. He touched her bare breast and she shuddered against him, her sigh lost in his mouth.

Adelaide's sighs were not so lost. Katherine peeked out to find that Graham was now taking her, hard and fast. He let out a garbled groan and then he collapsed over her. Her hands smoothed over his back and their panting breaths were the only sound in the quiet room.

Roseford's hand stilled, he pulled away, his lips sliding to Katherine's neck as she froze. They'd be heard if they did anything now.

Graham flopped on the settee next to his wife. They were fixing themselves, tucking in, rolling down. Adelaide's hair would not be repairable, of course. But her wide smile told Katherine she didn't care.

"How is Maddie?" Graham asked, referring to their daughter.

Adelaide's face lit up. "She is well, as always. Beautiful. But she has missed you. I cannot wait to see the look on her face when she wakes to find you here in the morning."

Graham's smile widened. "I want to go upstairs and look in on her. Once I have, *wife*, I want to do what we just did all over again," he said as he leaned in to kiss her. "All night."

She pulled away, cupping his cheeks, searching his face. "And you don't care if everyone knows we snuck out so you could ravish me?" she asked, her tone laced with teasing and love and connection that made Katherine shiver.

"I would take it as a wound to my honor if they didn't think I couldn't wait to ravish you," he teased back. He got to his feet and tugged her to hers. For a moment, they stood, face to face, eyes locked. Then he leaned in and kissed her. It was gentler this time. "I love you."

She lifted on her tiptoes and kissed him harder. "You and you and you forever. Now take me upstairs."

He caught her hand and the two fled the room like young lovers, rather than a respectable duke and his bride of several years. Katherine remained where she was, frozen in place by their passion and their love. Unwilling to move away from the man who still had his hands on her.

"They closed the door," Robert said.

She nodded. "Yes."

He stroked his fingers between her legs. She rocked against him. "Say it again. Mean it. Or tell me no, Katherine, and I'll walk away."

CHAPTER EIGHT

Katherine licked her lips. Roseford was offering her two devilish options. Say yes and give herself over, even a tiny bit, to his schemes. His wager. Say no and walk away from the kind of passion he inspired. The kind she had just witnessed and longed for in the core of herself.

He was the first person who had ever told her that the longing wasn't wrong or dirty or something to cover in shame.

Could she do either?

"Say it," he repeated, his breath warm on her skin. "Say *something*."

She swallowed hard and turned to face him. In the dim light behind the curtain, his face was shadowy. Wicked. She should have backed into the light, away from all he would do and say and make her feel. Instead she caught his hand and gently lifted it, setting it against her bare neck, gliding it lower so it closed over her breast.

He shook his head. "It has to be yes or no, Katherine," he pushed. "I can't have questions. You have to tell me what you want."

"To come," she gasped out, her cheeks so on fire that she felt like she might glow in the darkness. "I want you to make me come."

His eyes lit up and he motioned his head toward the settee where Graham and Adelaide had made love. "Like he did?"

Her breath shuddered in. She had never had that pleasure, a man's mouth on her. She jerked out a nod. "Yes. Like he did. With his…his tongue."

He said nothing else. He teased no more. He simply used the hand on her breast to gently guide her through the curtain into the brighter parlor. He pushed her back onto the settee and she fell into place, staring up at him as he crossed to the door and locked it.

Her heart was beating wildly as he watched him stride back to her. He stood over her, blocking the firelight. A dark outline of male virility and promises of passion unlike any she'd ever known.

A promise of all she'd ached for and thought she couldn't have.

That was all this was. It didn't have to be anything more. It wouldn't ever be anything more. It was a moment, and she would walk away from him. She knew what he was—it couldn't be that hard.

He dropped down on his knees, like she'd watched Graham do with Adelaide. Slowly, he caged her in with his arms and leaned up, brushing his lips back and forth against hers until she parted them and offered herself. He chuckled as he took, kissing her once more. This time it was different, though. He traced her lips, flicked his tongue in. He was showing her how he would kiss her in that other place.

She squirmed at the realization, lifting to meet him, opening her legs to give him more space there. He ignored the invitations and just glided his mouth down her throat. Over the revealed skin below her collarbone. He traced the neckline of her gown, then put his hands beneath it again. He teased her nipple, lifting her, and suddenly the warm air in the room was against her skin.

She looked down and watched as he traced her exposed nipple with just the tip of his tongue. He looked up at her, smiling as he teased her. Smiling as she gasped with electric pleasure that jolted down between her legs and made her hot and needy for him.

He didn't linger, though. He crested lower, his mouth warm even through the silk of her gown as he pressed his lips along her stomach. He was hitching her skirts up as he did so. She felt the warmth of the fire against her calves, her knees, her thighs.

Finally, he pulled away and looked into her eyes. He held there, his expression daring her to refuse. Daring her to end this. She didn't. She couldn't. She was on fire and she needed him to extinguish the flame. To show her how because there was no way but him.

He caught her knees, cupping the backs of them with firm enough pressure that she felt the weight of every finger. He stroked her, making her body shake with sensation. And when she gasped out pleasure, he slid her forward on the settee. Her backside came to the edge and her legs fell open. He looked down at last, smiling as he saw her drawers. They were flimsy, silky things, and in this position they were parted so they did very little to cover her. Still, he tugged and they came off. He tossed them aside and she was bared to him.

She should have felt shame in that, she supposed. Her husband had seen her this way, of course. She'd always felt ashamed then. Humiliation came with the ache, she knew that.

But she felt none of that now. Roseford stared down at her, licking his lips, his eyes wide and his hand trembling ever so slightly as he reached out to trace her sex with just the tips of his fingers.

"So lovely," he muttered, she thought more to himself than to her. It didn't matter anyway, because when his fingertips stroked her naked flesh, her mind emptied of any questions, all concerns, all doubts.

She lifted against him, pressing his hand harder, forcing his fingers past her lips just a fraction and increasing the heat of his touch. He smiled, not mocking, but accepting. Pleased.

"You've waited a long time, I think," he whispered, almost soothing. "I won't make you wait anymore."

He bent his head. His fingers pressed her open, holding her in place. And then his mouth closed over her. She cried out at the heat of him steaming over that sensitive flesh. His tongue was firm as he pressed it to her, stroking her entire slit in one long lick.

She spasmed at the outrageous pleasure that ricocheted through her body. Her fingers dug into his hair, holding him steady, pushing him away, urging him on all at once. He smiled against her—she felt the expression. His hands held her still and he devoured her. Every lick woke that wicked part of her she'd always tried to hide, control, destroy. As if he knew that, he moved harder, faster, sucking her clitoris and sending her body to ever rushing heights.

But it was when he added his fingers that she lost all control. He glided two inside her long-empty sheath, stretching the channel, reawakening any pleasure she'd ever found from sex. She bucked against him, dropped her head back as the orgasm began from deep inside of her. He licked her through it, tormenting her with pleasure as she cried out again and again and again.

It was only when she went utterly limp against the settee, her shudders subsiding slowly, that he ceased his tongue's exploration, withdrew his fingers and stared up at her with a satisfied smile.

"I hope that was worth the wait," he said as he leaned over her body, kissing her. She tasted her release on his tongue, and her body quaked with renewed desire at that salty-and-sweet flavor.

He drew back and looked down at her, exploring her face like he was trying to see something, find something. And in that instant, her relaxed, lazy pleasure faded and was replaced by something else. She remembered what he was. Remembered what he wanted. He hadn't pleasured her as some selfless act. He wanted more. To win his little wager, to claim that he could have the woman who had killed with pleasure.

She pressed her hands to his chest and pushed. His brow wrinkled, but he drew back from her and watched as she got to her feet, shoving her skirts down and spinning away from him so she'd no longer have to look at that thick hair she'd mussed or those wet lips that had touched her so intimately.

"What is it?" he asked.

She refused to look at him as she moved to the mirror above the sideboard and looked at herself. She was still mostly in place, save for a few wrinkles in her gown and some strands of hair that had fallen from her chignon. But she was flushed with pleasure, her expression wanton. If anyone saw her...they would know. They would know what she did.

And even if they didn't, she would.

"Katherine," he said, sharper.

She faced him, forcing calm onto her expression. Forcing coldness and collected boredom, like what had happened meant nothing.

"*That* was a mistake," she said, hardly able to form the words.

His lips parted. "I'm sorry?"

"I was overwrought after what I witnessed," she explained, hating that her cheeks filled with color. "And swept away by...by everything. But I should not have allowed you such liberties, Your Grace."

He folded his arms, his irritation clear on his face. "I think it's a bit late for formality. Robert will suffice."

She tensed. She'd never thought of this man as anything but Roseford. Until now she hadn't realized how much that title was a safety net for her. A barrier. Robert was a man. A man who had pleasured her in a parlor with a hundred people just down the hall.

She didn't want to think of him as Robert.

"Roseford, don't make this harder," she said. "We did what we did. But it is not something we shall ever repeat."

She moved toward the door, tensing for the moment when he would follow. Would catch her arm. Would demand or yell or even force. After all, she had left him in a state. She'd seen the outline of his hard cock against his trousers. She knew what he wanted. What he likely thought he'd earned.

And yet he didn't do any of those things. He stood exactly where she'd left him, staring at her as she unlocked the door and fled the chamber. She was too cowardly to look back. Not just because she feared the rage she might find on his face.

But because if she did, there was a good possibility she would go back, fall into his arms, and give him the prize he'd wagered on. And that would be a colossal mistake. So she escaped, like a thief in the night, and had no idea what the consequences of her foolish surrender would be later.

Robert stared as Katherine left the room, her shoulders straight and her stride certain. He was…stunned. He'd spent a life as a libertine. Some used that word as a slur, but he'd always embraced it. Pleasure was not a negative, no matter what Society tried to argue. He gave, he received, no one got hurt. In fact, some were even advanced by their affiliation with him, found longer term lovers who provided well for them.

He didn't pursue women who were innocent. Partly because he had no interest in the noose of marriage. Mostly because he didn't think they could adequately make a decision about whether or not they wanted something they'd never experienced. Something that could ruin them.

And so, because he was choosy and careful, he had never had a lady refuse him. At least not like this. The occasional woman who was loyal to her current lover, certainly. But not an unattached woman who clearly wanted him. Not a woman to whom he had given oral delights upon a settee, certainly.

And yet Katherine had looked him in the eye, her stare as cold as ice, her tone even more bitter, and told him it was a mistake. That she didn't want him, at least not for more than what she'd already gotten thanks to his tongue.

She sounded like she meant it, too. Like she was dismissing a servant who had brought cold tea, not a man offering to be her lover. Offering to give her all the pleasure she could stand and more.

It was utterly confusing. The dichotomy of her vocal and enthusiastic orgasm and her harsh dismissal. The first was why he was still rock hard. Her body was a pleasure. She was so damned responsive. Just the graze of his hand or the touch of his tongue and she was arched beneath him, begging, panting, whimpering. He'd always like a woman who came hard. He liked watching his lovers take pleasure. That was nearly as satisfying as taking his own.

Now, as he relived those moments of her beneath him, his cock throbbed.

"Fuck," he muttered, exiting the room at a swift clip. He strode down the hall, up the back stair and down the hall to the room where he had been placed by Emma and James. He burst inside, barely taking in his surroundings. He kicked the door shut, moved to the bed and unfastened the placard of his trousers.

He spit on his palm before he stroked himself. His body twitched and he leaned against the high mattress with one hand as he worked his shaft swiftly and with purpose. When he shut his eyes, he pictured Katherine, leaning against him, her body gently grinding as they watched Graham and Adelaide's passionate reunion.

Katherine spread out before him, her sex glistening with desire as he bent his head to lick her. Her flavor still burst on his tongue, and he increased the pace of his hand as he relived the power of bringing her to powerful completion.

And then his mind took him to fantasy. Of sliding up her body and pushing into that sweet, still rippling channel. Of pounding into her until she screamed down the house. Of marking her with his mouth and his hands and pouring every drop of his release deep inside of her.

The pleasure he imagined in that act combined with the pleasure of his hand, and he grunted as his seed spurted from his cock, relieving, at least for a moment, the tension of need that Katherine had stoked in him down in the parlor.

When his mind stopped spinning, he pushed from his slumped position against the side of the bed and tucked himself back into place. He glanced in the mirror, tidying up his tangled hair, rearranging his twisted waistcoat. Eventually he looked like himself, rather than an animal who had just rutted out back.

He blinked at his reflection. In his own eyes, he saw need still there. He felt it in his edgy body. It wouldn't be satisfied until he felt Katherine ripple around him in powerful release.

An odd thing considering how he had been so soundly set down not a quarter of an hour before.

"Bollocks," he muttered, and exited the room to return to the ball and act like none of it had ever happened. If that was what Katherine was doing, he could certainly manage it.

And yet, he still needed to purge her from his blood. Which meant he had to figure out why in the world the woman hated him so much.

CHAPTER NINE

Katherine stood at the window in her chamber, looking out over the lovely view of the orchard. There was something soothing about that tangled grove of trees that were just starting to drop their leaves. As if she could just step into the sheltering darkness of their branches and disappear. Away from the prying eyes of Society, away from the watchful stare of Roseford and away from her own memories of what she had allowed him to do to her twelve hours before.

"Eat your scone, my dear!"

She turned from the scene outside and forced a smile for Aunt Bethany. She had been doting over Katherine since she claimed a headache the night before that had allowed her escape from the ball before Robert returned. Thankfully, she had been left alone since then.

Alone with her memories of last night. Her dreams. And this morning, alone with her hand. Not that she had been even remotely as satisfied with touching herself as she had been beneath his mouth.

Dastardly man.

"Honestly, you look as though you've seen a ghost," Bethany said, patting a seat at the small table in the corner of Katherine's room. "Sit down and eat before I request a doctor to check you for a fever."

Katherine pursed her lips and did as she'd been told.

Bethany gave the scone before her a stern glance, and Katherine laughed as she tugged a piece of the pastry free and popped it in her mouth.

"Good," Bethany said with a sigh. "And while you eat, I think you and I should have a talk."

"A talk?" Katherine said, pushing away troubling thoughts and trying to focus on Bethany. She always liked her talks with her aunt, though this one sounded ominous, indeed.

"I realize it is none of my business. After all, you and I have only been reunited as aunt and niece for a few years."

Katherine reached out to touch her hand. "And I feel close to you. You may speak to me about anything. Goodness knows we've talked about a great many intimate things in the past year since Gregory died."

Bethany cleared her throat and shifted in her seat. She glanced over her shoulder, as if she wanted to be certain the room was empty. "I have noticed several of your exchanges with the Duke of Roseford."

Suddenly the delightful scone tasted like sandpaper, and Katherine stared at her aunt in horror. She drew a few long breaths before she said, "I'm not certain what you mean."

"Back in London I noticed you talking to him once or twice. I realize you danced with him the night I did not accompany you. But that is London. I am thinking more of the exchanges I have witnessed between you here, since our arrival yesterday."

"Exchanges," Katherine said, trying to keep her tone light. "You make it sound like we have had our heads together for the twenty-four hours since our arrival. I have spoken to the duke all of twice."

Bethany nodded. "Yes, I suppose that is technically true. But I watched you when we arrived and he was on the drive. There was something about the way you two interacted. And at the ball last night, there was an intensity to your body language that I could not pretend didn't exist."

Katherine pursed her lips. Blast it all. She was only making things worse if her interactions with Robert felt intense to an observer. His reputation would do nothing to save her own. And if the truth of what they'd done in the parlor came out? Well, she was done for. She doubted that gaggle of duchesses downstairs would want her to be a friend if they knew she had opened her legs to him so willingly. They were too ladylike to accept that.

So was the rest of good Society.

"There is nothing to what you saw, or think you saw," Katherine said softly. "Roseford is no more than a thorn in my side, I assure you."

She had somehow expected Bethany to dismiss the topic when it was put in those terms, but instead her aunt's expression grew quizzical. "A thorn? How is that possible. You hardly know the man, don't you?"

Katherine froze. There she went again, placing importance on Roseford that could be misconstrued. Or perhaps seen properly, and that was worse. She shook her head. "I only mean he is a cad."

Bethany seemed to ponder that a while. "Yes," she said slowly. "He is that. He is known as far worse." Her aunt blushed deep red and Katherine felt her own cheeks heat as well. "But I don't know why he should upset you so with his behavior. Unless there is something between you that you might want to share with a most beloved confidante."

Katherine looked at Bethany, her expression that of deepest sweetness and light. She couldn't help but laugh a little at the look. And yet, she didn't want to say too much for fear of losing the only family she truly had left.

"You are looking for more scandal for me, aunt?" she teased. "Gracious, you'll have me banished before supper."

"No," Bethany said, taking her hand. "Of course not."

Katherine gathered herself with a sigh. "I assure you, *dearest confidante*, that I am not going to do anything to endanger myself socially."

"Well, that wasn't exactly what I meant," Bethany said with another strange expression. She pushed to her feet and walked away slowly to stare at Katherine's orchard.

"Then what?" she asked. "What could you mean except to warn me away from such a man?"

Bethany turned with a shake of her head. "If you were still a blushing eighteen-year-old debutante, of course I would throw up a wall between you and a man such as Roseford. But you aren't."

"Thank you?" Katherine said, wondering if she had just been insulted.

Bethany laughed. "I only mean that you have been married. You've been through hell thanks to that marriage. Oh, I'm explaining my thoughts all wrong. Let me start over."

Katherine stared as Bethany seemed to regather herself. Then her aunt said, "Your mother had a free spirit. She was lively and fun. Watching her be destroyed by the weight of your father's disregard was a nightmare. Especially when I was not allowed near her, or you, to offer comfort or advice."

Katherine nodded. "And that has to do with my situation...how?"

"I see her in you." Bethany reached out and touched her cheek. "Sometimes it steals my breath when I catch you from the corner of my eye and feel my sister is back with me. And it isn't just your lovely face or your eyes. It is your spirit. When you were married to the earl, I was happy to be allowed to reunite with you. But I was also devastated to see you crushed beneath a man's judgment the same way my sister was. His death was not something I grieved, I will put it that way."

Katherine gasped. "You never said anything."

"Because it is a terrible thing to think, let alone say out loud." Bethany shivered. "I shall surely have a place in hell for it. But that is something for another day. Right now, you are *free*, Katherine. Yes, there is a scandal, and I know that troubles you. Embarrasses you."

"Their whispers make everything seem so hopeless," Katherine admitted, blinking at the tears she just could not let fall for fear they would flood her entire life.

"But it's *not* hopeless," Bethany said. "You are in a unique position as a widow with a bit of money, that you do not have to rush back into the marriage mart. So you do not have to overcome your scandal immediately in order to save yourself from ruin. This gives you options."

"Options?" Katherine repeated, utterly confused.

Bethany's cheeks darkened again. "Options when it comes to what you would do with a man like Roseford. His reputation as a libertine does not include any cruelty. Nor abandonment of his obligations. What is whispered about him involves only the most wicked of pleasure."

"Bethany!" Katherine said, jumping to her feet and backing away.

Her aunt smiled. "I was married, wasn't I? As were you. Why should we not be a little more blunt about this topic?"

Katherine couldn't stop blinking. This was just another dream, brought on by the outrageous things she had done the night before with a man she considered an enemy. Her aunt was not truly talking to her about Robert and pleasure and what sounded like permission when it came to those other two things.

"What are you saying?" she asked. "I cannot even fathom what you are saying."

Bethany cleared her throat. "Well, to be indelicate about it…if the man has an interest in you…why would you not allow that to happen? You deserve some pleasure, some fun, after all your father and your husband put you through."

Katherine's mouth dropped open and she stared her aunt in the eyes as she gathered a bit of skin on her arm between her fingers and pinched hard.

"What are you doing?" Bethany asked in surprise.

Katherine shook her head. "Pinching myself because I know this must be some very odd dream. Perhaps I ate some bad fish."

"Of course not," Bethany said, coming across the room to her. "You are awake and so am I, and this conversation is very real. Why wouldn't you consider some kind of…oh, I don't know what to call it…"

"Affair," Katherine said. "You are implying you think I should start an affair with *Roseford*!"

"Why not?" Bethany asked.

"Because of his reputation and my own. Because I do not trust him, nor think that he can be depended upon. I know what he is, down to his core."

Bethany wrinkled her brow. "So you wouldn't marry him. Gracious, you don't need to think he is your prince if you are only going to bed him."

Katherine's eyes boggled. "Perhaps *you* had the bad fish. You are practically my guardian and you are encouraging me to fall into a shocking arrangement with one of the biggest libertines in all of England."

"And have a fine time doing it, I hope. Clear your head, heal your body. And come back to London for the next Season without the horrible events of the earl's death hanging over you."

Katherine shook her head. Her aunt was giving her the most dangerous kind of permission. To do exactly what her aching body wished to do. To do it without fear or judgment. To have what she wanted, something just for her…as Robert had said last night.

And yet Bethany didn't know about his cruel wager. Katherine wasn't about to repeat that particular humiliation, even to her aunt. So how could she both punish him for his past crimes against her and yet have exactly what Bethany was implying she could take? Was that even possible?

Was it even wise to have this conversation in her heart, in her mind, with her companion or just in her own head?

"Have I gone too far?" Bethany asked softly. "I see I've shocked you into silence."

Katherine blinked. "I suppose that I'd be lying if I said it wasn't something I'd *considered*. Roseford has been blunt about what he would want. I have been equally blunt in my refusal."

"Because you fear the consequences."

"Yes." Katherine shivered. "They are very great if this were to go wrong."

Bethany nodded. "They could be. But I would think that a person such as Roseford would know that better than most. If it is something you are considering, you might think about simply setting some boundaries with the man. Limits that will keep a new scandal from taking hold."

Katherine drew back. Boundaries. In a way, she'd already been setting those by utterly refusing his advances. *Almost* utterly. And yet Bethany was talking about setting a boundary that wasn't all or nothing.

But would Robert agree to that? If he wanted so desperately to claim her body, would he settle for an affair where he did not get to do that?

She smiled a little. If he did, he would do it with the idea he could convince her to surrender more. What tortures she could put him through. It would serve him right.

"I'll think about it," Katherine said.

Bethany smiled. "Good. Now, the Duchess of Abernathe said something last night about lawn games before a picnic. Why don't you come down and join the fun? Forget all about this troublesome subject."

Katherine nodded, but as she moved to find her bonnet, she knew that her aunt's last statement was incorrect. If Robert was amongst those playing games, there would be no forgetting anything. Especially since the possibility her aunt had just made her see would now play endlessly in her head until she decided what to do next.

Robert stood to the side of the bowling green, watching as the tournament Emma and James had proposed played itself out. He'd never been the biggest fan of the game, but he had to admit, he was having a fine time watching it all. Emma had insisted that the husbands and wives be separated, so the teams who faced each other were couples intermixed and squaring off against their spouses.

"Not fair!" Adelaide cried out as Meg leaned up to whisper something to Graham before he took his shot. "You two were engaged once—you ought not be on the same team."

Robert shook his head as the group of friends erupted into riotous laughter at that uncouth point. Two years ago, her words might have resulted in a fight, but today Meg stuck her tongue out at Adelaide. And her husband, Simon, nodded. It seemed love could solve all matter of problems.

"Emma put them together to give them an advantage because she fears the strength of *our* team, Adelaide," Simon said sending a fake glare toward Emma.

Robert stepped away from the group as they continued to bicker playfully, and when he did, he found a clear look at Katherine. She was standing on the other side of the field with her aunt. And she was looking at him.

But then, she had been doing that all day. Not an expression of anger, nor of shame…but something different. Something that felt like she was rolling an idea around, judging him for his fitness.

How he felt about that, he didn't know.

When she realized he was looking at her, she blushed and jerked her gaze back to the field. Graham and Meg had won the round and the couples were shaking hands. Now a new set of couples took their place. Katherine had been matched with James, while Baldwin, the Duke of Undercross, paired with Isabel as they began.

He watched Katherine play for a moment. James said something to her and she laughed. Robert's stomach clenched. She was very pretty when she laughed. She had hardly smiled at him. And yet James, who would never look at another woman outside of Emma, could inspire a laugh.

He didn't like being jealous, especially when it was so silly to feel that sharp emotion.

"Who do you think will go to the final in Emma's little

tournament?" Graham asked as he stepped up next to Robert and began to watch the round.

"She's stacked the deck, just as you implied," Robert said. "You and Meg will likely make it, against either James and Lady Gainsworth or Emma and Ewan."

Graham chuckled. "You wound me with your implication. It cannot be true that she thinks I'm such an inferior player that she would wish to play against me to win a nonexistent prize."

Robert shrugged one shoulder. "If the terrible aim fits."

They were both quiet a moment, then he cast a glance at Graham. His friend didn't know he and Katherine had spied upon his intimate moment with his wife. He had no intention of telling him, either. "I can't believe you did not protest being separated from Adelaide. Your reunion at the ball last night was..."

Graham glared at him. "Did our love intrude upon your sensibilities, my friend?"

Robert kept the smile on his face, but he felt the sting of the question, even if it was only meant as a teasing statement. In truth, that had been the hardest thing to watch for him, both in the ballroom and in the parlor. Graham and Adelaide's passion was obvious. Their love even more so.

"You and your love have nothing to do with me," he grunted, perhaps a little more sharply than he intended.

"You've had this same conversation with so many in our group," Graham said, pivoting to face him fully. "Are we going to do the same?"

Robert pressed his lips together in annoyance. "Why bother? I know every line of the song you are about to sing. *Be better, Robert. Be different. You don't belong anymore, Robert.*"

Graham shook his head. "No one feels you don't belong."

"Of course you do—you are a band of married men now. I do not doubt that Kit will join you once his father is gone and he has settled into his role of duke. So that will leave me. And some part of you all must bring me to heel."

"By asking you to be better than your worst impulses?"

Graham asked, his tone suddenly very gentle. Like Robert was a child who needed soothing.

The effect was the opposite. He stepped forward, holding Graham's gaze evenly. "You know what I'm doing right now?"

"Enlighten me."

"What I want. Perhaps that is difficult for all of you because you've placed yourselves in scenarios where you no longer have the ability to do that. To pursue your own pleasure however you see fit."

Graham arched a brow. "My pleasure is taken care of, thank you."

Robert bent his head, thinking again of Graham's expression as he made love to Adelaide. No one could say there wasn't pleasure there. Passion. All the things he'd told himself could not exist in a marriage.

"I'm so tired of everyone pushing me to fit into their mold," Robert spat. "So why don't we just skip it, eh?"

He didn't wait for Graham to respond. He turned on his heel and headed away from the party, down the hill toward the lakeside. He felt their stares as he disappeared from view. Felt their judgment, which he was certain would be discussed with clucked tongues once he was gone.

What he'd said to Graham was true. He felt himself on the precipice of losing his friends, his brothers. If he didn't want to fall over it, he would have to change. It was obvious his true self was no longer good enough. That what had once been seen as harmless, fringe behavior was now seen as reason for expulsion from their ranks.

Worse, that judgment sat in his chest like a rock. Made him question himself on the deepest level. Made him think of things he didn't want to think about. Hate himself the way he didn't want to hate himself because it made him feel like a man he despised.

He reached the lake and bent to pick up a stone. He was the champion of skipping rocks across the water. No one could beat him. But today when he tossed the rock out, it sank rather than skipped.

"Apropos," he muttered.

"Your Grace?"

He froze and turned. Coming down the hill was Katherine, her stride filled with purpose and her face lined with emotion. There was no doubt she was coming down here to lecture him. Her expression said that even before she spoke something more than his name.

And he was not in the bloody mood.

"Lady Gainsworth," he growled, picking up another stone and making a second attempt at skipping it. Failing again. "What is it?"

She stopped three feet from him and folded her arms. "We need to talk."

CHAPTER TEN

Robert tried to contain his suddenly bubbling emotions as he pivoted and glared at Katherine. His breath caught despite everything. Why did she have to be so beautiful? So alluring? So tempting? Why did his pursuit of her have to feel so…different? Beyond just the fact that she pulled away from it and from him, the way no other woman ever had.

"You know," he snapped, "for a person who wants me to leave her alone, you certainly keep popping up next to me enough."

She blinked at the aggression in his voice and stepped back a fraction. For a moment, he thought she might run. And part of him knew that would be better for them both. Something dangerous was happening here. For her. For him. Cutting it off would be best for all involved.

But she didn't run. Instead, she swallowed hard and an intriguing steel entered her expression. A strength that increased her beauty even more than her smile had earlier. Something that made him lean in a fraction, against his will.

"You and the Duke of Northfield were having an intense conversation," she said. "I think I deserve to know if you told him about what you and I…what we saw last night."

Her hands were shaking, despite her strength. Her voice, too. But beneath her fears and the courage to overcome them, he saw something else. Her gaze slid over him, her cheeks pinkened.

Desire was there. Crackling between them despite his annoyance at being seen at this vulnerable place and her refusal to surrender the prize he desired.

"You want to know if Graham is aware that you and I made a show out of him fucking his wife?" he clarified, enjoying how she blushed dark before she turned her face at his crude description. "Or that you rode my tongue to completion afterward?"

She caught her breath. Her gaze refused to return to him. "I suppose *yes* to both. My reputation relies on some secrecy being maintained about what we…shared."

He shook his head. Her *reputation*. Her bloody reputation. Fuck, *his* reputation. He was tired about talking about any of it.

"You'll be pleased to know that you did not even come up in conversation, my lady. Nor did our little observation party in the parlor last night." He sighed. "Graham wanted to talk to me about what a disappointment I am. Which has been true since long before you returned to Society."

As soon as he said the words, he wished he could take them back. They were laced with a pain he'd always kept private. A fear he didn't reveal to anyone and only allowed himself to feel in the most private of circumstances.

Now he had laid it bare, and from the way her expression shifted, she understood what he meant. Understood what was beneath his words. He felt more stripped naked than he ever had with any lover. Revealed on a core level that could never be unseen.

"Oh," she said, the pepper gone from her tone now. Replaced by something softer.

"Is that all then?" he asked, turning away from her and picking up another rock. He pitched it and it sank like all the others. Somehow that made this worse.

She cleared her throat. "I'm—I'm sorry if you quarreled with your friend. I can imagine that is difficult, considering how close everyone knows you are."

He squeezed his eyes shut at that observation. "They are close to each other," he muttered. "They tolerate me."

She caught her breath, and suddenly her hand closed around his arm. He opened his eyes and glanced down, staring at the fingers that now clenched his forearm, denting the line of his jacket. Slowly, he lifted his gaze to her face and found an expression he'd never seen on her face. At least not when she looked at him. There was no disdain. There was no wall there between them.

There was only empathy. As if she could understand being cut away, feeling like an outsider with the only people he'd ever considered family.

"I'm certain that is not true," she said, her voice soft in the quiet by the lake. "Roseford, every person in your circle who has spoken to me about you has done so with great *love*. You must know that and not feel that whatever upset they may be experiencing about you now and again is not a permanent affliction."

He hated how those words soothed him, hated that a little peace entered his wild heart when she touched him as she was now.

As if she sensed that, she pulled her hand away and he was briefly bereft.

She bent and picked up one of the rocks by the shore. He stared as she threw it and it skipped once, twice, three times before sinking beneath the surface.

She glanced over to find him staring and shrugged one shoulder. "My cousins taught me when I was a girl."

He arched a brow. "Perhaps Emma could arrange a rock skipping contest. We'd enter you as a ringer."

She bent her head with a laugh and he tensed at the way that sound settled him even further. He didn't want that. Not with her. Not with anyone. If she could give peace, that meant she could take it away. Not a risk he wanted to take, because he knew how badly that could all end.

He folded his arms and hardened his heart and his tone in

equal measure. "But I don't think probing into my personal life or skipping rocks is why you hustled after me this afternoon, angling to get me alone."

The smile on her face, that first one that hit him in the gut like a sledgehammer, fell away and a flash of hurt replaced it before she hardened herself as he had. The walls between them returned, erected by them both.

"I didn't angle to get you alone," she said, her tone sharp again. "You are wrong to suggest otherwise."

He tilted his head. "You followed me down a hill away from the others. What would you call it?"

Her lips pressed hard together and she shook her head. "I only wanted to speak to you. Don't you think we must after what happened between us? We will be here together for more than a week. We cannot simply stay in opposite corners, can we? Clearing the air is the…the only option."

"Not the only one," he growled. "And not the one you actually came here to pursue."

"You think you know my mind?" she asked, laughing again but this time with no pleasure. "Do edify me."

"You followed me here to wave your arms around and preach to me about reputation and propriety. You came to pretend that you didn't want last night, just as you did immediately after your orgasm faded. You came to order me not to do anything like that ever again, even as you stare across the bowling green at me like I was some sweet treat you wanted to…" He leaned in and took a whiff of her spicy scent. "Lick."

The wall she had built a moment ago crumbled as he said that. The desire she felt flared high, mixed with that contempt that crossed her face whenever she looked at him. Her breath caught and she shook her head. "You couldn't be more wrong, Your Grace."

He lifted his brows. "No. Did you come to rut with me by the lake, then?"

"No," she said. "Last night I *did* tell you what we did could never be repeated. I believed it at the time. But the more I have…" She trailed off with a blush.

"Don't stop now," he said with a wave of his hand. "Do continue."

"The more I pondered what we did, how it made me feel, the more I have wondered if it is something I could experience again. With you. No matter how wrong that desire might be."

Katherine shifted as Robert stared at her in utter silence. She thought it might be *shocked* silence, and that was something she couldn't help but be proud of. Roseford was jaded, everyone knew that. He practically wore it as a badge of honor. A cloak of protection. But in that moment, *she* had shocked him into silence.

He overcame it at last and said, "I want to be clear on this. Are you saying you would consider trysting with me again?"

She drew a long breath. Her mind took her back, to her father, who had cursed what he called her nature. To her husband, who had used that same nature for what he desired, but never given much in return. To her aunt, who had just hours before given her a sort of twisted permission to take what she wanted, just this one blessed time.

And she thought of the ripples of pleasure this man had drawn from her. Almost effortlessly and without demanding she give him something first or in return. Even now that wasn't what he taunted her with or asked her for.

Her pleasure hadn't come with a price, despite the bargain she knew he'd made. Or at least it hadn't yet.

"Yes," she said, answering his question at last.

He blinked at her and his expression of confusion would have made her smile if she weren't shaking so hard in pure terror at what she had just admitted. To this man, of all men. Even knowing what he wanted from her, even knowing why.

She still said yes because there was no other word to say.

"What?" he asked.

She placed her hands on her hips. "Of course you would make me spell it out. Very well. I *want* something. Something just for me. But I'm not certain you would honor that, nor allow it."

"Something just for you," he repeated slowly. "You are talking about your pleasure given without mine taken."

She nodded, shocked that he would even say those words. "Yes. Something that is all for me. And yet I doubt that I can trust you with that need. You would demand. *Take*."

He arched a brow. "You mean like I did last night?"

She flinched at the sarcasm that dripped from his tone. The vulnerability and warmth she had sensed in him when she asked him about his friends was gone. Back was the hard man. A man she realized was pulsing with emotion just beneath the surface.

But that didn't matter to her. He *couldn't* matter.

"Are *you* saying you would even consider entering an affair with me that wouldn't involve…full completion for you?" she asked.

His eyes widened, and there was no denying the concern that flashed over his face. And yet he didn't deny her out of hand, which meant he was contemplating her outrageous demand. Despite the bet he had made to have her fully. One he couldn't win under her terms.

And *that* would be a little punishment alongside her own pleasure. Yet she couldn't smile about that fact.

"I could consider it," he said. "If I would be allowed to try to convince you otherwise."

"Force, or convince?" she asked, setting her feet wider, as if she might have to fight. It felt like she did.

He shook his head. "*Convince*," he repeated. "Great God, Katherine, whatever monster you have built me to be, know that I have never and would never, *never* force you or any other woman to do anything she did not wish to do. Any man who does that is a craven coward who deserves the most brutal of punishments."

She drew back at the flash of fire in his dark stare. The anger that bubbled up past the carefree exterior, just as his pain had earlier. She wondered where it all came from, those emotions he was usually so capable of controlling.

"Very well," she said. "In truth, I've never heard anything untoward about your behavior with any woman. That has never been your reputation, nor has it been what I've observed myself."

"Observing me, were you?" he asked, giving her another of those cocky smiles. When she glared at him, he laughed. He seemed to like sparring with her. And some small part of her liked it, too. "What you've asked leaves me a great deal to consider."

She swallowed. "Yes. Despite it being my suggestion, it is not a decision easily come to. If we were to enter into some kind of…arrangement, there are risks, more for me than for you I think."

"Then perhaps we should take the rest of today to consider those risks, and the benefits." He stepped toward her. "Come to my chamber tonight, after you've thought about it." He winked. "Or should I come to you?"

She set her jaw. "For all the world to see and for you to crow about?"

"You truly despise me."

"You make it easy to do so."

She waited for him to argue with her or try to excuse himself from his behavior. Instead, he reached out a hand and traced the line of her jaw with his fingertips. She shivered at the touch, so gentle and yet so heated as he held her gaze with his dark one.

"That must create quite a conflict in you, my lady," he whispered. "To want what you hate. In truth, it isn't the worst thing in the world. Passion is passion, and what you feel could make things all the more…intense. If that helps you make your decision."

She wrinkled her brow. He wasn't even trying to make her

like him. He wasn't defending the indefensible or telling her some story to get what he wanted. There was an honesty to his interaction with her. A space for her to feel whatever she felt without judgment.

She wasn't certain anyone else in her life had ever given that. And it felt so dangerous now, because she wanted to lean into it, give herself over to it. Forget everything she'd experienced with this man, everything she knew about his motives, and just…bathe in his experience and his passion.

She stepped away from him and from that wild desire. "If I want this, I'll come to you," she said.

She turned on her heel and walked away from him. And just like he had the night before, he let her go without comment or attempt to control what she would do. He just watched her go.

She crested the hill so she was out of his sight and saw the party just ahead. She had to gather herself now, forget the conflict that Roseford had stoked in her, at least for a while.

She doubled her efforts to do that as Meg came racing down from the bowling green, with a wide smile on her face. "There you are! James was about to send out a search party rather than forfeit. Your next round is about to begin."

She forced a smile. "Excellent, and I am ready."

Ready to play games. But not the ones Emma had set up for the party's enjoyment. If she understood anything now it was that she was about to enter a very dangerous game with the Duke of Roseford.

One she had to win.

CHAPTER ELEVEN

Robert entered the dining room at the end of the group of his friends and scanned the table for the arrangement. He smiled as he saw his name card and stepped over to stand just beside Katherine.

She jolted as he caught the back of her chair and gently slid it out for her. "My lady."

For a moment her lips pursed, and then she actually smiled as she took the place he offered and watched him settle in beside her. "Your Grace. Not that I am complaining, but I find myself a little surprised that you and I would be seated together, considering we were each invited here in an attempt to avoid the other."

"I will tell you a little secret," he said, leaning in close to her ear and just controlling himself from pressing a kiss there. "*I* moved the arrangements so we would be placed together."

She pulled away and stared at him. "You did not!"

"It's why poor Emma is glaring daggers at me at the end of the table," he said, and leaned around Katherine to wave at their hostess. Emma shook her head, but there was undeniable mirth to her expression. "She tolerates me."

Katherine placed her napkin in her lap. "I suppose every court needs its jester."

He snorted out a laugh of surprise at her cheeky retort. "You think that is what I am?"

She shrugged. "You are entertaining, that is certain."

"I can be," he said, arching a brow toward her. She blushed, as he hoped she would.

Her gaze dropped to her empty plate. "I may regret asking this, but is *this* your version of allowing me space to consider our arrangement?"

He frowned at the lilt of desperation that was in her tone. He'd heard it earlier, too, when she talked about being controlled or forced. He could imagine there had been little choice in her life. That was the way for ladies in any rank. He had watched it many a time, sometimes far too closely.

"We spent an afternoon in opposite corners," he said. "Though I did heartily applaud your win with James in the bowling tournament."

She laughed again and her face relaxed. "Thank you. I think the mantle of champion may be a hard one to bear, though. Graham and Meg have already challenged us to a rematch, claiming the windy weather was the reason for their failure."

He nodded with false solemnity. "Yes, I can see that. They're both rather competitive souls. I assume we will witness a battle royale over the next week or so."

"So you think an afternoon is enough space?" she asked, returning to the subject she had broached earlier.

He turned a little to look at her more directly. "Katherine, everything doesn't have to be about some arrangement. You and I are two of the only people at this party who are not married. And I happen to find you very charming. As I know you find me, else you wouldn't despise me so much."

She drew a breath. "Is that your logic? What does that even mean?"

He smiled at the laughter in her tone. "Finding me so utterly delightful is what makes many a person hate me. The emotion is just too intense."

Her smile fell a little and she turned her face. He watched her. *That* had struck a nerve, even if he'd meant it as a foolish statement. So, whatever she felt or desired was too intense for her. It frightened her.

At least they were the same when it came to that. The intensity with which he wanted this woman was not easy for him, either.

"Let us put it this way," he said gently. "Why don't we try to be friends, no matter what we decide to arrange outside of the public eye?"

She hesitated a moment, worrying her napkin in her lap as she pondered that suggestion. Before she could respond, the Duke of Tyndale, who was seated across the table with Isabel at his side, leaned closer.

"I'm sorry, my lady, is this gentleman bothering you?" He said it with a wink, a tease, and Robert smiled at him. The two of them had shared that terrible little exchange before they left London, but Matthew was not one to hold grudges. He'd accepted Robert's written apology and his gaze held no inkling that he was still upset.

That was a relief, at least.

Isabel shot Robert an uncertain glance, but she didn't seem angry either.

Katherine laughed. "Only in the slightest way, Your Grace, I assure you. I was just telling him what an entertaining gentleman he was. I assume you must have stories to prove that point."

Matthew arched a brow and his expression grew wicked. "Stories about Roseford? Oh, there are *dozens* of those. Let me think of the one that will humiliate him most."

"When he lost his clothing at your father's ball," Charlotte offered from down the table with a sly look at Robert. "That is my favorite. I think it is Ewan's, as well."

The Duke of Donburrow grinned and nodded, signing a few words. Charlotte took a breath to translate, but Robert lifted his hand. "I'm certain I know exactly what my friend was going to say. No need to translate."

Charlotte laughed and the rest of the table now joined in. Robert shook his head. These were the moments when he felt so at home with his friends, his family. At a time when he was alone, frightened, uncertain, heartbroken, they had loved him despite all his faults. And their shared memories of their youth buoyed him on days when everything just felt…heavy.

"Well, do tell the story," Katherine encouraged as their first course was laid out by the servants. "It sounds the perfect way to bring the duke down a notch or two."

"I will start by saying that I was told there would be swimming the lake sans clothing," Robert said. "And that *all* my friends would be participating."

Matthew grinned. "We did tell you that, yes."

Ewan signed a few things and Charlotte smiled. "Ewan says that you were very happy to leave that stuffy party and that was when the plan was hatched."

Robert glanced over to find Katherine staring at him, appraising as she ate and listened. "How many at the party?"

Matthew leaned back and seemed to be trying to recall. "It was the annual summer soiree. That has always been my mother's crowning achievement. How many attend, Isabel? A hundred?"

"About a hundred and fifty earlier this year," Isabel said. "I have not heard this story, so I am as on the edge of my seat as you are, Katherine."

"So they tell me we are going swimming au naturale," Robert continued. "Unsurprisingly, I am all for the idea. When offered the choice of something wicked or something staid—"

"Always choose wicked," Baldwin finished with a side glance at his wife that turned Helena's cheeks pink. "Not a sentiment I always agreed with but find much more merit in now."

"We went to the lake and everyone ducked behind bushes. I had no idea why, but I stripped down to what God had given me and turned to see what in the world was taking everyone else so long…"

"Only to find my father and fifteen of his cronies standing there with drinks and cigars in their hands." Matthew began to laugh. "Mother *hated* when he smoked in the house, so she had banished his friends outside, and Papa was thrilled to show them the new boat dock that had just been built there."

"Which *he* knew about," Robert said, pointing at Matthew with an accusing shake of the head.

"But the best part," James said, his eyes watering from laughing so hard, "was Robert's reaction. What was it you said?"

"Well," Robert said with a wink toward Katherine. "I was standing there, shocked to have all these very proper, very *old*, very disapproving faces looking back at me. What else could I say?"

"Did you apologize?" she asked.

"No," he said. "What fun would that have been? I asked who wanted to join me and said the last one in lost a shilling. Then I got in the water."

Katherine tilted her head back, and her peals of laughter filled the air with the rest of them. "The gall," she said, swiping at the tears streaming down her face. "What Tyndale's father must have thought!"

Matthew's expression softened and he and gave Isabel a loving glance. "Oh no, my father had the best sense of humor of anyone. He turned to the group and asked if there were any takers. I think a few of the gentlemen considered it even. But eventually they went inside and we came out of the bushes."

With that first story told, the table continued sharing their exploits of the past. Since, aside from Katherine and her aunt, everyone here was part of their greater 1797 Club family, there were things told that might not have been recalled in Society as a whole or with too many strangers in attendance.

Robert watched as Katherine took part it in all. She laughed at the right parts of every story or threw in a witty comment that brought the rest of the party to even more laughter. She asked questions and seemed truly interested in whoever was speaking at any given moment.

It was impossible not to like the woman. That was what he discovered as their supper went on. She was so sharp witted and unfazed by anything she heard. It seemed passion was part of her very nature. She laughed with it, she ate with it, she glanced at him and there it was, bright in her dark, sultry eyes.

And there was no denying her beauty. It seemed to increase the more comfortable she became with his friends. She relaxed, her walls dropped and there was a glimpse of the real woman beneath the shame she had carried into Society. The hesitation she showed with him.

The dessert plates were at last taken away and their party began to rise, separating off so that the men could take their port before they joined the ladies for whatever entertainment would follow that night.

Robert shook off his thoughts on Katherine as she stepped away, linking arms with her aunt as the ladies left in a giggling, chattering group.

"Hmmm," Matthew said as he came around the table and nudged Robert with an elbow.

Robert jerked his attention from the spot where he'd last caught a glimpse of Katherine. Matthew looked awfully smug. "Hmmm? What hmmm?"

Matthew shook his head. "Oh, nothing. Just observing you, that's all."

Robert narrowed his gaze. "Oh, that's all, is it? And what do your observations reveal, Tyndale?"

Matthew laughed as he gently shoved him toward the door. "Nothing I'm inclined to share yet. Now let's get to the port, shall we?"

Robert fell into step beside his friend, letting Matthew talk about something to do with his estate as they followed their friends to James's study for their drinks. But he felt a strange discomfort as he did so.

Like something had been revealed that he hadn't wished to share. A genie had been let out of a bottle and he had no idea how to put it back where it belonged, nor what would happen now that it was on the loose in his world.

Katherine stood up from the chattering group of ladies and walked to the sideboard to refresh her glass of sherry. At least it gave her something to do. Since the men and women had separated, not even the lively, friendly conversation of her aunt and her new friends could adequately distract her.

She kept watching the door, anticipating when Robert would return. It was a strange thing. When she saw him the night of her return to Society in London, she had wanted nothing more than to flee from him. Her memories of the night on the terrace when her father had decided to marry her off added to other thoughts of Robert, things he didn't even seem to remember, she had wanted distance.

And when she found out he had wagered on bedding her? Oh, she could have clawed his eyes out. But since then, since coming here, she had begun to see him in a different light. Of course, there was their passionate encounter in the parlor the night before to consider. But it was more than that.

There was more to *him*. She couldn't stop thinking of the emotion he had shown her earlier in the day. Or that fact that he didn't demand reciprocity for the pleasure he had given her the night before. And the stories told by his friends were all charming, revealing a side to the duke that went far beyond cad. He was cocksure, certainly, but he was also clearly loyal and loving to his friends.

Which left her conflicted and confused and longing for the arrangement he kept telling her they could make.

"If you want something stronger, I have other options."

Katherine jumped and turned to find Emma standing at her elbow. Katherine blushed, for she realized she'd been standing there, holding the bottle of sherry, just staring at the door for heaven knew how long.

"I must have been woolgathering," she said, tilting the bottle and filling her glass at last before she offered the same to

Emma. She shook her head with a little smile.

"I wanted to tell you again how happy I am you joined us. I know you came in part to avoid Roseford, and I do apologize again for the misunderstanding. But it seems you two are getting along."

Katherine ducked her head and hoped that her blush wasn't too revealing. Emma was one of the quieter duchesses, but she had the impression that the pretty woman was always watching and listening. "We are making the best of the situation," she said at last.

Emma nodded. She said something then, but Katherine didn't hear it. At that same moment, the parlor door opened and the gentlemen streamed back inside, filling up the room with masculine presence and laughter. The last to enter was Robert and his gaze scanned the room until he found her. He nodded a fraction, then entered the room and crossed to speak to the Duke and Duchess of Sheffield on the opposite side of the chamber.

"I want to say something," Emma said softly. "And it is violating the bounds of our very new friendship. But if I don't, I will worry about it."

Katherine shook off her obsession with Robert and refocused on Emma. "Oh, that sounds dire. Please, do say whatever you need to say."

Emma glanced across the room and Katherine blushed as he realized she, too, was looking at Robert. "Roseford is a good man, beneath it all. I believe that. But he is…fire. And that can be a very good thing, many of my friends have married fire and learned to dance within the flame. But if you don't learn, fire can still burn. Do you…understand what I mean?"

Katherine stared at the duchess, taking in her words and trying to find a response that didn't reveal too much or put her on the outs with her new friends. None of them could truly understand, after all, what she was about to do.

"I can fight fire," she reassured Emma. "You needn't worry about me."

Emma wrinkled her brow, but James said her name in that

moment and she excused herself before the conversation could continue. Katherine took a breath as she departed, happy for the privacy as long as it would last.

Emma wasn't wrong that Robert was fire. Katherine had felt that fire, never more than last night. But she had no intention of fighting it, not anymore. She just had to figure out how to dodge the flames to get only what she wanted and not a bit more.

CHAPTER TWELVE

Katherine's hands shook as she made her way down the dark and empty hallways of the guest wing of the house. Robert had whispered which room was his as everyone was saying their goodnights, and now she counted doors from her chamber to his as she prayed no one would come out of any of them.

Not that it seemed likely. The rooms were filled with dukes and duchesses, and in the quiet of the hall, she sometimes heard murmurings from behind the doors. Even little moans.

All it served to do was put her on edge in the most shocking way.

At last she reached the seventh chamber from her own. She had to smile, as it was almost as far removed as they could be from each other in this wing. Emma was true to her word that she'd been trying to separate them.

And yet here Katherine was, standing in front of the beautifully carved door, ready to knock and place herself in the immediate path of a man who knocked her off kilter. A man whose actions had led to her marriage years before, a man she had tried to hate for that.

A man she knew she couldn't trust because of his wager, his reputation, his...everything. And yet if she knocked and gave him just a little, she could take so much more. Take the pleasure she'd sought all through her marriage. Take the wickedness she'd been told was her nature. Take the sensations she had experienced last night at his hands and tongue.

"Just don't forget to take," she muttered, and finally forced her shaking fist to tap the wooden surface before her.

It took him less than a minute to answer the knock. When he opened the door, her breath vanished. He was undone. His jacket, cravat and waistcoat had been discarded. His shirt, too, and now she was staring at an expanse of muscled perfection like nothing she'd ever seen before.

Being a libertine normally meant overindulgence in everything under the sun. Clearly Robert did it very differently, for his body was carved from stone.

He could not have been more different from her husband, and she stared because she couldn't look away. Slowly she forced herself to look at the rest of him. His hair was mussed. His trousers slung low on his hips, revealing the most fascinating curves and lines. He was wearing no boots.

And he was smiling at her. Not smug, not challenging, not even teasing. It was a smile of...welcome.

She gaped, trying to find something clever to say to break the tension when her mind was now entirely empty. He didn't wait for her to find words, he simply caught her hand and drew her into the room.

He released her and then turned, locking them into the chamber, locking out the world that would judge her for what she was here to do. Now it was only the two of them.

"You came," he said softly.

Well, now she had to find her voice, for it was clear he expected some kind of response beyond gaping at him like a fish out of water. She swallowed hard and forced herself to say, "I think you knew I would."

"Drink?" he asked, motioning to a little table in his sitting room. There was a bottle of scotch there.

Normally she was not a fan, but in that moment, she needed liquid courage. "Yes," she squeaked.

He moved to the table and poured them each a portion, then turned back to hand over the glass. When she'd taken it, he tilted it toward her in salute. "To tonight."

Her scotch sloshed as she tried to make it reach her lips. She hated herself for revealing how nervous this made her.

"Katherine," he said, setting his glass aside without drinking. He moved closer and took her glass, too, placing it beside his and taking her hands. "Relax."

She blinked up at him, outlined in firelight. Standing in his chamber, he felt so big. So all-encompassing. All the emotions she'd ever felt toward him crowded in together, shouting for her attention and memory. And above it all was the loudest voice that screamed *desire* and *whore* at once.

When his hands gripped hers, when his thumbs smoothed over her flesh gently, the cacophony faded a little. She swallowed. "How can I?" she asked.

"Sit down, please," he said, drawing her toward the settee in the middle of his antechamber.

She blinked in confusion. The door to his bedroom was in her line of vision behind his head. She could see the bed over his shoulder. And yet he wasn't hustling her in there to get this job done. It was very confusing.

"You must be filled with regret asking a ninny such as me to come to your chamber in the middle of the night," she said, turning her face.

"On the contrary, I am very happy you came," he said. "I worried as the night went on that you had changed your mind."

"I almost did," she admitted. "I stood in my chamber for three-quarters of an hour after the party retired, trying to convince myself what to do. You can see my wanton side won out in the end."

He frowned and his dark gaze searched her face carefully, closely. She tensed beneath the unexpected regard that had nothing to do with desire. There was something else there. Something she didn't want to experience or see.

He drew a breath and touched her chin, tilting her face so she was looking at him. Then he asked her a question she would never have expected in all her life. A question she had been avoiding for months.

A question he had no right to ask and yet he did, his face close to hers.

"Katherine, what did he do to you?"

Beneath his fingers, Katherine jolted, and Robert watched as her facial expression went utterly flat. It was a defense mechanism, of course. He'd seen her use it in the ballroom the first night she reentered Society. Put up a shield to the pain.

But he knew from bitter experience that the shield didn't soothe the underlying agony. It just kept the world out, for good or for bad.

"Why do you want to know about *him*?" she asked. He noted she didn't seek clarification. There was only one him.

He shifted. It was a good question. This entire endeavor, the pursuit of this woman, it was for his pleasure. And his ego, if he recalled the wager that seemed so far away. He was not meant to dig deeper. He never did. And yet here he was, pressing her to develop the connection.

The *why* was more complicated than he was willing to admit. Not even to himself.

"You want something from me," he explained softly. "And I want to give it to you, more than you could possibly understand. If I understand your physical past better, then it will help me understand your needs, as well."

"And use what I tell you against me." Her chin tilted up, defiant, accusatory. "How could I *ever* trust you?"

He bent his head closer, drawing in that cinnamon scent. Driven by a need to know more about her even if that scared the hell out of him. "I swear to you on—"

She interrupted him with a laugh that cut through the quiet. She backed away. "There is nothing you could ever swear on, Your Grace."

He pressed his lips together. "My mother," he said softly, letting the pain rip through him when he said those two tiny words. When he thought of the woman who'd loved him, just not quite enough that she'd stayed. "Gone for far too long and much beloved. I swear to you on my mother that whatever you tell me here in this chamber will die with me."

Her lips parted and she looked at him with a bit of new understanding. He wasn't sure he liked that. No one truly understood what he'd been through. Even his friends only knew snippets. Not the worst of it. Never the worst. He had never been able to say that out loud.

She sighed, the sound shuddering from her lips. He saw her soften in emotional surrender. It was better than the physical to watch her walls come down. Well, almost as good anyway.

She reached over to the table and took one of the glasses of scotch. She sipped it and then said. "I was forced to marry him."

Her gaze held steady on Robert. Almost accusatory. He wrinkled his brow, for there was a flicker in his mind. A memory he couldn't quite access. An itch. But then it was gone.

"For his money?" he asked. "His position?"

"No, that would be a normal reason for a father to trade his daughter," she said. There was no mistaking the bitterness in her tone. "My father believed my nature was wanton. And as a man of what he considers a godly bent, he had to crush that in me. He believed that marrying a man like the Earl of Gainsworth would put me in line. Break me, I think he put it."

Robert froze. There were a great many ways to break a person. He'd watched some of them, watched his friends endure horrible childhoods. He'd felt some, too. From his father. When his mother died. When he found out why.

The idea that Katherine's father would want her unique spirit broken made him hate a man he'd never met. And it tugged him toward her. To protect her. Hold her where no one like her husband or her father could ever touch her again. He wanted to close her wounds and tend her scars.

He shook away those unexpected needs that roared up in

him like a tidal wave that had been constrained but now burst through the dam. This conversation was about understanding, nothing more. What he would share with her could heal some of this pain, but that was not his responsibility.

It never would be. This was a temporary distraction and it would end.

"*Did* he break you?" he asked.

She sucked in a sharp inhalation of breath. "My husband turned out not to be the man my father believed him to be. Oh, he looked as pious as my father, but he was not. He liked a young wife. Liked having me on his arm and implying what his prowess was to have me. And he liked my body. He used it, training me in what he liked. Wanted."

Robert tensed. "Forced?" he asked, thinking of her earlier accusation that he would simply take what he wanted if she didn't offer it freely.

"No," she said swiftly, and to his great relief. "I *was* titillated by what he desired. What a man and a woman shared in their marriage bed. And at first, I was an eager student. But as weeks passed, I began to feel more and more empty. He had pleasure, that was clear. But for me? There was never anything but flutters. A tease of something more that he never allowed."

Robert shook his head in disgust. Katherine was so damned responsive, it was incredible to him that a man would not tend to her pleasure. Seeing it last night was like watching magic.

"He never brought you to completion?" he asked.

Her cheeks brightened with embarrassed color and she darted her gaze away swiftly. "Can I—do I—must I…"

"No. Not if you don't want to share."

She kept her gaze from his for what felt like an eternity. Robert so wanted to touch her. To kiss her. To take away these painful memories, wash them clean with sensation. And yet he didn't. He waited for her, as patiently as he could.

She finally glanced up. "I began to touch myself."

He blinked in shock. *There* was an image. Katherine splayed out before him, hands between her legs, eyes locked with his as she pleasured herself. Readied herself for him and what he would do to her.

"There was pleasure then," she admitted softly. "But Gainsworth discovered what I was doing. He accused me of being just what my father had always said. A whore. Dirty. Wrong. *Wanton*."

She emphasized the last word sharply, leading Robert to wonder how many times it had been spat at her. By her father, by her husband. No wonder how she recoiled when she heard it whispered by those in Society.

"He was a bastard," he said.

She shrugged, but there was a flash of gratitude to her expression. As if she was pleased to find an ally in her tale. He supposed she would be. So many were against her. Both in truth and in her mind. The fact that she was telling him this at all took so much courage.

And trust. Which he hadn't earned. Which he vowed now, just to himself, never to betray as she had been betrayed before. Loyalty, at least, he knew he could give.

"I suppose you wonder about the night he died," she whispered.

He did wonder, though he'd never considered asking her. That night was a private moment that had already been dragged into the light in the worst way possible. It had buckled her beneath the weight of gossip and half-truth. It had brought her to this place where she could hardly breathe, couldn't look at him, believed that anyone who knew her only saw her as the countess who had killed her husband with her wanton needs.

"Of course you do," she said, almost beneath her breath. "It is all anyone wonders when they look at me."

Her cheeks darkened again, the color of humiliation. The color of pain. The color of desperation.

He waited, holding his breath, as she struggled. At last, he moved just a little closer. "Tell me, Katherine. Not to satisfy my curiosity, but because I can see it devouring you from the inside. Tell me so it doesn't destroy you."

CHAPTER THIRTEEN

Devouring her from the inside. Yes, that was the most apt description Katherine had heard to describe what she felt. Those feelings rose up all the higher as she confessed to Roseford. She hadn't meant to do that. She'd been determined to keep the wall up between them, to only allow herself a bit of pleasure.

And yet, once she'd started talking, saying those words she'd kept to herself, stories she hadn't even told her aunt, it was like a spigot was turned on. She couldn't stop.

That was shocking enough, given what she knew about the motives of the man standing before her. But more than that was the fact that he took in what she said. Solemn but without judgment. He didn't tease her or play off her words.

He just *heard* her.

And that was like a gift she hadn't realized she needed so desperately.

"He was tired that night," she whispered, trying not to follow her mind down its path to her worst memories. "But demanded his pleasure regardless. He asked me to be on…"

She stopped. This was too much. Too intimate. Too private.

Robert leaned in, his gaze never leaving hers as he reached up to stroke her cheek with the back of his hand. "You needn't be embarrassed. I've seen it all, remember. Biggest cad in London. I am not capable of being shocked. Nor of judging you, which I would like to reiterate, I do not."

She shut her eyes. He made this too easy. How could it be so easy with him? And yet it was.

"I was on top," she finished without looking at him. Of course with her eyes shut, she could see Gregory now, laid out on their bed like some ancient king demanding tribute. "And as I moved, I began to feel that flutter of pleasure I wanted so *damned* badly."

Robert took her hand, his thumb sliding over her skin gently. "You reached for it."

She still didn't open her eyes. "God, yes. Harder and faster. In control for the first time in a very long time. I saw his eyes go wide, saw him gape with what I thought was surprise. And then he went so stiff beneath me. I could see something was wrong. He was not well. I screamed for help immediately. I wasn't thinking of how it would look when the servants burst in. Me naked over him, him sprawled out on our bed. Dead."

She heard her voice getting louder, more hysterical, as it had that awful night. Robert tugged her and she fell into his arms. Warm arms, comforting beyond measure. He smoothed his hands across her back, whispering empty words of comfort against her hair as he just…held her.

Some part of her screamed in to pull away. Run away because this felt too, too real. But she was exhausted by confession, broken by reliving all that pain in the past. Knowing all the pain still yet to come as she navigated her way through Society and their judgment.

And his arms were so strong. She leaned into his chest, shuddering as she fought tears. "It was awful," she whispered against his skin. "He died, and I recognized immediately that his death would be the end of my life, too. *Everyone* would know what had happened. Everyone would see I was exactly what my father always accused me of being."

She felt him stiffen and his arms tightened around her. Like he could protect her from her words. Like he wanted to.

"That's all of it," she whispered.

She stayed there in the cocoon of his warmth for a moment,

then began to pull away. He held her tight, not forcing her, but not letting her get away either.

He looked down into her face. His was just inches from hers. His gaze was firm on hers. "This was *not your fault*."

She jolted at the words, at how deeply they touched her even though she couldn't trust him. Didn't trust him. Didn't *want* to like him or see him as a person she could curl into and surrender her fears just as she had.

"Look at me," he said gently. "Really look at me, Katherine, without thinking about your next move."

She froze in the midst of her struggle to escape this connection and forced herself to take a long breath. To come back to this moment rather than let her fear take over.

"What happened that night is *not your fault*," he repeated. "Gainsworth was wrong not to teach you how to harness your own pleasure. He was certainly wrong to tell you that the desire for that sensation was dirty. He should have celebrated your responsiveness. Nurtured it."

She felt a tear slide down her cheek and gasped at the heat of it. He wiped it away with his thumb and then pressed a kiss to her forehead.

"You were never, never wrong for what you wanted, Katherine."

He released her when she pulled away this time. Only she didn't race across the room as she had thought to do at first. She stood before him, still warmed by his presence as she stared at him. "No one else but you would ever say that."

He shook his head. "Not true. Any person who'd ever experienced pleasure would say the same. Every duchess in this house would tell you the same."

Terror raced through her. She had so little—the burgeoning friendship with the duchesses was so fragile and precious to her as she came to know them.

"You would not tell them what I said? Your friends? Their wives?"

"No," he said immediately, with strength. Almost with

shock that she would assume that. "Never, Katherine. Here in this room, between us, it is private. It will remain so."

She sighed. "Trusting you will never be easy."

"But I will prove you right in doing so."

She turned away, staring into the fire as she thought about that night all those years ago. That encounter that had started her road to marriage. And the other encounter that had sealed her fate. He remembered neither, and they were so pivotal to her life.

"Please, Katherine." His soft words broke into the cloud of her doubt. "I see now why you would want something that was just for your pleasure. I understand your desire. I want to grant you that."

She faced him and lifted her chin. "You understand that I never want to be someone's plaything ever again?"

"You won't be," he said, then cupped the nape of her neck and drew her forward. His mouth dropped and he kissed her.

She didn't want to melt into him. She didn't want to give herself without a hesitation or without setting further boundaries, but she did. She lifted a hand to his bare chest, settling it against the planes of muscle there. He continued kissing her, drawing her further and further into his spell, further and further into her every desire.

Her fingers clenched against his skin, tracing the lines of his chest, lower to his stomach. Great God, but the man was a specimen. She didn't even know men could be made like this. It had always seemed a flight of fantasy in painting and sculptures, but here he was. Real. And hers, apparently, if his words could be believed.

He nudged her back to the settee where they'd begun and lowered her there. She glanced toward the bedchamber as he leaned away, but he made no motion to take her there. To bring her to his bed. She almost felt disappointed, but then he pressed a finger beneath her chin and lifted so she was looking at him.

"I want to undress you, Katherine. See you, be able to touch you far more than I did last night. May I?"

She blinked. "You are asking me?"

He nodded. "I told you that you would be able to trust me. That despite what you think of me, I am not a man who takes and takes and takes. You are in control of whatever happens here."

She gaped at him in shock. She had never known a man who would cede any kind of power or control to a woman. And yet here this man was. A man who would do whatever he liked, with whomever he liked. A man who had done both those things.

And he was asking her permission.

Her head spun as she tried to recategorize him from the cad she had always believed and experienced him to be. Where did she put him now that he was proving to be so much more than that?

"Katherine?" he said softly. "You can tell me no. There's no punishment." He smiled. "I would be disappointed, of course. But you owe me nothing."

She swallowed hard, refocusing on this moment. There was only this moment, after all. She caught his hand and lifted it, settling his fingers at the line of buttons along the front of her gown.

"Yes," she breathed, her cheeks flaming as she surrendered once more. "Please."

The corner of his lips tilted into half a smile and he leaned in, putting his mouth against the side of her neck. He licked and sucked, wild sensation bursting through her entire body. She was aware of his fingers moving, and suddenly her dress gaped.

She struggled to find words. "So easily, eh?"

He lifted his mouth from its trail along her collarbone and grinned. "You will find there are many benefits to asking a libertine to pleasure you, my dear. Experience has its benefits."

She couldn't help but laugh along with him, though the sound was quickly transformed into a moan when his mouth returned to her flesh. He pushed her gown open and his mouth moved between her breasts, steaming breath through the thin fabric of her chemise.

Her fingers slid into his hair and she shut her eyes as she

surrendered, once again to all he would do to her. For her. He said this night was for her. And she wanted it so badly. If he was willing to meet her terms, why shouldn't she give in? Enjoy every second since it would certainly not be repeated. He would want more.

She couldn't give it. Not with so much on the line.

But *this* she could take. And she did as she rested her head against the settee arm and let go of everything in her mind.

Robert felt Katherine's surrender in the way her body went liquid beneath him. Her breath exited her lungs in a shaky sigh and she shut her eyes. He took the opportunity to look at her face as he slipped a hand beneath her gown and lowered her sleeve and chemise strap at the same time.

There was normally a tension to everything Katherine did. With him, yes—of course he felt it. She was conflicted whenever she was with him. Torn between wanting him and hating him for those unnamed crimes he hadn't yet determined.

But he saw that tension everywhere else, too. He understood it more now. She was always waiting for an attack to come…because in her past it always had. How he despised her father and her husband, men who had convinced her that her desire was to be hidden. Quashed.

She had deserved so much better.

And this was to be her reward.

Oh, he still wanted her. He wanted to take her and make her see that sex with him would be something for them both. But not tonight. Tonight was about her. Even if his cock was hard as stone and aching to plunge into her heat and mark her forever.

He jolted at that unexpected thought. Then shoved it away as he pushed the opposite arm of her gown down and bared her, at last, from the waist up.

She had small breasts with dusky pink areolas and hard

nipples just begging to be sucked. He covered each one with his hands and felt her lift beneath him, arching to get more, demand more.

Oh, he was going to give that to her. Carefully. Gently.

"I want to take the rest off," he whispered.

Her eyes opened, and once again she looked at him with the same confusion as the first time he had asked for her consent. His heart hurt at the expression. Clearly her wants had never been on the top of any man's mind.

She nodded. "Yes. Please."

The *please* was needy, plaintive. Wanton. And he liked that sound so very much. He liked making her long for what would come. Needed it like breath. That was his job tonight, after all. To make her anticipate and then quake with release. One thing he knew—he was very good at doing *that*.

He stood, drawing her to her feet in one smooth motion. She steadied herself by placing a hand on his chest, and he felt the burn of her skin against his. God, but when she touched him. He wanted to feel it all over.

He pushed that desire aside. Holding her gaze, he hooked his thumbs into the folded fabric of her tangled gown and pushed, drawing the entire contraption down around her feet. She stood naked before him now, save for her drawers and stockings and slippers.

He stared. She was a goddess. Meant to be worshipped exactly as he intended to worship her. Meant to be surrendered to and offered whatever she desired.

What she desired was pleasure, release, orgasm. That was easy.

"Did he ever tell you how beautiful you were?" he asked.

The flicker of pain over her face was enough to give him the answer even before she choked, "He liked my looks until I belonged to him. Then he would accuse me of using them to tempt others."

"You are beautiful, Katherine," he whispered as he smoothed his hands along her naked sides and up over the flimsy fabric encasing her round hips. "The kind of woman men used to go to war for."

She swallowed hard and he thought he saw tears in her eyes before she turned her face away. He pressed his mouth to her flesh as he dropped to his knees. Now his face was even with her stomach, and he sucked and licked there as he untied the little ribbon at the waist of her drawers. He lifted his gaze. "Yes?"

"Y-Yes."

He tugged, gliding the drawers down to join at the pile of fabric at her feet. He let his mouth trace the line of one hip, then across her thigh. As he brought his face across the apex of her thighs, he breathed in that cinnamon scent that so enraptured him. She made a little moan above him and it was like music to his ears.

He cupped her bare backside, kneading his fingers into the soft flesh. Pulling her against his mouth and steaming warm breath over that most sensitive place. Her fingers came into his hair again and she let out cry of pleasure as she massaged his scalp.

He smiled against her, darting his tongue out to just tease her mound. She buckled and he shifted so he could place her into a seated position on the settee. Her eyes were glazed as she stared at him, wedged between her legs. The legs she'd had to open when she sat.

Revealing that pretty pink sex just as she had the night before. He reached out to trace her lips with his index finger, and she shuddered and lifted toward him.

He shook his head at her silent demand. "First, your stockings."

Her eyes were wild as she stared at him. Watching as he rolled the flimsy silk away and then gently removed her slippers. He tossed first one then the other over his shoulder, and she was naked. Completely naked, splayed out on the settee before him like an offering.

He wanted to do so many things to this woman. Lock them both into this chamber, heedless of every other guest, and spend a week exploring every inch of her. Take her in every way, learn what made her gasp. Teach her even more. Let her learn his body.

A week? He wanted a month. A year. A decade. But he had tonight. And that would be enough. It had to be.

"Before you ask," she gasped, lifting herself toward him. "Yes. The answer is yes. Yes, yes, yes."

He smiled at her desperation. The need that laced every word from her lips. He had no intention of denying her. "If the answer changes to no, say the word," he whispered.

She murmured some incoherent noise and he laughed as he pushed up on his knees and cupped her breasts. He had so wanted her naked last night, so he could touch and tease and pleasure. Now he had her that way. And in his chamber, where no one would interrupt. No one was waiting for them, watching for their return in the ballroom. This was all there was.

He massaged her breasts, squeezing them, letting his thumbs graze her nipples as he watched her reaction. She bit her lower lip, muffling a moan, and her head tilted back. He smiled, marking the sensitivity to his mind as he lowered his mouth to one nipple. He licked her, letting the flat of his tongue smooth over the peak gently.

"Yes!" she cried out, fisting her hands against the settee cushion.

He licked again, this time harder as he continued to squeeze and pluck the opposite breast. She was lifting her hips now, grinding her lower body against his still-clothed one as he began to suck. Harder and harder, letting her nipple slide free with a pop every now and again.

She was shaking beneath him. He felt her wetness, knew it would leave a mark against his trousers as she sought release by rubbing against him like a cat. It was torture, of course. Because it would be so easy to loosen the front fall of his trousers and slide home into her. Let her grind against him from the inside and give them both a sweet release.

He had promised, though. Despite his reputation, he kept

his promises.

He licked the nipple he had been neglecting, and now she writhed, her body lifting against him as she keened in pleasure at his teasing.

"Please, please," she whispered.

He nodded, putting his hands back on her breasts to replace his mouth. Massaging as he licked a trailed down her body and nudged her legs wider with his shoulders.

Her slick sex was just before him now, and he let his hands come down so he could press his thumb there, parting the folds, finding her center, feeling her wet heat against his skin. He could drown in her.

He wanted to do so.

Instead, he spread her lips, revealing his prize. He couldn't help it—he had to taste. He leaned in and glided his tongue across her, reveling in the sweet flavor of her as it burst on his tongue. Her desire, her need, it was a feast. He was a starving man. Only one thing would set them both free.

And yet he wanted more. He wanted to remind her how good a man could feel inside of her. Not with his cock. God help him, he wouldn't do that.

But there was something else. He pressed a finger to her entrance as he leaned in for a second lick. She gasped as he gently breached her, her body rippling around him, tight and hot. He watched as he pushed his finger into her, thrusting, probing, reveling in the hot grip of her.

And knowing that if her husband had refused her pleasure, punished her for seeking it, she had probably never been touched the way he was about to touch her. He slid a second finger inside of her and gently curled them both, finding the rough little section inside her body that could bring her as much pleasure as her clitoris could.

Her eyes flew open wide as she stared at him in a combination of surprise and panic.

"What is…" she gasped.

He stilled his fingers. "Too much?"

She shook her head. "More."

He smiled. God, it had been a long time since he'd played with a lady who felt so innocent and so wicked all at once. It was an intoxicating combination.

He leaned in to press a kiss to her thigh, licking her, watching her, curling his fingers all at once. She began to grip him with her sheath, rocking her hips in time to his movements. Her eyes squeezed shut, her legs began to shake, her body grew hotter, wetter, tighter around him. And then she let out a keening, desperate cry and her body began to ripple around his fingers. He leaned in and sucked her clitoris and she jolted harder, her back curving and her fists gripping against the settee as she came.

Katherine flopped back, her body limp and sated, as the crisis faded. She looked down at Robert through a hooded gaze and found him smiling up at her. Gentle, but also filled with pride. Because that was him. A dichotomy of cocksure arrogance and tender generosity. She had no idea which was real. Or could they both be? And where did his wager about her fit with it all? Or their past exchanges?

He withdrew his fingers from her body and kept his gaze on her as he licked them clean. She shuddered with desire at that action.

He leaned up, caging her in with his hands as he looked into her eyes. She could see his desire there. Feel it in the hard cock that was now pressed into her thigh. The cock she very much wanted inside of her, no matter what hesitations she had about him.

And now he would ask her. He would try to seduce her into changing her mind about their arrangement. He'd told her he would, after all.

So she tensed, trying to find the strength to refuse. Or to

surrender. She didn't know which would be her response at this point.

He nuzzled her neck, nipping her skin gently. His kisses feathered up her jawline, across her cheek, and then his mouth found hers. She tasted herself on his mouth and sighed as she cupped the back of his head with one hand.

To her surprise, he pulled away at last, then shoved back from her and got to his feet.

"Let me help you dress," he said.

She blinked at the hand he extended. Was he *not* going to try to seduce her? Not going to take her at all?

What did that mean? That he didn't want her? That she had disappointed him somehow? Bored him?

"You look like you're upset," he said, pulling her to her feet and into his arms. He held her there, her naked body pressed to his half-clothed one. "Want to discuss something?"

"You don't want me?"

He blinked, then cupped her backside and rotated her hips against his hard cock. Both of them shivered together. He kissed her and backed away.

"I definitely want you," he said as he bent to grab her chemise.

She tugged it over her head and took the gown he offered to do the same. "But you aren't trying to, er…"

He laughed. "For a lady who told me in no uncertain terms that she would never open her body to me, you are quite passionately trying to convince me to make the attempt."

She smoothed her gown and went to work on her buttons. At least the action allowed her to glance away from him as she said, "I suppose I was only expecting you to press your case more. Make demands."

He shook his head. "I told you a dozen times tonight, you can always say no and I'll respect it. But if we do this again, I do not think I'll be able to resist asking you very sweetly if I could show you that a man's body joining with yours can be as pleasurable as his mouth or his fingers."

She swallowed hard as she pictured just that. She wanted to see him, to touch him as intimately as she had been touched, to feel his weight over her as he slid home into her body. To look into his eyes as he lost control.

She shivered. "If that's what you want, then why haven't you asked for more?"

"Because no matter what happens next," he said as she took her stockings and stepped barefoot into her slippers, "I want you to know that you are owed nothing less than pleasure, Katherine. And if anyone ever suggests otherwise, then he is a fool who is not fit to shine your boots, let alone touch you."

She stared at him, shocked by his words, shocked more by the tingle of tears those words created in her eyes. What he was describing was a gift. One given without thought of what he'd get in return.

And as he led her to his door and pressed one last kiss to her lips, the power of that gift made her knees tremble. She stepped into the hallway and looked back at him. "G-Goodnight," she whispered.

"Goodnight," he said, and then he shut the door, leaving her to ponder not just the passion he had shared with her, but the meaning of it all.

CHAPTER FOURTEEN

Robert stepped from the house and squinted at the morning sun. God's teeth, but one had to be mad to regularly get up this early. Normally he didn't. But today he'd been awake at dawn, restless and troubled about what he and Katherine had shared.

It hadn't been the plan. The plan was to give her pleasure, to be certain, but then to seduce. To convince her to give herself to him completely. That was how he'd win his wager. Only he hadn't recalled that little detail until she was long gone and he was alone with a rock-hard cock that needed tending to.

He pushed out his breath in a huffy sigh and started across the garden. He needed to clear his head. It was too full of memories of Katherine's soft confessions about her awful marriage. Full of real empathy for what she'd been through.

He didn't want empathy for her. That was not how he operated.

He turned a corner into the maze of the garden and came to a full stop. Of course she was there. She would be. That was fate, it seemed, to find her standing there, autumn leaves fluttering in the air around her.

She fit there, amidst the reds and oranges and yellows. They were colors of fire and she was fire. Even her gown matched, for it was a sunny yellow with a fall of stitched butterflies along the skirt. She clutched a shawl around her shoulders, a rich red color.

She hadn't noticed him yet. She was too busy examining a

pretty bush with bright red berries that was filled with chirping birds. He had time to turn tail. To escape her and all the very odd things being around her made him feel.

Only he didn't. He stood there, dumbfounded, locked into place as he tracked her like a fox might track a rabbit in the woods. Only he didn't feel like the predator. Around her, he was as much prey as she was.

Another odd feeling for a man who had never been in anything less than full control.

She froze in her examination of the bush, and then she turned. She caught her breath at the sight of him a few feet away. Her expression was unguarded and, since she wore no hat, unimpeded. She lit up, and for a brief fraction of a moment, it was clear she was happy to see him. Worse, he felt the same joy in his own chest. Felt himself smile without hesitation.

Then she caught herself and the walls came crashing down once more. That was his impetus to move and he came toward her, a sailor lured by a siren. At this rate he would be lost.

"Good morning, Katherine," he said.

She swallowed hard. "Good morning, Your Grace."

He arched a brow at her formality. Normally she called him Roseford, if she called him anything at all. But somehow he'd expected a little more freedom since they'd shared so many intimacies. He found himself longing for her to say his name. His given name, not the one that was related to his title or his family or his position in life.

"Is that where we are?" he asked softly. "After the last two nights, am I still Your Grace when we're alone?"

She blushed and dropped her gaze away from his. "Robert," she whispered.

The sound almost didn't carry on the breeze. yet it hit him like a rifle blast to the chest, nearly knocking him back. He shut his eyes briefly, reveling in the way his name sounded coming from her lips. Wanting to hear it more, in all kinds of scenarios. He wanted her to say it warmly, gently, he wanted her to use it when she was angry with him, through tears. When she was shaking with pleasure.

"Robert?" she repeated, this time as a question.

He jerked back to reality and smiled at her. "Katherine. Shall we walk together, since we are clearly the earliest risers of our little group?"

He expected her to hesitate, just as she had every other time he'd asked her a question like this. But this time, she didn't. She didn't even look irritated as she slid her hand into the crook of his elbow. "Lead the way," she said.

He somehow forced himself to do so, guiding them farther into the garden, past the maze of hedges, onto the long expanse of grass that would eventually lead to the woods and beyond.

They were quiet at first. Robert had never liked the quiet overly much. With strangers, at least, he tended to fill the silence with chatter. He was good at entertaining with his wit, as exhausting as that could sometimes be.

But as they walked, he didn't feel that pull to talk that he often did. Being quiet with Katherine was actually...*comforting* in some way.

"You know, you do not to seem to be the kind of man who is early to rise," she said after they'd walked for a while.

He found himself laughing and shot her a look. "Depends upon what I am *rising* for."

She shook her head, and to his surprise, she disengaged her arm from his and turned to face him. "You are amusing, as you know. But you deflect with flirtation and sex so easily."

He shrugged. "It is the best way."

She held his stare for what felt like a very long moment, and then she sighed softly. "Roseford, I poured my heart out to you last night. I told you things I have never repeated to another soul on this earth, despite my misgivings about you. Can you not tell me *anything* real about yourself?"

He gaped at her quiet, calm question, and her statement that what she'd told him about her husband was a secret she had kept inside all this time. That meant something. He knew it did.

"You are so direct," he said.

She smiled a little, and this time it was she who flirted. "You like it, I think."

Her teasing, so gently placed in the midst of her serious query, did its job. He softened toward her, even if he didn't wish to. What harm could there be in talking to her a little? He'd already accidentally done so when they spoke about his strained relationship with his friends. She hadn't held that over his head.

His sleeping schedule was certainly not so fraught as the other topic.

"I admit there are many mornings I've spent snoring in my bed far too late. A late night can be hard to overcome, and I've had many of those."

She tilted her head. "Like last night."

He nodded. "Yes. But it was worth any exhaustion I might experience today. Would you agree?"

Her cheeks brightened again, but she was smiling as she dropped her gaze. "I would, yes."

He took her arm again and they began to walk a second time. "I would not say I woke early today, though. In fact, I couldn't sleep much last night after you left." He glanced at her from the corner of his eye. "I couldn't stop thinking about you."

She jerked her gaze to him in surprise. He couldn't blame her. Making such a confession was a surprise to him, as well. She brought out such honesty in him.

"You couldn't?" she asked, breathless. "I'm surprised to hear that. I didn't think I would matter much to you."

"No?" He stopped again.

She faced him slowly. "Please don't play a game with me. I know you've had a great many women. You'll forget me before tomorrow. Just as you have in the past."

He wrinkled his brow at the odd turn of phrase. "You are so certain?"

"Yes." She said it softly, but firmly. There was no doubt she meant it not as a flirtation or a challenge, but as a statement of what she believed was fact.

And it would have been a fact not so long ago. Now it

felt…different. She felt different.

He shook his head. "I have always sought pleasure, that is true. At the expense of all else, some would say."

"Why?"

He blinked at her. She was staring at him evenly, her gaze clear and wide. "Why?" he repeated in surprise. He had not expected the question. Almost couldn't fathom giving her the answer.

She cocked her head. "I have no illusions about men of power. Your friends all seemed to have their dalliances before they settled down into what appear to be very happy marriages. But you have said it yourself—you are not like them. You've made seduction into an art form."

"Compliments, compliments," he drawled, teasing in order to press a wall down harder between them.

She seemed to recognize the trick, for she didn't respond, but just stared at him. Waiting for his answer. His explanation that was so much more complicated than she knew. Than he had ever said to anyone, even his friends.

There were some secrets no one knew.

He cleared his throat. He intended to say something flippant. Something meaningless. But that wasn't what fell from his lips when he spoke.

"It has always been a way to do exactly as you said earlier. It's a way to keep people out."

Her lips parted in surprise. He felt the same emotion. He hadn't meant to share that with her. He hadn't even allowed himself to think about it much over the years.

"Robert…" she breathed at last.

He shrugged, shifting beneath her regard and the fact that she now knew something so personal. "You wanted honesty, didn't you? There it is."

"How do you mean?" she asked. "Talking about sex as a shield is one thing. It's a topic that is meant to make others uncomfortable. But to use the act itself as a barrier feels…it's so intimate."

He swallowed. Yes, it was that. With her it was that. With her it was something beyond a natural need for pleasure. Something deeper that both drew him in and made him want to run. Run back to London to bury himself in meaningless pleasure with ladies who made him feel nothing.

He cleared his throat. "Passion is control."

Her eyes widened. "I might beg to differ."

"It feels like it's not sometimes," he admitted. "But you have that control as well."

She shook her head. "The thing that frightens me most, that kept me up last night, was how much that statement isn't true."

"You offered me your pleasure, but you put up a boundary, didn't you? A line you told me not to cross. If I want the pleasure, I must respect the line. It's no different with anyone else who engages in an affair. When the lines are drawn, there can be no confusion. No one expects more."

Her gaze held on him and something in her expression changed. Before she had been open, interested, engaged in this exchange. Now that wall came back up. He didn't understand why, but there it was. She drew back from him a long step, her eyes grew colder.

There was something more to this conversation for her. And he had no idea what it was.

"What if someone asked you for more?" she asked. His lips parted in shock, but she held up a hand to keep him from responding. "Not me, don't worry. I mean anyone."

He pondered that question. Over the years, of course, there had been woman who had angled for more than just his cock. Women he'd liked, even, but had balked at the idea of granting more. He had lovers, not mistresses. He did not court.

"If someone asked for more, I would push them away. Gently, if possible," he said.

Her lower lip trembled a fraction and she nodded slowly. He couldn't tell what that statement meant to her, nor why she had asked it. But it was clear it elicited some kind of response.

"Yes," she said at last. "I suppose you would." She glanced

back at the house. "You know, I think it would be best if I returned. Please continue with your walk, Your Grace. Good morning."

"Katherine," he said, longing suddenly to keep her with him. To find out how this conversation had turned so suddenly and bring her back to the easy connection they sometimes shared.

But she ignored him. She walked away and kept walking. And she never looked back. A fact that felt like someone had pressed their fist through his chest, gripped his heart and squeezed.

He'd had that feeling only once before in his life. Now he clawed to make it stop as he struggled to find another emotion to replace it. Another thought to keep the darkness out.

Katherine was dangerous. It was in his best interest to cut her away now before she wiggled her way even further into his mind, his heart. And yet all he wanted to do was chase her.

He wasn't certain whether to hate her or admire her for that.

The morning had been bright, almost too bright, but now, several hours later, it had turned. Rain streamed down the windows, keeping the party inside.

Katherine had no idea what the rest of the group was doing, but at present she was tucked into a quiet parlor, book in hand. A book she wasn't reading. Instead she stared at the inclement weather and scowled. It reflected her heart, really, and she resented that. Bright after her night with Robert. Cloudy and uncertain after their troubling conversation that morning.

He'd said that if someone asked for more, he would push that person away. That statement cut her deeper than she'd wanted to admit. It made her think of her encounter with the man. Not when he'd almost kissed her years ago. The one after. She'd gone to him to ask for his help after her father arranged her marriage.

And he'd done exactly what he described earlier today. Pushed her away. Not gently as he'd said he'd try to be. It had not been gently. She knew he'd been drunk when he'd done it. Now he didn't recall it.

She was just another lady he'd escaped. She would be again once he was finished with this painful connection they were now exploring. She couldn't be so foolish as to forget that.

The door to the parlor clicked shut and she pivoted to find Robert standing at it, leaning against the surface and staring at her. He looked...ragged. Worn out. She'd seen his emotion before when he talked to her about losing the attachment to his friends, but this felt different.

"I don't know what I did to anger you today." He moved forward and she scrambled to her feet, ignoring it when her book clattered to the floor. "But I don't want whatever it is to come between us."

She stared at him, uncertain of how to respond. "Robert—" she began.

He cut her off by taking a long step toward her, gathering her into his arms and dropping his lips to hers. She wished that she were strong enough to freeze. To refuse when she'd just been considering the folly of this affair and all it could lead to.

But she wasn't. She wanted him, and when he touched her everything else fell away. She opened her mouth to him, eagerly welcoming his tongue as it swept against hers. She lifted against him, losing herself in desire, in longing, in pleasure.

He cupped her backside, grinding her against him as he moaned low and insistent into her mouth and let her know he was as moved, at least physically, as she was.

She had no idea what would have happened next, in those desperate moments where all her hesitations faded and were replaced by the uncontrollable feelings he stoked in her. She didn't get a chance to find out.

The door to the parlor opened behind them.

"Katherine, we heard you were in here and thought you

might want to join the duchesses for—oh my!"

Katherine pulled away from Robert, staggering back and staring over his shoulder at the door. Emma and Meg stood there together, eyes wide as they looked from Katherine to Robert and then back again. Katherine knew what they saw. She could guess what they thought.

Shame rushed up in her, erasing all the pleasant feelings Robert had stirred in her with his passionate embrace. She glanced at him. His expression was stricken.

"Katherine," he said softly.

She ignored it. Ignored her friends, and did all she could do. She ran.

Robert stared as Katherine raced past Emma and Meg out the door of the parlor. He strode forward, ready to stop her, but Meg placed herself in front of him. "No, don't," she said, placing a hand to his chest.

"Why?" he snapped, unable to temper his tone even though he'd known Meg for a very long time and had always liked her. "You all wanted so desperately to protect her from me—is this the next step in the evolution of your plans to separate us?"

Meg blinked up at him and Emma caught her breath. He felt their regard heavy and hard on him, and his face suddenly felt hot.

"No," Meg said carefully. "You are both adults and there is nothing any of us would do to break apart what is clearly a consensual and mutual attraction. She's upset."

"Yes, and that upset seems to come from embarrassment at being caught," Emma said gently. "If you follow her, that will not ease her mind. She will still believe she's being judged by our group."

He blinked. "Y-Yes. She does fear that if the duchesses recognized her true...I think she refers to it as her nature...that you would despise her."

Emma pursed her lips and glanced at Meg. "It is *exactly* as I told you."

"Then we must do the other thing you said," Meg said with a nod. "Check to be sure her aunt is resting so we won't be interrupted, then go tell the others. I'll find Katherine and bring her to you."

Emma gave Robert a long look and then slipped from the room.

Meg tilted her head. "I recall the first time I met you. What was I? Ten?"

He forced a smile. "Yes. A most annoying sister."

She laughed. "I think you must still think that, considering how you are glaring at me so angrily."

He turned away. "Then I am being rude. I would not wish to bring down the wrath of either James or Simon. Your brother and husband have enough issues with me currently."

"Yes, your wager. Except I think you aren't so invested in that anymore. You need to evaluate the fact that you care about Katherine."

He spun back. "I beg your pardon?"

Meg rolled her eyes. "'I beg your pardon?'" she mimicked before she put her hands on her hips. "You like her. I think you might more than like her, judging by what I've seen."

"I've no idea what you're talking about," he said. Lied. He lied.

She shook her head. "Great God, Robert, she would be a good match for you. She never lets you have even a quarter and that is exactly the kind of woman you need to keep from getting bored. But I know you. You're about to buck and run like an unbroken stallion, in order to escape what you truly desire. And that could get you both hurt. So I beg of you, fight your impulses to be an utter ass."

He stared at her. Meg had always been direct, but this was far even for her.

"Is that all, Your Grace?" he asked, trying to keep his tone icy but only managing to sound as flummoxed as he felt.

"No, but I have a lady to comfort and right now that is more important." She smiled at him and reached up to pat his cheek. "You know we all adore you, right? Get yourself together."

With that, she turned on her heel and marched from the room, leaving him to gape after her. Not only had Meg been shockingly direct, but what she said didn't feel too far off the mark. And that was abjectly terrifying.

CHAPTER FIFTEEN

Katherine could hardly breathe as she stumbled into her chamber and raced for the settee. She threw herself into it, trying to calm her throbbing heart. Trying to fight the tears that clouded her vision.

What had she done?

Her blossoming friendship with the duchesses was something she enjoyed so much. She'd been isolated all her life—being around them now felt like finally having the connection she'd lost when her mother died. That she was just barely reestablishing with her aunt.

Now with one foolish loss of control with Robert she had probably not only threatened her relationship with the women, but destroyed it. And if they broke with her, especially publicly? All her hopes of even the smallest return to Society would be dashed.

There was a light knock at her door, which she ignored. She didn't want to see anyone. Didn't want to see their judgmental stares or hear Robert try to explain how she should just surrender to the life of a wanton and forget everything but pleasure.

"Katherine, please may I come in?"

She shook her head as she rose. She recognized the Duchess of Crestwood's muffled voice in the hallway. Of course Emma would not come. *She* was likely horrified. From Katherine's observation of the women, Meg was one of the most direct.

Likely she had come here to ask Katherine to leave.

She deserved no less, though she had no idea how she would explain it to her aunt.

Resigned, she got to her feet and trudged to her fate. "Your Grace," she said as she opened the door, refusing to look at her visitor.

"Katherine," Meg said, touching her hand.

Katherine forced herself to look into the duchess's eyes and was surprised to see kindness there. That empathy broke the dam of her emotion and the tears she had been fighting began to fall.

"Oh, what you all must think of me!" she burst out.

Meg's expression softened further and she drew Katherine in for a hug. "Dearest, oh dearest, you mustn't. If you believe I came up here to chastise you about a kiss, or even more than a kiss, then you are wrong."

"You didn't?" Katherine asked, confusion cutting off her tears as she stared at Meg in disbelief.

"No, I didn't. Emma and I were looking for you in the hopes that you'd join the ladies for tea. I believe your aunt is resting, so it would just be the duchesses." Meg squeezed her hand tighter. "Please, won't you come?"

Katherine found herself nodding, though she wasn't certain it was the best idea. After all, Meg might be kind, but that didn't mean anyone else would understand what she'd been doing in the parlor.

She was in no less danger of being ostracized by her new friends. Yet she could not refuse, so she followed Meg through the hall and down to the parlor where the other ladies had gathered. They were talking all at once, but when Katherine entered, it stopped.

She froze at the entryway, heat flooding her cheeks. This was the worst part of being a pariah. Either conversation went on about you, around you, or it tellingly stopped the moment you entered a room.

"Good afternoon," she said, not lifting her gaze from the floor as she awaited the hissing, the tone of voice to tell her she didn't belong.

Instead, as Meg stepped in to join Adelaide, Charlotte, Helena and Isabel, Emma rushed forward and took Katherine's hands. Katherine dared to look at the duchess and found Emma with the same gaze of understanding that Meg had on her face when she came to Katherine's chamber.

"Come in." Emma drew her into the room and ushered her to a place in the middle of the settee. She was now surrounded by the duchesses, who were all watching her, save for Emma, who had hustled off to get her tea.

When she rejoined the group, Meg gave the ladies a look and said, "I have always believed that directness was the best policy, assuming it is directness that is kindly meant."

"Here, here," Adelaide said as she raised a teacup as a toast.

Meg arched a brow at her friend. "Katherine, I think you know we're as much like sisters as our husbands are like brothers. I believe the ladies already know what Emma and I stumbled upon a little while ago in the parlor."

Katherine bent her head lower, wishing she could disappear into the settee and never come out again. Although she supposed she appreciated the fact that the women weren't wasting too much time talking about her behind her back, she could also see her hopes spiraling the drain.

"I see," she said. "It was an unfortunate thing that you and Emma walked in on such a scene. I recognize it was shocking and scandalous. I could understand if you wanted me to leave and removed all your...I don't know, is it patronage? Removed your support from me."

Adelaide leaned forward. "I would call what we offer friendship."

"Yes," Charlotte said with a frown. "I always enjoyed our talks all those years ago when there was so much unhappiness in both our marriages. We're *friends*, Katherine. No one is being so condescending as to believe it is anything less."

Katherine dared to look up. Everyone was leaning in now, a group expression of empathy and care in their eyes. Were they truly...*accepting* her? Despite her bad behavior? The kind that so proved her father's slurs right?

"You are all so kind," Katherine began slowly. "But you are also sophisticated and elegant. How in the world can my kissing Roseford in a public parlor in Emma's home be acceptable? Especially considering the stain that is already on my reputation thanks to my late husband's death. None of you could want to associate with that kind of scandal."

For a moment the room was quiet and then, to her surprise, Adelaide began to laugh. That opened the floodgates and very quickly all of the women were giggling around her. Katherine blinked. She did not see the humor of the situation.

Emma edged closer. "We aren't laughing at you, my dear. It's just the idea that none of us would want to be associated with scandal is ludicrous. We have all been scandalous in our lives, most especially with our husbands before we were married."

Katherine's mouth dropped open. "What?"

Meg shook her head. "You don't believe us. Well, I'll start since my scandal was most public. You must know that I was first engaged to Graham for a long time. But I was in love with Simon and we, er...well, we handled it badly."

Katherine caught her breath. That had all happened at the apex of her worst time with Gainsworth. When she had been at her most isolated. She'd known a little about it, but had honestly forgotten the details.

"*Everyone* talked," Meg said, lifting her chin. "It nearly destroyed us. But we kept being...scandalous. And ultimately we are here and we are happy."

Adelaide nodded. "And for my part, the scandal Meg and Simon created threw poor Graham into turmoil and brought him to me. Do you recall that actress that was in the news two years ago? Lydia Ford?"

Katherine sat up a bit straighter. "Yes, I heard she was a wonderful performer. I so wanted to see her final play, but Gregory would not allow it. He hated theatre."

Adelaide smiled. "If you'd like, I could try to recall the lines

I had in that play. You see, Lydia Ford was my stage name."

Katherine pushed to her feet and backed away from Adelaide. "*You* were Lydia Ford?"

"Yes. Masquerading as a famous actress by night, a mousy little wallflower by day."

"As if *you* ever could have been mousy," Helena muttered, and Adelaide glanced at her with a smile.

"Graham fell in love with us both and it was all very torrid and shameless and romantic and terrifying. So in the race for who has the greatest scandal, I think that might be me."

"Er, wasn't there a murder?" Katherine whispered.

Adelaide shook her head. "A friend of mine from the theatre was attacked and her lover killed the bastard. Once Graham and I were to marry, Lydia had to disappear, so her confession and disappearance were meant to save our friends. So you see, my scandal has many levels and not one of my friends has ever judged me for it."

Emma stood and came to put her arm around Adelaide. "Why would we? You are wonderful. As for me, James and I pretended a courtship so that I would garner the attention of other men. And then we had an affair." She blushed. "Here, actually." She looked around with a sigh. "I have always loved this house."

"I'm American," Helena offered, and the group laughed, including Katherine, despite her shock. "And if that isn't enough of a scandal on its own, when I came here I was my cousin's companion. A servant, really. Baldwin and I were instantly drawn to each other, but we couldn't be together because of…well, he had his own scandal he was trying to subvert. We worked it out in the end, but there was some vicious talk when we returned to London last year. Some of *them* still glare at me for taking a duke from market."

Katherine shook her head. "I had no idea. I was so removed from Society by my husband that I missed all this. But surely that is all. Isn't it?"

"No," Charlotte said with a soft smile. "You and I were

once in an unhappy marriages club. But my scandal was that I have been in love with Ewan since…forever. Since I was a girl. When I came out of mourning last Christmas, I decide to seduce him. We ended up trapped in his estate by a storm, and seduce him I did. We were nearly killed by his own brothers, who have always despised him. I must be in the running, dear Adelaide, for biggest scandal."

Adelaide tilted her head. "The brothers do make it more complicated. But I think if there is a second to my scandal, then it is Isabel."

Isabel had been smiling through the entire recitation of all the head-swimming scandals, and now she stood and looked around the room. "I met Matthew at the Donville Masquerade."

Katherine covered her mouth. She had heard of that place. Sometimes Gregory had thrown its existence up in her face. Taunted her with his membership, told her she belonged in its halls like the rest of the whores.

"Is it terrible?" she whispered.

Isabel's face softened. "No. It's a place for pleasure. Matthew and I connected there, and it was only after that when his identity was revealed. He was once engaged to my cousin. She died, very tragically, in an accident."

"You didn't know it was him?" Katherine gasped.

"Not at first." Isabel took a deep breath. "When the lie came out…well, there were other circumstances and we were forced to marry. It's complicated."

"But he forgave you for the lie," Katherine said. "I've seen him with you—it's clear he adores you."

"Yes, I'm lucky."

"He's lucky, too," Meg said, taking a sip of tea. "You saved him, we all know it."

Katherine wrinkled her brow at the reference. "I cannot believe so many of you have had scandal."

"All of us, really. Even the couples not here at present were embroiled in it. You'd have to ask Amelia and Diana about that, but I'm certain they would confess with just as clear a conscience as we have," Emma said. "Because the fact is, my dear, that scandal doesn't mean a thing."

"The best couples seem to begin with one, that is for certain," Helena said with a smile.

Katherine froze as she realized they were comforting her because they thought her kiss with Robert meant more than it did. Perhaps if they understood the truth, all this acceptance would fade.

And yet she didn't want to lie.

"Roseford and I are not a couple," she said slowly.

Isabel folded her arms. "That cad. Honestly, it is like he is determined to snatch defeat from the jaws of victory. So Robert tells you that a future cannot be?"

Katherine shook her head, thinking of what he wanted, thinking of what she withheld. "No. Both of us. *Me*."

There was silence in the room for a beat, and then Charlotte got up. "I know what it's like to be unhappy in a marriage for so long. Your circumstances seem to be far worse than my own were, and I can well imagine that would leave you…uncertain of making a new future."

Katherine bent her head. "I suppose that is part of it. There are other reasons."

"Is it the bargain I told you Robert made?" Isabel asked.

"That's another part of it, yes."

Isabel's shoulders rolled forward. "Oh, Katherine, you must know that for all his eccentricities, Robert is a good man. I was angry with him for that bad behavior and thought you should know the truth, but I would never discourage you from taking a future with him."

"We've all watched you with him this week," Emma said softly. "And have commented to each other more than once that you two seem a good match."

"Do we?" Katherine said with a shake of her head.

"You do," Adelaide said. "You do not let him run you over. It's terribly confusing to him and amusing for us. But that is what he needs. Someone who doesn't give him much quarter, makes him work for what he wants. He…*smiles* more when he's with you."

"He is the real Robert, which you hardly ever see in mixed company," Meg added. "Normally he is the Seducer at full force, but when he's with you, I see *him*. The man we all care for. The man who would die for his friends."

"From the outside, it *does* look like a good match," Helena said.

Katherine's hands began to shake and she shoved them behind her back as she paced away from the group and stood at the window looking down at the garden. She didn't see it. Her mind was too busy spinning, her eyes blurred.

What they were saying…it was almost impossible not to allow it to put thoughts in her head. Dangerous thoughts of a future she didn't want. A life she couldn't lead. A man she couldn't love. *Wouldn't.*

"Well, I thank you all for your candor," she said, hating that her voice was shaking, too. "I clearly have a great deal to think about. Perhaps you'll forgive me for being rude and excuse me."

Emma stepped forward. "Oh, Katherine, we didn't mean to overwhelm you."

Katherine tried to smile, but it was almost impossible as she faced the group of duchesses, all looking at her like they believed she would one day soon be one of them. But they didn't know the truth. They didn't know she could *never* be with him.

"You haven't," she managed to say.

It was true to a point. She was overwhelmed, but it wasn't entirely by them. It was her own heart that overwhelmed her. Her own mind. Her own desires, that whispered, then spoke, then screamed in her head that what these women described was something she couldn't deny.

"She looks like she'll faint," Helena said, getting up. "Katherine, sit down. Drink your tea. We are all going to stop regaling you with competitive stories about our scandals and trying to convince you that Robert is a safe bet for a future. Instead, we are going to talk about Emma's gown, which is brand new and beautiful. Emma, where did you get that fabric?"

Katherine thumped back into the settee and half-listened as her friends loudly changed the subject for her benefit. But in her mind, the subject would not be changed. And she would have to face the topic soon enough when she came face to face with Robert again.

CHAPTER SIXTEEN

Katherine had been avoiding him since their kiss in the parlor. Robert supposed he should be accustomed to that. After all, this was the same woman who had fled from him after her return to Society weeks ago. The woman who had set him down and thrown him aside and denied him ever since, even though she clearly wanted him.

If avoiding him were an art, she would be a proficient.

At first, it had created amusement and interest in him. But now, watching her across the room as she played a hand of whist with Meg, Emma and Charlotte, the fact that she would not look at him was…

Well, annoying was the word. It sat in his gut, making him think about her face earlier in the day when they were caught together. His imprudence had caused that sick expression, that dull fear, and he felt…guilty for it.

Guilt was not an emotion he normally let take root in his mind. Too dangerous.

"You look mightily aggravated," Simon said as he moved to Robert's side and observed the room with him.

"*You're* here," Robert muttered. "Who wouldn't be aggravated?"

Simon grinned at his ill-natured quip but didn't back away or press him on it. At least for a moment.

"I'm fine," Robert added when the silence became too

much. When he felt Simon's questions and judgments hanging in the air like a noose between them.

"Good," Simon said. "Never implied otherwise."

"Yes, you did." Robert turned toward him, folding his arms in what he knew was a display of petulance that was far beneath him. "You said I looked aggravated."

"You *are*," Simon corrected him. "You are practically throwing yourself on the floor and having a fit like Bibi does."

"You compare me to an eighteen-month-old child," Robert asked, thinking of James and Emma's little girl. Although none of the children in attendance had been to many of the events, he knew they were around. Saw them with their parents from time to time.

"I suppose that's unfair," Simon said with a smile. "Bibi at her worst is more charming than you are at present."

Robert turned away from him with a harrumph and hoped his friend would go away. Instead, Simon bumped him shoulder to shoulder. "Should I guess what is bringing on this little fit?" he asked.

Robert ground his teeth. "Have you nothing better to do?"

"Nothing at all." Simon laughed. "You like her. And it's driving you *mad* that this is becoming more to you than just some wager."

"Like who?" Robert grumbled.

"The queen of bloody Spain," Simon huffed. "Katherine, of course, you great idiot. Everyone can see it."

Robert squeezed his eyes shut. He didn't want everyone to see what he was having a hard time admitting to himself. "You and Meg," he snapped. "With your stupid theories."

Simon nodded. "Ah, so you *don't* like her. Then you won't mind if I invite her to join Meg and me for a few weeks after the party here is over."

"Of course not," Robert said, ignoring the twinge that accompanied the idea of the party ending. When it did, he wouldn't see Katherine every day, no matter where she went. "I'm sure she'd love the country. You have a pretty estate."

"Thank you. I'll pass along your compliments," Simon said with a chuckle. "Meg enjoys her company, of course. No need for her to go back to the lion's den that is London so quickly, eh? Only bad influences there."

Robert pursed his lips. "You are trying to get a rise out of me. It will not work."

"No, because you don't like her. So you will be happy to know there is a viscount who lives two estates over in Crestwood. Perhaps Meg will invite him to a cozy supper one night. He might be a wonderful match for Katherine."

Robert pivoted, and his expression must have looked as fierce as it felt, for Simon took a long step away from him and his eyes went wide as saucers. "Would you like me to ask you my first question again?"

"I don't *know* if I like her," Robert growled. He had never wanted to throttle a person so much in his life. Simon stared at him for a beat, two, long enough that the silence became uncomfortable. At last, Robert threw up his hands. "Out with it."

"You've avoided entanglements for a long time," Simon said gently. "I'm concerned."

Robert's heart sank. It was one thing to guess how little his friends thought of him. Quite another to see it, to hear it.

"You fear what I'll do to her, cold-hearted snake that I am," he sneered.

Simon shook his head. "No. I am concerned about what you'll do to *yourself.* Opening your heart is well worth the risk. But there *is* a risk. Meg and I know that fact as well as anyone."

"Well, I'm not interfering with anyone's engagement, so how would my risk be the same?" he asked.

Simon ignored the barb. "There will still be a part of you that you put on the line. You're good at that in some ways. But never this one."

Robert glared at him. He hated to admit that Simon's words had struck upon the very fear that gripped him when he thought of taking a leap with Katherine. That the risk would not pay off. That both of them would be destroyed by love, just as he'd seen his mother destroyed.

He didn't want that pain. He didn't want to be responsible for what it would do to her. But what did that mean? Would it be best now to walk away from her? To end this affair and go back to what he was before?

Was that even possible?

"Robert?" Simon said softly.

"I've already risked something," he admitted slowly. "I didn't know I was doing it, but I did. And here I am. With all of you lot making eyes at me and asking me about Katherine three times a day."

Simon nodded. "So what will you do?"

"Dance with her," Robert said with a sigh.

"Dance?" Simon repeated.

He cast a side glance at his friend. "Ask your wife—I'm sure she remembers what it is to dance."

"You know that's not what I'm saying. You're just going to dance with her. Make no other decision?"

Robert looked at her across the room again. She was on her feet now, the whist game over. Charlotte had moved across to the pianoforte, settling in with Ewan at her side to play a duet so the couples could dance.

He knew nothing more except what he'd admitted to Simon already. When he looked at Katherine he saw desire and beauty, he saw connection that he didn't fully understand. He saw terror and hope, wound into one woman.

And right now all he wanted to do was dance with her. Let the rest fall away, be determined later.

"Dancing is a decision," he said softly. "Six months ago, I would have just run."

He met Simon's eyes evenly, and his friend nodded. "Then go dance."

He strode away toward her. She looked at him as he approached. There was that combination of happiness and anxiety that always mixed on her face when he came near her. He wondered what his own expression looked like.

But she didn't run, just as he hadn't. She shifted in her place beside her aunt and waited for him.

"My lady," he said as he reached them. "And Mrs. Sambrook. How lovely you both look tonight."

Mrs. Sambrook inclined her head. He could see the uneasy examination she was making. Just like his friends, it was clear she was aware of the circling he and Katherine were doing. Aware of how badly it could all end.

"You did not play cards," Mrs. Sambrook said at last.

He smiled, forcing himself back into his mask of charisma and flirtation. His most Roseford of looks, rather than Robert. He was beginning to feel they were different people now, when once they'd been the same.

"I did not. Though I saw that Lady Gainsworth and the Duchess of Donburrow won." He winked at Katherine and appreciated her little blush. "It seems you are quite the expert at cards."

"She is," Mrs. Sambrook said with a laugh. "If you are ever in a situation where you play whist with her, be sure to pick her as a partner. You do not want to play against my niece."

Katherine shook her head. "You make it sound as though I would roundly trounce him if he were not my partner."

"That sounds about right," Robert teased.

Mrs. Sambrook glanced from one of them to the other, that appraising gaze more focused now. "Well, I think I shall get myself some punch. Will you two be fine if I leave you?"

Robert could tell that the question was truly aimed at Katherine. A way to suss out if she wanted to be alone with him. He waited her response and was pleased when she nodded. "Of course, Aunt Bethany."

"I actually came to see if Lady Gainsworth might wish to dance with me," he said.

She glanced over at where Charlotte and Ewan were playing. Their choice was the perfect song for a country jig. There would be little touching, at least nothing intimate like in a slower dance. But it was better than nothing.

"I would like that," Katherine responded.

He nodded to her aunt, then extended a hand to Katherine. She took it, electricity leaping between them. He guided her into the space on the floor meant for dancing and joined in on the dance in progress.

When they swung in close together, he smiled. "I'm glad you accepted my invitation to dance, Katherine. I thought after earlier that you might run."

Her smile faded. "Why would I do that?"

They parted and he waited to respond as they each performed their complicated steps and then stepped in together once more. "Because you've been hiding from me all day."

She blushed. "That isn't true."

He arched a brow and they separated. Her cheeks held their flush as she twirled and then returned to him.

"Very well, I *might* have been avoiding you," she admitted. "I was embarrassed that we were caught in such a state by Emma and Meg. I worried they would not like me anymore. But they quickly disabused me of such a notion."

Her eyes were a little clearer as she said that, and he relaxed. He'd never believed the women would not be kind to Katherine in her upset, but to see that she had been calmed made him love his friends' wives even more.

They returned to each other, and he said, "I am sorry that I caused you grief even for a moment."

Her eyes went wide and she stumbled in the steps. "You? We were both in that room, Robert. We were kissing each other."

He licked his lips and couldn't help but think about doing the same right this very moment. "Yes, we were. And now I must ask you a question."

Before he could, the dance dictated they part again. She kept her gaze on him, confused and concerned before they returned and touched hands. "What is your question?"

The music ended and he executed a bow. "Come to me tonight?"

She caught her breath, and for a moment he saw all the conflict in her mind play out across her features. But it took her only a few seconds before she nodded.

"Yes," she whispered.

Something in him buckled at her acquiescence and his stomach flipped. He was so tangled up in her now. His happiness was starting to be bound to her presence.

"You two just danced the most serious jig in history," James said as he approached them, arm around Emma and a grin on his face. "Charlotte has said she will play a quadrille. May we trade partners so that poor Katherine will not have to continue in whatever dour little conversation you were sharing?"

Katherine laughed and sent Robert a side glance. "His Grace and I finished our dour little conversation. I would be pleased to dance the quadrille with you."

She flitted off with James to her place in the line beside him, but even as all their friends began, he couldn't stop watching her. And knowing that whatever was between them was growing. If he was not careful, it would soon be out of control.

CHAPTER SEVENTEEN

Katherine stood at Robert's door for the third occasion in as many nights. But this time she didn't feel nervous. No, that old anxiety had faded. What she felt was slightly more terrifying.

She felt peace. With this man. This man who did not love. Who did not stay. A man who would seduce. Who would make a wager because he was so convinced he could do so. A man who would run as far and as fast as he could from a future. But when she was with him, she didn't care.

"What do you want?" she murmured.

That answer leapt to her mind so easily. She wanted Robert. Only him. Despite the contentious element that came into their interactions. Despite the pain he had caused her in the past and the wager she still knew existed…or did it? After all, Robert had made no move to take her.

In fact, she was the one who longed for that now.

She shook away her troubled thoughts and knocked on his door, at last. It opened in a moment and Robert stood there. Tonight he was still formally dressed in his evening clothes and she almost felt disappointed. She was getting very accustomed to enjoying the view of his muscular chest and touching his warm skin while he pleasured her mercilessly.

He stepped back and motioned her into the room, shutting the door behind him and leaning back against it as he stared at her. "I wasn't sure you'd come," he said, his voice heavy with strain.

She wrinkled her brow. "Why?"

"You have to ask?" he said. "We talked about it while we danced. There was such…tension between us today. I didn't like it."

"I didn't either," she admitted.

He stepped forward, and it was clear he wanted to address their kiss, the interruption, her reaction. And she…didn't. Talking wasn't what she'd come here to do. Especially about such troubling topics. She feared if she started telling him about her heart, it would open her up to spilling it all. Including how connected she was beginning to feel to him.

How much she wanted him, not just in this chamber, but in her life.

She wasn't ready for that. She wasn't ready for him to turn away from her as he had on a night that seemed like a lifetime ago.

"Katherine—" he began.

She moved toward him and lifted her hand, covering his lips with her fingers. She felt the warmth of his breath against her flesh and it took every ounce of her control to speak.

"I didn't come here to do anything but touch you," she whispered. "I came here to let you touch me. Please, Robert. Let's leave the rest of the world outside for a while. Let's just give each other pleasure."

His eyes widened and he kissed her fingertips before he caught her hand and moved it aside. "You want…to touch me?"

She nodded slowly. "Yes. I do. Tonight I want to touch you as you've touched me. Please."

She didn't have to ask him twice. He caught her waist, dragging her against him and lowered his lips. "I am at your command, my lady."

She shivered as he kissed her. At her command? She could not imagine that. She'd never had a man at her command before. Her husband had certainly never allowed her any power, alongside his denial of pleasure.

And Robert? Well, he was a force of nature. She'd been swept up in him for days, never expecting he would allow anything but that.

She pulled away, even though his kiss was heaven, and looked over his shoulder toward the bedchamber. The one they'd never made it to before. Shaking, she took his hand and drew him into that adjoining room. She stopped beside the big bed and took a long breath that did nothing to calm her racing heart.

"Take off your clothes?" she asked.

He smiled. "All of them?"

Her heart stuttered. She'd not seen the man naked yet. An imbalance in the power of their relationship that matched all the others. She wanted to now. Wanted to desperately.

"For what I want to do, you can't have anything on."

The smile faded from his face. So did the brash swagger. He nodded and she watched, motionless, as he slowly shed every item he wore, starting with the jacket. He moved with grace, elegance, strength. She stared at rippling muscle that she wanted to trace with her fingers and then her tongue. She watched the casual way he tossed aside his expensive waistcoat. The way he held her gaze as he tugged his shirt over his head.

And then he was naked from the waist up, as he'd been the first time she came here. She caught her breath, stepping forward to lay her hand on the plane of his chest.

"Katherine," he whispered.

She blinked, forcing herself to look into his face and not at the body that drew her in to places that were frankly terrifying to go. "Yes?"

"I may need help with the boots," he said, one corner of his lips lifting.

She laughed, she couldn't help it. The man was so...easy. So comfortable in his own skin. He made it all a game, only there would never be a loser. No wonder it was impossible not to surrender.

He made it that way.

"Sit down," she said, motioning to the chair before the fire.

He did, slouching low on the seat and watching her as she dropped down and began to unbuckle the boots. She tugged and one slid away. Then the other. She was on her knees before him now, and she smiled as she positioned herself between his legs, just as he had done in the parlor, in the antechamber, in her dreams.

She caged him in with her hands, mimicking what he'd done so many times before, and then settled herself over him, straddling his lap. It was wicked to do so. She was entirely dressed. He was half naked.

And she liked it. Liked the way his gaze went hazy as he stared up at her.

"Do you really intend to let me be in control?" she whispered.

He smiled again. "I think you already are."

"Am I?" She shook her head. "We both know that in an instant you could reverse our positions and just have what you wanted."

"If I was going to simply take what I wanted, I would have had it nights ago," he drawled. "Wouldn't I?"

She tensed. Yes, that was true. She would have given herself to him any time he asked. She never would have refused him, even if she'd claimed she would.

She ground down against him a little and his breath went short as he strained up. She smiled and then slid from his lap. "Stand up. Let's remove the rest."

He moved to his feet and stood watching her. He reached for the fall front of his trousers, but she batted his hands away.

"My turn."

He held his hands up. A tiny surrender. He was not moving, not breathing, not stirring as he watched her tangle her fingers in the waist of his trousers. She glanced down, struggling with the buttons. The fabric strained thanks to the erection beneath. Her fingers felt thick and useless with anticipation.

Together it made for far more of a production than it might

have under other circumstances. But at last she loosened the buttons and let the flap fall, revealing his hard cock for the first time.

She stared, knowing it was silly and girlish to do so, but unable to look away. Her husband had not looked like this. Not like velvet over steel. Not like a divining rod to pleasure rather than water. Robert was thick, the skin darker at the base of him than at the mushroom head of his cock.

She glanced up, at last breaking her gaping stare and found him watching her.

"And what is your verdict?" he asked softly, not teasing, but still easy in his manner.

She shook her head. "My education was sorely lacking before. But I want to do things, Your Grace. And now you're going to get onto that bed and let me."

He laughed and the tension bled from the room. He shifted his trousers from trim hips, kicking them aside, and then he did as she'd ordered. He settled back on his bed, hands behind his head on the pillows, staring up at her in challenge and question and desire.

"I'm all yours."

She tensed, halfway up on the bed. All hers. That was most decidedly not true. Robert wasn't hers. He wasn't anyone's. He'd told her that once, that he would not be seduced to marriage. To commitment of any kind. He didn't remember that night, but she did.

Only he didn't mean hers to keep. He meant hers to enjoy. She pushed the first away and focused on the second.

She was on her knees now. Settled between his calves, and all she could do was stare at his naked body.

"Once my husband asked me to do a thing," she whispered, reaching out to trace his cock with her fingers. "Only he didn't like it when I did it."

"What did he ask you to do?" he asked, breathless.

She leaned over, little tendrils of hair loose from her bun tickling her cheeks and tangling around his cock. She darted her tongue out and let it flick over the head.

He sucked in a breath through his teeth. "He didn't like it?" he choked.

She smiled at the tension in his voice and looked up at him with a tiny shrug. "He said I did it wrong. And he said that if I did it, I was a whore. Which is an odd thing to say to someone who you asked to do a thing."

"I hate him," he muttered, arching as she stroked her hand over him. "I'm glad he's dead."

She shook her head. Right now she was very glad of the same, even if she would surely rot for such an uncharitable feeling. After all, his being gone allowed her to do…this…

She licked Robert a second time, loving the softness of his skin, the underlying hardness beneath. Loving the flavor of him, male desire and clean flesh. Loving that this man who was so capable of retaining all this control at all times arched beneath her touch and gripped the coverlet like it was the only thing keeping him sane.

"Katherine," he groaned. "You are not doing it wrong. Don't stop."

She smiled against him and licked again, circling the head of him gently before she finally dropped her mouth over him and took him inside. He was bigger than her husband—she'd never had to maneuver so much. She took him as far as she could comfortably go, gripping the base of his shaft and stoking it as she withdrew.

He mumbled garbled, helpless sounds and they drove her on. She sucked him deeper, watching up the length of his body as his face grew lined with tension. With pleasure. With sensation. *She* was doing this. Making him moan. Making him arch. Making his feet flex.

She was doing it and it made her whole body tingle, the same way it did when he touched her. When he licked her. When he made her come. She moaned against him and he cursed, his eyes squeezing shut.

She knew then what she would do. What she wanted. What

she needed. She stroked him one last time and then she slid up his body. Her dress tangled around him, one of her slippers clattered to the floor, but at last she straddled him once more. She was pushing at fabric, trying to get to the naked flesh beneath, for she had not worn drawers tonight.

She positioned herself about him and looked down to find his eyes wide. "Are you sure?" he asked.

She nodded, pushing away any doubt. Pushing away the wager that had kept her from this before. Pushing away memories of the night her husband died.

And she glided down, her wet sheath taking him, stretching and aching with pleasure as he filled her completely. Together they shivered, and she rested her forehead against his as their ragged breathing began to match. They were one now, joined in a way that could never be undone or forgotten.

He glanced up at her and smiled. "You're wearing too many clothes."

She laughed, shocked one could find humor at the same time that sensation ripped through her whole body. There was nothing dour or serious about this moment. Not like it had been before. This was no duty. It was something magical.

He caught her hips, dragging her forward and kissing her. She drove her tongue into his mouth, rotating her body, squeezing him inside of her. He moaned and she did the same as the pleasure ricocheted through her, hitting parts of her she didn't know existed until this moment.

She was vaguely aware of his fingers flitting along her spine. Her dress opened in the back and gaped forward. He tugged at it, pulling it over her head. She heard the delicate fabric rending before he tossed it aside.

"My maid will not be happy," she giggled. She grabbed the hem of her chemise and yanked it off her head, letting it join the dress on the floor.

Now she was naked, save her stockings and the one slipper that had stayed on her foot when she straddled him. He glided his hands up her sides, staring at her as he cupped her breasts and squeezed, massaging the flesh there.

She shut her eyes, dipping her head back as her hips thrust of their own accord. He grunted out his satisfaction, lifting to meet her as she rode him. She thrust harder, faster, feeling the pleasure build in her. She was just on the edge of it, ready to fall, when her mind yanked her back to that night just over a year ago.

The night when her husband had died in just this very position.

Her eyes flew open, pleasure gone as she stared down at Robert in horror. His face had been lined with satisfaction, but when he saw her expression, that faded. Concern replaced everything and he settled his hands onto her bare hips.

"What is it?" he said, his voice strained.

She shook her head, trying to make those images go away. "Just…he…I…"

He nodded slowly. "That night," he whispered. "You're remembering."

She gasped out a sob and leaned down against his shoulder. "I'm sorry. I'm so sorry."

His arms came around her, gentle as he smoothed his hands along her bare spine in comfort. "Why are you apologizing?" he asked against her ear as he kissed her there. "Of course you would experience memories, considering our position. Had I known you were going to do that, I might have moved us this first time."

She pulled back. "You aren't angry?"

"No." He traced her face with his fingers. "Never. But I need you to listen to me, Katherine. You didn't do anything wrong. The night that he died, it had nothing to do with your prowess."

"I know," she said.

He cupped her chin. "You say it. But *do* you know it?"

Her bottom lip began to tremble as she relived not just the moment Gregory had died, but the moments after. When the servants had come in to find her screaming over him. When the doctor had hissed at her to put on a robe. When everyone in the world, it seemed, judged her and whispered about her and the worst moment of her life.

"You married an old man," Robert said gently, "who obviously had a great many health problems. But I'm not an old man. You can't hurt me. What you were doing just now, riding me, felt like heaven. And watching you edge up to release as your body gripped me, that was something I will never forget."

She stared down at him. He was taking care of her so sweetly, not angry their interaction had been interrupted. And he wasn't lewd about what she was capable of doing to a man, as so many might be. Nor was he teasing her, instead taking her pain seriously. No one had ever done that. No one had ever done anything that Robert had done in the time they'd been here in Abernathe.

In that moment she realized she didn't just want him. She didn't just like him despite all the reasons she had to put walls up between them.

She was in love with him.

And she blinked down at him in shock that the feeling existed, growing now that she'd named it in her heart.

"Will you let me take over?" he asked. "And show you that you can have pleasure and I can bear it?"

Her throat was thick and she couldn't speak, not without confessing the thing she now knew. And he couldn't love her. That much was clear. So she simply nodded. She would take this connection of bodies, even though she might not ever get a connection of souls.

He gripped her hips and rolled her to her back. Their bodies stayed connected, and at first she thought he would just start thrusting. But he didn't. He withdrew, leaving her bereft until he began to trace his mouth down her naked body.

"This has been so worth the wait," he murmured before he began sucking her nipple.

He was hard, firm, and her thoughts left her mind as she trembled at his expert touch. She drove her fingers into his thick hair, lifting her hips to his as the pleasure began to grow deep inside her once more.

He shifted, one hand gliding between them, and he positioned himself back at her entrance. She gasped as he speared her, filling her completely in one long thrust. He brought his mouth back to hers, devouring her with kisses as he circled his hips in long, slow, almost languid thrusts.

She was drowning. In his kiss, in his touch, in the intense sensation that flowed from their joined bodies through her entire being. All her fear, the terror that had gripped her, it faded as he brought her focus back to their joined bodies. She was with no one else but him, there was no moment but this one.

When she surrendered to that fully, that was when her orgasm began. She'd had them before, of course. Alone in her bed as she furtively touched herself, from the expert skill of Robert's mouth and his fingers. But this…this was something different. Her body began to ripple, her sheath squeezing out of control. But this time he was inside of her and she had something to brace against as she cried out his name into the quiet room.

He continued to thrust, pulling his mouth from hers as he watched her arch and writhe beneath him. His pace increased. She felt that through the haze of her pleasure. When she opened her eyes, she saw the strain on his face, the edge of that control he always maintained.

"Please," she whispered, begging for his pleasure now that she'd had her own.

He let out a low, raw sound of animal pleasure and then he withdrew. His seed splashed between them as he cried out and she lifted up to kiss him.

He collapsed over her, their tongues tangling wildly, then slower, then sweetly as the high of passion faded. Only then did he gather her in his arms and roll to his side. She was splayed half on top of him, their legs tangled as he just…held her, his fingers combing through her hair gently. Almost hypnotically.

"If you keep doing that, I shall fall asleep," she said with a nervous laugh.

His fingers didn't stop. "And what would be wrong with that?" he whispered.

She tensed and looked up at him. In the heat of a moment, she had declared to herself that she loved this man. In this new moment that felt even more true.

"I-I would think a man like you would normally be pushing his lovers out the door after he…finished," she said.

He cupped her chin and drew her up for a kiss. She relaxed against him, the storm in her mind quieted for a moment by his touch. At last he drew back.

"I suppose normally I would. But these aren't normal circumstances." He shifted beneath her. "Stay with me tonight, Katherine. Let me make love to you over and over again. You can sneak back out before the servants begin their duties for the day. No one will be the wiser."

She swallowed hard. He was offering her more passion. More connection. More of everything but his heart, which she could not dare ask for.

And she wanted to give it. Soon enough this would all be over and she knew what she would regret if she walked away tonight.

"Yes," she whispered, then braced herself on the pillows to kiss him again. "Yes, yes, yes…"

Words she kept saying as he rolled her on her side and took her once again.

CHAPTER EIGHTEEN

Robert had been trying to deny it to himself in the three days since Katherine surrendered her body to him, but the truth was impossible not to feel. He had a spring to his step as he walked beside her now, trailing behind the group of their friends and her aunt on their way to a picnic by the lake. She laughed at some silly thing he'd said and the music of that sound tickled his ears.

He was becoming far too comfortable with a woman in his life. That should have terrified him, and yet it...*didn't*. The days with her felt peaceful, easy. The nights filled with passion as one of them snuck to the other's chamber so they could make love until dawn. Leaving her as the sun rose and pretending it had never happened was the only pain he felt in the affair.

He shook his head at that thought. Desire had always been something he could rely upon. Control, even. It came, he slaked it, it faded and he was finished. But with Katherine something was...*different*. His body might be satisfied as she drew his pleasure from him with her sultry, sensual passion, but his mind?

That *never* seemed fulfilled. He always wanted more. More and more of her.

Something about his demeanor must have changed, as well, for his friends had stopped haranguing him about the wager he'd made and teasing him about her. Oh, they still watched. They seemed patently incapable of not watching, but they did not interfere. Which made him just as nervous as the fact that he desperately wanted to hold Katherine's hand right now.

"Oh no," she whispered, leaning closer and making him so very aware of the sweet scent of her hair. "You are disappearing into your head, Roseford. Do come back."

He blinked. She knew him so well now that she could see that too. See it and draw her to him with just a whispered word. Part of him wanted to turn tail and run away from that realization. The other? Well, that was the part that seemed to be in charge and it forced him to stay just where he was.

He leaned in closer. "Perhaps I am simply reliving every moment of last night," he whispered. "Especially the part where we pleasured each other with our mouths and then you begged me to take you from behind."

Her eyes widened, and she glanced up at the group ahead of them. But *that* was another thing that had changed. While Katherine was still proper, of course—she could be nothing but—she no longer scolded him about potential damage to her reputation.

"You are a shameless cad," she whispered, laughter thick in her voice.

"And you love it," he retorted, then edged away to a more proper distance as they reached the picnic blankets that had already been laid out by servants earlier in the day.

He stared at the scene before him. Although most of the party events had been reserved for the adults, today the families were together. Bibi toddled around the blanket in front of Emma and James. James smiled at the little girl, laughing at her endless chatter, coaxing even more from her. From time to time, he leaned in to kiss his wife's neck and rest a hand on her belly.

Isabel was moving to take her place on a different blanket. Matthew held her arm, easing her down as they both laughed at her increasing size. Helena was sitting on the same blanket and she smiled at Baldwin, something knowing that made Robert wonder if they, too, would soon have an announcement for the group. The foursome was sharing their blanket with Katherine's

Aunt Bethany, and Robert's gaze moved to her. She was important to Katherine, a slender tie to the mother she had lost as a girl. And he liked the woman. She was as sharp and kind as her niece. And protective. He knew she watched him, and he didn't mind it as much as he once might have.

As for the others, they were scattered on another two blankets and seemed to be making a game of passing Charlotte and Ewan's gurgling five-month-old son, Jonathon, and Simon and Meg's nine-month-old son, James, back and forth between them. Meanwhile, Graham reclined with his head in Adelaide's lap, their seven-month-old daughter Madeline curled up sleepily on his chest, sucking her thumb and patting his face from time to time.

Once upon a time, Robert might have found this wholesome, family scene a bit stifling. It was why he'd initially turned down James's invitation to this event. Where was his place here? And yet now he felt something else stirring in his chest. He might have called it longing, but that was ridiculous. Wasn't it?

"Katherine!" Charlotte called out from one of the blankets. "Come and sit. I want to talk to you about Christmas plans."

Katherine gave him a little look, her face bright with happiness, then slipped off to take her place beside Charlotte and Ewan. Robert remained standing, staring as Charlotte handed off Jonathon to Katherine.

She shifted the child into a more comfortable position and began to talk to him. Baby talk, though Robert could not hear it from this distance. In that quiet moment, a wave of emotion slammed into him.

Could he have this? This thing that had bewitched his friends, his family? He'd never been able to picture it, so he always avoided the exercise. But now…there it was, ten feet away from him, holding someone else's child.

He saw a lifetime in Katherine face. He saw her expression as he took her around the world, sharing all his favorite places with her. He saw her smile as they shared their home with their friends and her beloved aunt. He saw her standing in his bedroom, ready for his touch, only she would never leave. He saw waking up beside her until he was gray and slow and forgetful of everything except for her.

He saw a *life*. And it was no longer stifling or unpleasant or constricting or terrifying. It looked…perfect.

Katherine kept glancing at him as she talked to Ewan and Charlotte. At last she handed over the baby and got up. He knew everyone was watching as she made her way to him. But he couldn't move. He was frozen.

She reached him and tilted her head as she looked at him. "I was teasing earlier about you being in your head, but you look like you've seen a ghost. Why don't we walk?"

He nodded. It was all he could do when the source of all his consternation was standing in front of him and the last thing he wanted to do was escape her. Escape *with* her—that was another story.

She took his arm, smiled back their friends and said, "His Grace and I will be back. Don't drink all the wine!"

There was laughter as the group went back to their lives and Robert stumbled after the woman who was becoming the center of his. They walked for a while. Normally a silence between them was comfortable. Today he felt the weight of it. It made him hear his own thoughts, and right now his mind was screaming at the top of its lungs about things he had never considered.

They turned onto a winding path that took them into the deeper woods. He felt her hand tighten on his elbow as he took her over fallen logs and down a little hill. In the distance, a tiny cottage roof peeked up over the bramble of trees, and he stopped as he stared at it.

"Meg and Simon's cottage," he muttered.

Her eyes went wide as she lifted on her tiptoes. "Is it? Meg has told me a little more about the beginning of her marriage to Simon. That caused quite the upheaval in your group of friends, didn't it?"

Robert pressed his lips together hard. "It nearly destroyed us. At the time, I was shocked that Simon would let such a thing invade his sense of brotherhood. Now…"

She tilted her head. "Now?"

He looked at her from the corner of his eye. Now he understood it more. He couldn't say that out loud.

"Well, they are happy," he said instead. "Graham suffered for it a while, but now he clearly loves Adelaide to distraction, as you and I were witness to. I suppose it worked out in the end."

She nodded. "It did, it seems. The friendship between the two men appears to have been repaired, as well."

"Yes. And better than ever," Robert agreed. "Like the place where they were torn apart, the injury to their friendship ended up healing stronger."

"Hmmm." She paced away from him, closer to the little cottage. "I wish all wounds healed that way."

He nodded, his mind turning on his own points of damage, as well as hers. He knew them well. She had confessed them, trusting him with them, trusting him not to make them worse. Had anyone else in his life ever done that so completely? Had anyone else ever believed in him the way she apparently did?

She faced him after a moment and said, "What was it that made such a terrible look come on your face a few minutes ago?"

He stared at her, with afternoon sunshine filtering down over her face. She almost glowed in it, like he'd pictured an angel would do when he was a child. But she was real. She could be his.

And in that moment, he began to speak. "There are so many rumors about me."

She blinked, as if surprised by that topic. Then she smiled slightly, pink entering her cheeks. "Yes."

He shook his head. "Not just about my…*expertise*. My past."

The smile left her face. "I suppose that is true. Though the ones about your sinful talents tend to outweigh the rest."

He looked toward the cottage again, lost for a moment in

thought, but never doubting what he was going to tell her. Why he needed to say it. The words were hard. Painful.

Necessary if there was to be any of that future that kept reaching out to tempt him.

"Yes, I suppose that is by design. I said it to you a few days ago, that sex can create a distance, a screen over what one might wish to conceal."

She was quiet a moment. Then she stepped toward him and reached up to cup his cheek. It drew his eyes to her and her dark gaze snagged his, holding there. Filled with warmth and empathy. "And what would you want to conceal?"

"My mother," he choked, hating the pain that tore through him as he said those two words. Knew what he would say next. "She is not buried in a proper place on my estate. My father would not allow it. She's buried at a crossroads instead. Someplace unmarked, I practically need a map to find her."

Her lips parted. "A crossroads," she repeated. "Robert?"

He nodded, for he saw she understood the meaning of that loaded statement. Saw it crash over her lovely features, reflect back his own pain.

"She killed herself."

Katherine stared at Robert, torn to shreds by the expression on his handsome face. He was so good at covering how he felt with a wicked smile or an arched brow or a playful laugh. But she saw through it all now, that charisma he used as a shield.

He lowered it and let her inside to where pain ruled.

"Suicide," she repeated, her voice shaking. "Oh, Robert."

He tensed and his gaze flitted away, like he was seeking a path where he could run away. But he didn't. He stayed before her, cutting his heart out and offering it to her. She knew what a meaningful gift it was.

And she drew a breath and took both his hands in hers. "Tell me," she whispered.

His breath went ragged and he eased down onto a fallen log. She took a place beside him, remaining silent as she allowed him a moment to collect his thoughts and find whatever horrible words he needed to say.

"Victoria," he whispered. "That was her name."

"Lovely," Katherine whispered.

"I knew she and my father were troubled. He was…well, I have inherited his worst qualities, I suppose. Philandering was what he did, his number of affairs uncountable in their number. Christ, there are nearly a dozen by-blows whose support my estate ensures."

Her lips parted. "Your half-siblings. Do you know them?"

"Some. In passing." He bent his head. "She knew about them, too."

There was bitterness in his tone, and she flinched at it. "Your mother. How?"

His gaze flitted up to her, his mouth turned down in a frown. "*He* told her. Crowed to her, that craven bastard. When they would argue, which was often, he loved to cut her with those facts."

"And you overheard them?" Katherine whispered, thinking of her own loud, ugly childhood.

He nodded. "Sometimes. But more often than not, she would tell me all about it herself."

"How old were you?" Katherine gasped, shocked to hear not only of the cruelty of Robert's father, but of the indiscretion of his mother.

He gazed off in the distance again, leaving her, returning to his childhood, reliving what she could not see but felt pulsing in him. "The first time I recall her telling me about it all I was five, maybe six. And I was ten when she died."

"For four years, she burdened you with her pain?" Katherine asked softly.

He looked at her, almost shocked, like he hadn't considered that part of it. But he didn't pull away. "I suppose now that I'm an adult, I can see that it would be a burden for a child. But when I was a boy, I only wanted to help her. Make her smile, make her laugh. Make her forget him."

"But you couldn't," Katherine encouraged gently.

"No."

Silence hung between them. Heavy. As meaningful as any words they had ever said. She drew a few calming breaths and then took his hands in hers.

"How?"

"She took laudanum. She said it was for the pain, and I suppose it was." He blinked, but the tears still gathered in his dark eyes. "The pain in her heart. It numbed her to it all. It put her into a stupor where no one could retrieve her. And it got worse and worse."

"She took too much?" Katherine asked. "Could it have been an accident?"

"No." He bent his head. "As a boy I didn't even realize what she'd done. My governess woke me one day to tell me she was dead."

Katherine sucked in a breath. "With no more delicacy than that?"

"Not much more. My father didn't hire servants to be soft on me. She woke me, told me to dress, and by the way, your mother is dead. Died in the night."

Katherine felt her tears begin to fall but made no effort to wipe at them. She clung to Robert instead, pressing any strength she'd ever had into him. Seeing how deeply he was hurting and how much he needed to say these things.

"My father was vague," he continued, his voice thick. "An illness, he told me. He hardly looked up from his desk to say it. I was not allowed to see her, to say goodbye, to be at her funeral, nor even to know where she was buried. I used to sneak out, searching for her in the family graveyard at my estate and she was not there."

"You must have been devastated," she whispered.

"I was, but showing it was not an option. It was not long

after that I was sent away to school. My father did not allow me to speak of her on the rare occasions I was let home. My questions went unanswered. Until I turned twenty."

Her breath felt heavy now, difficult to draw as she waited for the next part in this terrible, terrible story. "You pressed him," she whispered.

"Yes. We were in London, and I admit I had been drinking. It was April—April is when she died, and I have never handled the anniversary well."

Katherine blinked as her mind was brought back to that night on the terrace three years before. That had been April, too. Robert had been drunk then. Had that been around the anniversary of his mother's death?

He was still speaking and she forced focus. "I was so bloody angry. I confronted him. I was screaming at him as he stared up at me, almost impassive. I vented all my rage, railed at him for probably five solid minutes with hardly a drawn breath. And when I had no more energy, he rose up before me and told me she had killed herself. He told me how weak she was, how worthless. He told me where she was buried and why she was buried there. Then he called me her son, told me I was as bad as she was."

Katherine jerked a hand to her lips, tears streaming over it as she stared at his blank face. "Oh, Robert. That is terrible. What did you do?"

"I hit him," Robert said softly. "As hard as I could. I spat on him. And then I walked away."

He pushed to his feet and paced off. She stayed where she was, despite how much she wanted to follow him. To fold him into her arms and hold him. Comfort him.

He leaned against a tree for a moment, his breath short. "I never saw him again. I left every letter unanswered. I avoided him strenuously. I threw myself into sin and sex to forget it all. He died three years later and I inherited."

She did stand now, stepping toward him. "Do you regret not talking to him in the final years of his life?"

He pondered that question a moment. "No. We had nothing left to say to each other. He wanted me to come back for control, not love. Whatever thin veneer of connection we ever had was dead long before he was."

She nodded slowly. She saw regrets on his face, perhaps ones he did not even recognize, but this was not the time to draw them out. He looked exhausted from confession. Ready to collapse.

"May I ask you a question?" she whispered, coming to him at last and reaching up to draw her thumb across his lips gently.

He shivered at her touch. "I have dumped an ugly pile of history on you. Ask away."

"Could he have lied to you about her death?" she asked. "Just to hurt her, hurt you, one final time?"

He sucked in a long breath. "I thought of that. Hoped it was true. But after he died, I was going through his papers and I found her suicide letter. He had filed it with her dowry and marriage contracts. Like it was a business transaction with the rest. I read it a hundred times. I could recite it to you word for word if it wouldn't make me—" He broke off and his head bent. "—choke."

Now she did wrap her arms around him, pulling him against her. His head dropped onto her shoulder and he went nearly limp in her arms. She held him, using all her strength to buoy his. Feeling this powerful man shake in her arms.

"Do they know?" she whispered when his breath returned to some kind of normal rhythm.

"*They*, the dukes?" he asked, his voice muffled before he lifted his head and stared down at her.

"You must have told them. They are your closest friends."

He hesitated and then shook his head. "They don't know she killed herself," he whispered. "Just that she died. Just that my father was an unrelenting bastard who deserves his cold grave."

Her lips parted. "Oh, Robert, to carry that pain all alone for so long. I'm so sorry."

He was staring down into her eyes now, his gaze intense. Unreadable. And her breath was stolen by how powerful her emotions were. Empathy, understanding and beneath it all, love. She so deeply loved this man, more every day. Despite their bad beginning, despite his terrible reputation, despite the bargain he had made that now seemed like it was leagues away.

She loved him. Maybe some part of her had always been drawn to him. That he made her nervous, fluttery, hadn't been something she'd understood. And yet now it all made sense. His soul, like hers, had been shattered for so long.

But when they were together, there was peace.

"Why did you tell me this?" she whispered. "When you have never said it out loud."

He swallowed hard, and for a moment she thought he might reveal the same feelings that now rioted in her chest. Love. A love that would be wild and free and passionate.

"I care for you," he said instead, and his gaze darted away.

Her heart sank a little. Not the declaration she had hoped for. And yet…it was clear it was one that was difficult for him to make at all. It was meaningful to him.

"You do?" she whispered.

He stared into her eyes. "Yes," he said softly, the sound barely carrying on the cool breeze. "I have always avoided such things. Entanglements of the heart are complicated. Even watching my friends marry and seem happy has not changed my opinion that marriage can be a very dangerous endeavor."

She blinked. He was talking about subjects that should have made her heart soar. But his choice of words, his tone…they were not particularly romantic. "I'm not certain what you want me to say, Robert, when you tell me that you like me despite your hesitations about matters of the heart in general."

He pursed his lips. "I wasn't clear. Let me try again. Katherine, I would like to…court you."

Her eyes went wide and she stared at him in shock. "I beg your pardon?"

"Yes, to court you," he repeated, hesitation thick in his tone.

She arched a brow. "Are you sure?"

"No, but yes." He smiled. "Not properly court you, though. At least not entirely. I will still want to do all those wicked things that we've been doing. I'm never going to be the man who simpers or smiles or thinks that kissing your gloved hand will be enough passion."

She shook her head. "Heaven forbid. But can you really mean that? Courting has an end, Robert, and it is the one you were just implying was still a mystery to you."

He glanced at the cottage once more, his gaze distant. Bleary. Then his gaze returned to her. "Marriage."

Her heart was racing but she managed to remain quiet as he processed that word.

"Yes, there is that," he said at last. "But it is something I must do at some point, isn't it? I do have obligations when it comes to my position. And I cannot imagine ever finding another person who challenges me or interests me or drives me as you do. Another person who I would feel comfortable telling my secrets to. Or a person whose secrets I, too, would wish to hold. If that is marriage, couldn't we be happy together?"

Once again she was torn. What he described sounded like it could be a happy life. And yet it wasn't enough. Because she wanted his heart. Now that she recognized it, she had never wanted anything more.

And yet she couldn't say that. Couldn't tell him that or he would run as surely as a spooked filly. What he offered was far more than she could ever hope to find. And perhaps, with time, it could become the thing she wanted most from him.

"Court me," she repeated, letting the words roll over her tongue.

He nodded. "Yes."

"Where are you two?" They both jolted as James's voice carried through the woods toward them.

"Perfect timing, as always, has my friend James," Robert said with a laugh and a roll of his eyes.

She smiled even though her heart ached, both a happy and

empty pain. "We have been gone a long time—they probably think we're doing something very wicked out here."

"We should have done instead," he retorted.

She stared up at him, seeing the core of his spirit in his eyes in a way she never had before. She shook her head. "No, we did exactly what we ought to have done. I'm glad you talked to me about your mother. And as for courting—"

"Katherine! Robert?" James's voice came again.

Robert furrowed his brow. "We're just returning, go find something else to do," he shouted out into the general direction of the voice. "As for courting...?" he encouraged her gently.

She smiled. "Yes."

His eyes went wide. "Yes?"

She nodded. "Yes."

His entire impossibly handsome face lit up and her heart warmed at the sight. Whatever else he did not, or could not, feel for her, he did seem truly happy that she had accepted his attentions. Happy enough that she lifted up to her tiptoes and brushed her lips to his.

His arms came around her and he tugged her closer, the kiss transforming into something deeper and darker and more filled with promise. At last she pulled away.

"We'll have to continue that later," she whispered.

He let out a playfully put-upon sigh. "I count on it. Now come on, before he sends out a party to drag us back to propriety."

He caught her arm and they walked back toward the group. And though Katherine was happy with what they had decided, happier than perhaps she'd ever thought she could be when she found Robert here at Emma and James's party, there was still a nagging doubt in her chest.

Doubt about him. Doubt about herself. Doubt about any future they could have, especially when the past still felt so powerful.

CHAPTER NINETEEN

Katherine pinched her cheeks and smiled at her reflection before she smoothed the skirts of her ballgown. As she did so, there was a light knock on her chamber door and then her aunt tucked her head around the barrier.

"Oh, you look lovely," Bethany cooed.

Katherine pivoted to face her. "Thank you. The brocading on this gown is my very favorite," she said. "Come in."

Bethany entered the room and Katherine smiled. "And don't you look lovely, too," she said, admiring her aunt's green gown, which brought out the highlights in her dark hair. The very same ones Katherine shared. "If you are not careful, you shall be mistaken for my sister, not my aunt, and some young man will sweep you into a scandalous affair."

Bethany began to laugh. "I doubt that. At any rate, I think the limit is one scandalous affair per family, isn't it?"

Katherine opened her mouth to deny the charge, but then threw up her hands. "I suppose there is no reason to deny it to you, Aunt Bethany. Robert and I are fairly obvious, I think, in our connection."

"I'm glad you took my advice to have a little fun just for yourself," Bethany said as she took a seat before Katherine's fire and smiled up at her.

"I am, too," Katherine said with a contented sigh. "The past week has been heavenly. I cannot believe we return to London tomorrow."

Bethany arched a brow. "And when you return? What then? You will break off the affair?"

Katherine worried her lip. "Well, it is…more than an affair now. You see, a few days ago Robert declared that he would like to court me. Officially."

Bethany's eyes went wide. "The Duke of Roseford asked to court you?"

Katherine couldn't help but laugh at the incredulity. "Yes. I was as shocked as anyone."

"And you accepted?" Bethany sputtered.

Now some of Katherine's pleasure was tempered. "You do not approve?"

Bethany pushed from her chair and paced the room. "It is just that the man has such a reputation! A courtship implies he would offer marriage. Would you want to be trapped in a life with a person like him? So driven by his baser desires?"

Katherine hesitated. What her aunt said was true, certainly, at least to the public perception. But she also felt protective. She knew Robert better, she loved him.

"Since his request to court me, I have felt a change in him," she said softly. "He is…well, he's not entirely proper, but there is something there that goes far deeper than mere desire. He makes me laugh. He makes me smile. He comforts me and has faith in parts of me that I hardly knew existed."

Bethany blinked at her in shock. "You are in love with him?"

Katherine ducked her head as she squeaked out, "I am."

Bethany was silent long enough that Katherine finally looked up at her to see if she had expired from shock. But it was concern on her aunt's face, nothing more.

"I have seen the connection between you two. And his friends certainly think highly of him. But I cannot help but worry. Your entire life has been tied to men who left you no choice for so long. I fear that you'll tie yourself to one who could break your heart. Before you do anything that will be permanent, please promise me that you will explore any concerns you have with the man. Promise me you will not be hasty just because he is handsome and charismatic and fabulous in bed."

Katherine sucked in her breath. "*Aunt Bethany!*"

Her aunt shrugged. "We must call a spade a spade, my dear."

Katherine laughed, but in her heart she knew her aunt was right. After all, there were three things that she had kept from Robert. Three secrets that she held close, at first so that she could use them against him. And now?

Well, she hadn't talked to him because she feared the damage they could do. But perhaps Bethany was correct. The time had come to open all the doors, to tell Robert why she had hated him for so long. To demand an explanation for what he'd done.

And to ask him if he could ever truly give her the future she desired.

"You've given me much to think about," Katherine whispered. "I know you're right."

Bethany linked arms with her. "I always am. Now, let's go down. You claim there is some young man who might be interested in me. I'd best find him before it's too late. And you have a gentleman of your own to see."

Katherine couldn't help but smile at her aunt's teasing, and yet deep within her anxiety bloomed. There were reasons she had hidden the truth from Robert. And there were stakes to telling the truth.

Like losing his love before she'd even determined if she could have it.

The last ball of the country party was in full swing, with what seemed to be every person in Abernathe and the surrounding counties in attendance. Robert found his foot tapping to the music as he watched the couples on the dancefloor. He'd always been good at dancing, of course. A gentleman was meant to be so, and he'd always felt that a dance gave him a good idea of a lady's behavior in bed. It was all part of the seduction.

Yet tonight, he wasn't playing a game. He watched those in attendance as they buzzed around each other, laughing and chatting, and he felt something…different.

Everything had been different, really, since three days before, when he'd confessed his darkest truth to Katherine and then asked to court her. It had not been easy. There had been times since then when he'd wanted to do nothing more than run as far as he could from her and all she represented. But she always drew him back. Gently, sweetly, and he could not resist her.

He would marry her. He knew that. And for the first time in his life, when he thought of that eventuality, it did not grip him in abject terror.

He was drawn from his thoughts as he watched Katherine spin around the dancefloor with James once more. She had been dancing with his friends and the other guests all night, and Robert couldn't help but puff with pride when he watched her.

She was something to behold, truly beautiful and graceful. Other men wanted her, but that didn't make him burn with jealousy. It was pride. *She* wanted *him*. She came to him. The others could rot, for all they would ever get was a dance.

And when she danced with his friends? That was even better. He loved how easily she fit into their ranks. She was a friend to the duchesses, and she was comfortable with the dukes. She belonged and that meant more to him than he could ever explain, no matter how long he had to write a treatise on the subject.

It was like nothing he'd ever felt before. And he never wanted to lose it. He never wanted to lose her. He didn't know what to call that feeling. He had an idea what some of his friends would label it, but he wasn't ready to do that yet. Not yet.

The song ended, and Katherine laughed as she curtsied and James bowed playfully. Robert stepped forward as they left the floor and met them at the edge of the ballroom, where they would part.

"I have watched this poor lady be manhandled by shockingly poor dancers long enough," he declared with a wink for Katherine. "Please, Lady Gainsworth, do allow me to offer you a far superior partner."

Her eyes lit up as she smiled at James. "Abernathe, do you think His Grace will introduce me to this superior partner soon? Is he here, Roseford? Have you been hiding him all along?"

James snorted out a laugh. "Never let this one go, Roseford. She is far too evenly matched with you."

Roseford glared at him playfully and then caught her arm. "Come along, minx."

She did not resist but returned to the dancefloor just as the orchestra began a waltz. Her smile softened and she stepped into his arms just as willingly as she did when they were alone and lost in each other.

"You know, you once tried to avoid this," he said, staring down into those dark eyes and feeling all the connection they shared pulsing back at him. Drawing him in.

She tilted her head. "Avoid what?"

"Dancing with me. Touching me at all."

He expected her to smile, to laugh, to be coy and playful. Instead her expression fell a little. "Yes, I did. I had my reasons."

He wrinkled his brow at the look. "Do you want to share those reasons, my lady?"

She swallowed hard and her gaze darted around the dancefloor at all the other couples. When her eyes returned to his he saw her hesitation. Her reluctance. It stoked a worry in him that he had never felt so powerfully before.

"Yes," she whispered. "But not now. Not here."

"Then what about our parlor?"

Now her smile returned. "Are you certain you don't just

want to be alone with me?"

He leaned in a little closer. Too close. Too obvious to the eyes watching them. In that moment, he didn't give a damn what anyone thought.

"Do you prefer me wanting you right here, right now, in the middle of this ballroom and in front of all these people?" he teased.

IIer eyes lit up and he groaned. Damn, but this woman. She truly was what everyone said she was. His match. She was his match, and that was wonderful and alarming all at once.

"I don't think I'm *quite* ready for that level of scandal, Your Grace," she said, slightly breathless. "So the parlor it is. I want to talk to my aunt for a moment first. Will you meet me there?"

As the music ended, he nodded. "Yes."

He so wanted to kiss her in that moment as she stared up at him, eyes filled with worry but also wonder. He wanted to kiss her for comfort, and to remind her that he...belonged to her. Because he did. He knew he did, he knew it like he knew his own face in the mirror.

Perhaps he would find the strength, the courage to tell her that tonight once she had made whatever confession that weighed so heavily on her mind. Perhaps he would be able to find words that weren't just that he cared for her, but that he felt something more.

She released his hand and smiled over her shoulder at him before she slipped through the crowd, disappearing from view. He grinned to himself as he went the other way. Past the other guests, his friends, down the long winding halls of James and Emma's estate and into the parlor where he had first kissed Katherine. First made her cry out with pleasure. He loved this room. He wanted to prepare it so it would be a comfortable, safe place for her.

He moved about the chamber, adding logs to the fire, fluffing pillows on the settee, pouring them each a drink in case she needed it to buoy her strength. In case he did.

"Preparing for a lady?"

He jerked his head up from what he was doing and found the Marquess of Berronburg leaning against the doorjamb with a drink in his hand. Robert straightened. He had not seen his...well, he supposed he ought to call the man a friend...since London. His cheeks flushed as he recalled their last conversation had been about Katherine. And the lurid wager Robert had declared he would win.

Now that memory turned his stomach.

"Berronburg," he said, holding out a hand in greeting. "I did not realize you were here."

"It's a crush," Berronburg said as he entered the room and looked around with a wicked smile. "And I'm fairly certain I was not officially invited. I may own an estate on the outskirts of Abernathe's land, but we are not especially friendly neighbors. His duchess thinks I'm uncouth."

Robert swallowed. "I thought you wore that label as a badge of honor."

Berronburg chuckled. "Men like us always do. I'm honestly surprised the lady still invites you. You are worse than I am."

Robert's mind turned instantly to Katherine. "I'm trying to be...better."

"Hmmm. In truth, I had to come. There was a rumor circulating in London that Lady Gainsworth is in attendance at this party, and of course it turned out to be true. You made a good move isolating her out here. And I saw you two dancing, so I must assume your pursuit of the wager is going well."

Robert's heart began to throb. This was a tricky situation to manage. If he told Berronburg to sod off, the marquess would never believe that he truly cared for Katherine. Robert's past behavior—toward lovers in general, but Katherine specifically—would not allow it. Berronburg would pursue her for the bet. They would *all* pursue her.

"It is progressing," he said softly.

"Progressing?" Berronburg repeated with a frown. "After ten days isolated on this estate, I would have thought you would have already bedded her and crowed to stake your claim. Are you losing your touch in your advancing years, my friend?"

"I suppose that is a possibility," Robert said, grinding his teeth.

Berronburg's face lit up. "Then that means the lady is still in play. The wager's amount has increased tenfold since she disappeared into the country. If you cannot land her, the winner will walk away with a tidy sum in his pocket. Perhaps I should play my cards, as well."

Robert's eyes went wide. Fuck it all, that was exactly what Katherine didn't need. To be stalked across the country by panting, leering men who wanted to bed her only to win a game. That he had ever been one of them made him hate himself.

"You assume I'm finished with the lady. I'm not by half. It isn't about not fulfilling the terms of the bargain, my friend. It's about fulfilling my own desires with the lady. You may tell the others that the prize has been won."

Berronburg's face fell slightly. "Bollocks. I knew it was too much to hope. You wanted her, of course you would have her. It probably wasn't even a challenge, was it? Are you going to give me any lovely details of the quest?"

Robert shook his head. "Not tonight, my friend."

Not ever, and this man was no longer his friend. But there was no reason to cause a ruckus now. To draw attention where it needn't be. When he returned to London he would ensure all talk of this shameful bet was erased from the mouths of his friends. That Katherine would never have to hear of it.

Or know what he'd done.

"Well, I hope you'll talk soon. You know how everyone loves the tales of your conquests."

Robert glanced at the door, anxious because he knew Katherine would be coming at any moment. Not that he thought Berronburg would be so uncouth as to mention their bet to her face, but he would leer and she would be uncomfortable.

"I see you counting the time," the marquess chuckled. "I'll be off and leave you to whichever lady you'll be rutting with tonight, be it the lovely Lady Gainsworth or another. We should go to the Donville Masquerade when you're back in Town. Catch up."

Robert pursed his lips. "Certainly. Goodnight, my lord."

"Your Grace," Berronburg said, and slipped from the room.

Robert let out his breath in a slow exhale. That unpleasantness was done. He didn't feel particularly good about it. He'd allowed the marquess the impression that he'd won the bet with Katherine. And he had. But that hadn't been on his mind for such a long time.

He heard the door behind him close and turned. Katherine stood there. He smiled at the sight of her, his thoughts of Berronburg vanishing at her entrance. But his smile fell as he read her expression. Cold. Hard. Broken.

And he knew in that moment that she'd heard everything the marquess had said.

She crossed the room in three long strides, her hands shaking. She stopped in front of him, dark eyes lifted to him. "How could you? You bastard, you bastard! How could you?"

CHAPTER TWENTY

Katherine had never wanted to strike someone so much in her life. To hit Robert because the pain that was bursting in her chest was too powerful to put into words. But she sucked in her breath to calm herself, remind herself she was better than that. And he did not deserve to see how deeply he had wounded her.

His face was ashen. "Katherine," he whispered. "Please, let me explain."

"Explain?" she repeated, jerking away from him and letting her gaze slide around the room. He'd been preparing the chamber for her. Laughing at her, she supposed, as he awaited Berronburg so they could crow over her foolishness. "How the hell do you think you can explain what I already knew? What I've known for *weeks*."

He stared at her, shaking his head. His expression was pained and confused. "You—you knew?"

"Isabel came to me even before I was invited here and she told me what a horrible bargain you'd made over bedding me." Her hands shook. "And I vowed I would *never* allow you near me."

He blinked. "That night at the ball when you said I didn't care what I did to other people. You knew then, didn't you?"

She nodded. "I did. When I was invited here, to escape you and your vile designs, I leapt at the chance."

"But I was here," he whispered. "And you were here."

"A test, and one I suppose I failed." She lifted her hands to her suddenly hot cheeks, letting the coldness of her fingers anchor her in some tiny way. "What an idiot I was, and how clever you were. To pretend to care as you did, to make yourself something I wanted. I-I wanted to believe you."

"I never made myself anything," he burst out, taking a step toward her. "Please, let me explain."

She stared at him. God, but he did look stricken. Such a big part of her melted at that expression of broken guilt and deep pain. But that was all part of his charade, wasn't it?

"Oh yes, please do." She folded her arms. "I would *love* to hear this."

"Back in London there were a group of...of..."

"Ungentlemanly bastards?" she filled in for him, shocked she could be so cold and direct when what she wanted to do was fall on the carpet and weep.

"Yes," he agreed. "We are idiots. *I* am an idiot. They knew your story, and of course it generated interest from them. You already knew that—it is no surprise. When I saw you that first night you returned, I was immediately attracted to you, Katherine. With a power that surprised even me. And I declared, in my own selfish, unthinking way, that I would have you."

"And you did *everything* in your power to make sure that happened," she hissed. "Perhaps you knew all along that I was invited here, even if James did not. Perhaps you maneuvered yourself to be here so that you could manipulate me further."

"No!" he said sharply. "No, that wasn't what happened. All the dukes found out what I'd done the moment the duchesses heard about the wager. They admonished me, none more than James. He begged me to listen to my better impulses rather than my baser desires. I came here, truly, to do as he asked and separate myself from you."

"But once you saw me, how could you resist such a challenge?" she snapped, hating the sharpness of her tone that revealed her emotions to this man who didn't deserve them.

"Yes," he admitted after a pause that seemed to fill the room. "You were my ultimate challenge. But I swear to you, Katherine, it was *never* about the wager. The moment I saw you, I knew I would not be able to resist pursuit, but it was never about winning anything except for your time and your attention. I craved that. Once I touched you, everything changed. What has happened between us is real. My desire to court you is real. The fact that I care for you is real."

"And *that* is why you crowed to your friend about bedding me and winning your wager," she whispered.

He dropped his head, shame flowing over his handsome face with an intensity that set her back a step. This was a man who did not allow guilt. Who did not come close enough to give a damn about what anyone thought of him.

And he practically dripped with shame.

"I did that," he admitted. "Out of a stupid, foolhardy notion that I could steer Berronburg away from you. I was taken aback by his being here at the ball tonight. And I was not ready for his questions. If I slipped into bad habits, it had everything to do with me and nothing to do with you. I promise you, Katherine, I was already planning how I would keep them from ever discussing you again when I return to London."

She shifted slightly. In some way she could understand his explanation. In some way she could forgive him for the wager she had already known about, already punished him for. In some way, she wanted to believe that what he said was true and that what they'd shared was as deep as she had believed it to be.

But now they were on a path, one she feared would destroy them. There was no escaping it all now.

"Do you know why I wanted to speak to you tonight?" she asked, steeling herself against all those things she wanted to believe. All those foolish things.

"No," he said.

"I wanted to tell you *why* I hated you when I returned to Society. Why I avoided you. I know you've wondered. I was going to confess to you tonight because I felt I was keeping a wall between us and I did not want it there anymore after all we shared."

His lips parted. "You were going to tell me you knew about the bet."

She nodded. "That was part of it, yes. But your disgusting wager is not why I hated you, Roseford."

"Please don't revert to my title." His voice cracked. "*Please* don't."

"I've hated you for three years," she whispered. "Because you destroyed my life."

Robert blinked, trying to clear his mind, trying to find something in his memories that would explain those harshly spoken words. He could find none. And yet there was no mistaking that Katherine truly believed what she said. Her lips were thin with anger, her hands shaking at her sides as she stared at him in challenge.

In hate.

"I'm sorry," he said, and meant it more than he had ever meant anything. "I don't know what you mean."

"Of course you don't," she said. "Because you don't remember what you did. I meant so little to you that you don't even remember that moment when you tore my existence to shreds."

"I recall meeting you," he said. "Was it Charlotte who introduced us?"

"Yes," she said. "Charlotte introduced us, but that was *four* years ago. What happened next is something else."

"Tell me," he pleaded. "Tell me what it is that I did to you."

She let out her breath slowly and paced away from him, stepping into the space at the bay window. He flashed back to the first night he'd kissed her. When they'd stood in that tiny space together, hiding from his friends, exploring…well, a future he hadn't understood at the time.

A future that was dissolving with every cold glare Katherine sent his way.

"I came onto the terrace for air," she said. "And you were there."

He swallowed. There was a tingle of memory when she said that. A bleary flash of Katherine's face looking up at him, trembling in the moonlight.

"Three years ago," he said. "Before you were married."

She didn't look at him still. "You were drunk. It was April, and I-I understand better now why that date might have meant something to you."

He pressed his lips together. He was always at his worst around the anniversary of his mother's death. "What did I do?" he asked.

"You were just…you," she said, peeking at him at last. Some of her anger seemed tempered then. "Flirted. Teased. And then you sort of…swung in on me and I knew, even in my innocence, that you would kiss me."

He recoiled in horror. "Did I force that on you?"

"No!" she said, pivoting fully and stepping toward him. "Drunk or sober, that is not who you are. I know that. I…damn it, I wanted you to kiss me. You have always been what I could not resist it seems, even before I understood fully what you were. What you could do to a woman."

"So we kissed," he said, confused again.

"No, we were interrupted." Her breath caught and tears flooded her eyes. "By my father."

He staggered back a step. He knew enough about Katherine's past, about her relationship with her father, to know what kind if damage such a thing would cause to her. "No," he whispered.

"He was so angry. After all, you were *you*, with all your reputation. Catching me almost in your arms was ammunition in his war to declare me a whore. And he did, loudly. Cruelly."

"Oh God." The weight of what his worst impulses had

caused crashed down on him.

"He threatened me with marriage," she said. "I'd been allowed freedom to find my match and he took that away. My marriage contract with Gainsworth was signed the next afternoon."

Robert couldn't help his mouth dropping open in shock at that horrible revelation. "You were forced to marry Gainsworth because...because of me?"

She nodded. "Yes." Her face fell. "No, not entirely. My father had wanted to do this for years. You were the excuse. *I* was the excuse."

Robert jerked a hand through his hair. "If I had known," he whispered. "If I had known, perhaps I could have done something to help you."

Her face twisted, and the anger that had been tempered flared back to full life as she staggered toward him. Her hands shook at her sides and she glared up at him. "But you did know, Robert. You knew because I told you."

CHAPTER TWENTY-ONE

Three Years Ago

Katherine shook as she climbed from the hack she had hired and handed over blunt to the driver. "Wait here for me and there will be extra at the end of your fare," she whispered.

The man looked her up and down, leering at her before he jerked his head toward the elegant townhouse they were parked before. "Why not? You're not the first chit I've brought here. His Grace pays well for his tarts."

Katherine flinched as she walked away from the chuckling man. His implication gave her no confidence in what she was about to do. There was a very good possibility she would only make things worse for herself, especially if her father ever found out she'd snuck from her rooms in the middle of the night to come here of all places.

But she was running out of time. Marriage contracts had been signed just hours ago and the Duke of Roseford was the only man who could help her. Save her. Surely when he discovered what their meeting on the terrace the night before had wrought, he would want to assist her.

He was a gentleman, wasn't he?

She edged up to the door and stopped. She could knock. A butler would come. He would look at her the same way the driver had, assume she was here for the same reason. He could turn her away. Worse, the duke's servants could talk and spread word of her actions. If it got back to her father…

She pushed at the door and found it open, despite the late hour. Her heart began to throb as she entered the quiet house and looked around the dim foyer. Gracious, but it was a sophisticated place. All marble and expensive art and cold detachment.

Rather like the man who lived here.

She glanced back over her shoulder. There was still time to escape. Run away and pretend she hadn't done this foolish thing. Hide away at home and merely accept the marriage her father had arranged with the Earl of Gainsworth. An old man! Older than her own father. A man who looked at her in ways that did not express the piety her father demanded of her.

She shivered and pivoted to walk farther into the house. Instead she crashed headlong into something solid, something warm, something muscular. Hands closed around her upper arms in the darkness, and she jerked her face up to find herself looking into the eyes of the Duke of Roseford himself. He was as close as he had been on the terrace the night before, smelling of whisky and male heat and danger.

Only tonight he didn't look like he wanted to kiss her.

"Who the hell are you?" he barked. "And what are you doing in my house?"

His words were slightly slurred and she realized that, like the night before, he was drunk. Was that his natural state? She shook off the question.

"I-I'm sorry, Your Grace. I realize I have done a foolhardy thing by coming here."

"Breaking into my house," he growled as he pulled her through the foyer and into an open parlor door. It was brighter within, and he released her, staring. For a moment, she thought there was a flicker of recognition over his face, but then it was gone. "Do not make me ask you again, miss."

She swallowed. "My name is Miss Katherine Montague, Your Grace. We met last night at the ball."

His expression didn't change. He folded his arms and glared at her. "Did we?"

Her lips parted. God's teeth, he really didn't remember. Here she had been reliving that wicked moment when he'd nearly kissed her over and over and he didn't even remember.

"Yes," she said. "We were on the terrace together. We were...er...talking."

One fine brow arched and a slow smile began at the corner of his lips. "Oh. Talking, were we? And you came here so we could keep...talking?"

She gasped. She might be an innocent, but his implications were not. "Oh no! I mean, you almost kissed me, but there was nothing more to it."

"Almost," he drawled, stepping closer. "How incomplete of me. You wanted me to finish the job?"

She stood there as he swung closer, and for a moment she pondered letting him. Kiss her, maybe more than kiss her. She wanted him to, after all. And it would solve her problems. If he took her virginity, surely the earl would not wish to marry her anymore.

She shook those wicked thoughts away and backed up. He immediately stopped advancing and looked at her with confusion and doubt.

"No, not exactly. You see, Your Grace...oh, I didn't think you wouldn't remember."

"I kiss a lot of women, my dear. An almost kiss isn't something that stands out." He turned to pour himself a drink at the sideboard. "Do explain yourself."

She flinched at his suddenly cold tone. "Well, my father interrupted us, you see."

He froze with his drink midway to his lips. "Yes."

"And now he has a terrible idea about a great many things. It's too complicated to explain fully, but he is marrying me off as punishment for my behavior. And I need your help."

He set the drink down on the wooden surface beside him with a loud clink and glared at her. "Ah, I see what this is. You do have guts, I'll give you that. Most of the ones who want to catch me just try to trick me into parlors at public events. I don't think any one of you has ever snuck into my home."

"Trick?" she repeated. "I don't understand. I'm not trying to trick you into anything. I just need—"

"You need a rake to ruin you so you'll get a better match than whatever one your father is arranging." He smiled. "The Duke of Roseford is a catch, despite my reputation. Perhaps because of it."

She stared at him as what he implied sank in. "No—oh no, I wasn't trying to force a match with you, Your Grace. Not at all. I only wanted to see if you might come and speak to my father. Explain to him that I was doing nothing wrong and—"

He folded his arms. "Just come and speak to your father?" he repeated, and now he laughed, but it was cold. "You are clever. I come to your trap? And then I suppose you tell him how you convinced me and he calls me out and we are married at the tip of a spear by Sunday next."

"No!" she burst out, stepping toward him.

His nostrils flared and his gaze swept over her, but then he backed away. "You are not the first chit who has attempted to steal my hand in marriage, my dear. You will not be the last. And while I applaud the boldness of your methods, you have failed. Go home, Miss Montague. Before I have the guard called and you are ruined in reality."

He turned to go and she reached out to catch his arm. He jerked it away in what seemed to be shock. She felt it, herself, for normally she would not be so bold. And yet panic and desperation clawed at her.

"This is my life," she whispered. "I cannot marry this man. Please."

For a moment there was a flicker over his face. Something deeper than the cad he normally showed the world. Then he hardened himself and she knew, before he even spoke, what he would do.

"That is not my problem," he said. "Now go home."

She stared up at him. So handsome and so emotionless. "You are as cold-hearted as they say."

He smiled, almost sadly. "I am. Proudly. Now goodnight."

He left the room and she stood where he'd left her, shaking, shocked. And as she trudged back out the way she'd come, back to the hack and its grinning driver, the desperation she'd felt that drove her here turned to resignation.

Her life was over. This man didn't care. No one did.

CHAPTER TWENTY-TWO

Robert's stomach turned as Katherine recounted the scene in his London home three years before, then turned away from him. Where there had been anger on her face at first, now there was a blankness. As if she were reliving those awful moments, reliving how she'd had to harden herself to the future that had been ripped from her hands.

A future he had made no effort to save for her.

For what felt like an eternity, the chamber around them was silent, and they each stood, separate as they pondered the facts of their shared past. A past he couldn't even recall, thanks to the man he had been then. The man he had chosen to become to protect himself from any pain, any injury, any connection that he perceived as dangerous.

In his haste to protect himself, he had destroyed her.

No wonder she hated him.

"Katherine," he said, his voice thick and heavy as he forced himself to speak. "Oh God, Katherine, I wish I could say I remember that night."

"That is the worst part," she whispered. "When you almost kissed me on that terrace, when you rejected me in your home the next night, those are two of the most pivotal moments of my existence. And you don't remember either of them. I was just another woman in a line of women who meant nothing to you."

He flinched. "That is how I lived my life," he admitted. "Encounter to encounter, using pleasure to mask the pain. Using seduction to keep anyone who could come too close at arm's length. I was…*am* a bastard. Like my father."

When he said that last sentence, his heart broke. He could see now how true it was. The thing he had been running from, the monster who had always lived beneath his bed, he hadn't avoided him. He'd become him. Hurting innocents.

And why could he see that? After all these years of his friends trying to open his eyes, to change his path, what made him so aware now? This woman. This amazing woman who had changed him long before she confronted him and made him look at what he'd become. Made him *want* to change what he was. Become what she thought he could be, or used to think.

"Your father was honest, at least, in what he was," she said, turning her face. "He did not pretend to change, at least not in any of the stories you have whispered to me in the dark. So you won your bet, Robert. Bully for you."

She moved toward the door and he panicked. She would leave. Tomorrow she would go back to London. This would be over, truly over, if he didn't stop her now.

"Please, Katherine. You are not about a bet for me. You never truly were." He caught her arm and turned her back toward him. "You must know that I—"

Her eyes went wide and she jerked away to interrupt his confession. "Don't," she whispered. "Don't you dare. Just let me go, Robert. It is what you are best at."

She said nothing more, but left the room, left him. And the heart that he had spent a lifetime stifling, putting up walls so he could pretend it did not exist, shattered.

Katherine stumbled, blinded by tears, as she careened through the halls toward the stairs that would take her to her chamber. She wanted to lock herself away. Away from her argument with Robert, away from his voice echoing in her ears. Telling Berronburg that she was a conquest, that same voice telling her she was more. She was so tangled by all that had transpired, she just wanted to hide from it all.

And knew she couldn't.

She raced up the stairs and turned toward her room. Just as she was about to reach it, the door across the hall opened and Isabel stepped out. For a moment the duchess smiled at her, but then her face fell. "Oh, Katherine," she said, racing to her. "What is it?"

"Nothing," Katherine muttered, fumbling with the door and finally getting it open. "Oh, nothing, please go back to the party."

Isabel followed her into the chamber, hands on her hips. "I will not. Not when you look so stricken. What is going on?"

Katherine faced her. She had become friends with Isabel in the previous weeks. With all the duchesses. That, at least, she knew was true. And she could tell her friend what had happened. There would be catharsis in that. And a good ear to help her sort through her tangled emotions.

But then she thought of Robert. He already felt on the outside of his group of friends. If they knew what had happened tonight, certainly they would all confront him in their own way. Katherine could not, would not, be responsible for breaking his world to pieces. For pushing him out of the only group of people he truly loved.

Loved. Was that what he was going to say to her before she pulled away from him and left the parlor? That he loved her?

"Katherine!" Isabel's voice was sharp and she caught Katherine's arm with both her hands. "Your look and your silence are frightening me."

She drew a few breaths. "It's nothing," she lied. "Just a bad night."

Isabel's brow wrinkled in confusion and deeper concern. "What happened? Is it Robert?"

Katherine flinched and knew that gave the answer she'd been trying to avoid. Still, she pulled away from Isabel and walked to her bed. She set her hand on the coverlet, trying not picture the nights she'd shared this room with Robert. Making love. Laughing. Talking long into the night with no thought of tomorrow.

Now she questioned if all those moments were just a lie, meant to manipulate her. They were soured. Ruined.

She bent her head. "I'm just ready to go home," she breathed. "Tomorrow cannot come fast enough."

Isabel was quiet for a long time. So long that Katherine thought for a moment she might have simply left the room. But at last she took a breath and said, "Katherine, please—"

She faced Isabel, loving that her friend was so concerned. Hating that this break from Robert would probably ultimately mean an end to her friendship with the duchesses, too.

"Don't," she whispered. "There is nothing that can be done. If you are my friend, and I know you are, you will just go downstairs and pretend you didn't see me. You'll make my excuses and you'll let this go. It is not something that can be fixed."

Isabel's expression softened and she nodded after a moment. "If that's what you want." She moved forward and caught Katherine's hands gently. "Anything can be fixed, my darling. Even at its darkest, night gives way to dawn."

"When dawn comes I'll be gone," Katherine whispered. "And it's for the best."

Isabel's expression saddened, but she didn't pry any further. She didn't push. She just kissed Katherine's cheek and left her alone. To think. To remember. And to mourn the moment when she'd believed her love for Robert could be enough.

Now she knew it wasn't, and her world would never be the same.

When the door to the parlor opened, Robert jerked to his feet and pivoted to face the intruder, praying it was Katherine returning to finish their conversation. Instead, Isabel stepped into the chamber.

He frowned and retook his place slouched before the fire. "I'm sorry to be rude, Your Grace, but I am not in the mood for company."

"I would assume not," Isabel said, looking around the room like she was seeking an answer to a riddle. "But I've been searching the estate for you in the last half hour and here I am."

He shook his head. He had one thing in common with his friends: not a one of them had been drawn to what was commonly called a biddable bride. Spitfires all were their loves and lovers.

"I saw Katherine," she said as she shut the door behind her and leaned against it.

He jerked his gaze to hers. "Was she...was she all right?"

Isabel's expression softened. "Physically, yes. I cannot speak to her emotional state, as she would not tell me what had happened. But it's obvious from your own broken expression that it has to do with you."

He stood up and walked to the window. As he looked out into the night, he said, "You told her about my wager."

Isabel was quiet a moment, and then she stepped forward. "Yes, I did. I will not apologize for it."

He faced her slowly, and the anguish of what he'd done felt raw and heavy in his chest. "I wouldn't ask you to. She had every right to know. Every right to destroy me for my cruelty."

"And yet she didn't. She came here and she made the best of it. You two were obviously involved in something far deeper than friendship certainly much more powerful than a bet. We were all thrilled to see you open yourself up." Isabel shook her head. "Robert, what happened?"

He shut his eyes, reliving those moments of confrontation with Katherine. Feeling himself burn in the fire of her contempt.

"She saw me. The true me," he said. "And that is what sent her away."

He saw Isabel's pity for him. And why not? He was pitiable. He had been thus for years, even as he strutted about reveling in his depravity. Crowing at the fact that he had erected a tower so high that no one would ever scale its walls and get to him.

Until one very unexpected woman had done just that. And what had he done? Burned everything down around them both.

"I would say you are right," Isabel said. "Katherine did see you. The true you. The good man you are deep in your soul."

He snorted out a pained laugh. "And you know so much, do you, Isabel? You have known me all of a few months."

"That would be a fair point, I suppose," Isabel said. "Except that my husband has known you almost all his life. My good, decent, steady husband has loved you through all your adventures and schemes. As has James, as has Ewan. These men who shy away from those who would proudly declare themselves libertines and rogues embrace you with the intensity of brotherhood. Why do you think that is?"

Robert poured himself a drink and downed it in one slug. "Every court needs its jester," he mumbled, thinking of how Katherine had gently teased him about his role in their merry group of gentlemen. Perhaps she had come closer to the mark than he had ever been able to admit.

Isabel was shaking her head. "Not true. These men see beyond the mask you wear. They see your true heart. You are the man who supports every piece of legislation in the House of Lords that gives freedom or hope to those beneath his station. You are the man who has stepped up and offered support to his friends. The man who welcomed me into this group despite the fact that you initially saw me as only a liar who was bent on destroying Matthew."

He jerked his face up. "He told you that?"

She shrugged. "You were decent at hiding it, but I felt your hesitance at first."

"Well, I've come to see you as far more over the months,"

he said. "I was wrong about you."

"You are wrong about yourself, as well. Robert, this woman brings out the best in you. She challenges you to reach for far loftier heights than you have dared to try. Matthew and I were talking about it just two nights ago—do you know what he said about you and Katherine?"

"That I'm an ass?" he asked. "That's what he says to my face."

She smiled but was undeterred. "He said to me that you *try* with her. That in all the years he's known you, you have never tried with any other person, save the others in your club. That the moment things get hard, you turn away. But with Katherine, you don't do that."

"And yet here we are," he said, holding up his arms. "So what use was it?"

She stepped closer, and her hand closed around his forearm. "You clearly hurt her deeply. I see how much that breaks your heart. Don't run away from that or you will regret it the rest of your life."

He knew she was right. "So what do I do?"

"Let her go back to London. A few days on her own, a few days to let this settle, that will do her good. But do not let another week go by before you try again to make it up to her."

He looked into the crackling fire. "I am in love with her," he whispered. Saying the words out loud was like falling off a cliff. And yet there was no fear behind them. Only truth.

"Then you have much to risk, but far more to gain." Isabel squeezed his arm gently and then backed away. "And there are nine other men and eight of their wives who would do anything in their power to help you. But only if you try."

She smiled at him and moved toward the door with a quiet goodnight. After she was gone, Robert let out his breath in a ragged sigh. He felt like he'd been torn into shreds, first by the pain he'd caused Katherine, then by the admission of how much of his heart she held.

And yet, when he thought of fighting for her, truly fighting for what he wanted, what she deserved…what they could have if he could just step forward instead of running away…

He knew it was worth the risk. And he had at least three days ahead of him to figure out how to make amends for what he'd done so that he could come to her as the man she wanted him to be. Not the man he was.

CHAPTER TWENTY-THREE

Robert strode into his foyer, tugging at his gloves as he did so. His butler, Jenner, was waiting, a grim look on his face. "Welcome home, Your Grace."

Robert gave him a cursory nod as he handed over the gloves. "Thank you. I assume you received my missive from the road?"

"I did, sir."

"And are they here?" He smoothed his jacket. His armor for the face-off to come. The one he had been planning in the four days since he last saw Katherine. Since she'd left James and Emma's home at dawn without so much as a word for him.

He'd ached for her ever since. And known he had no right to long for her, not after what he'd done in the past and the present. He had to earn that right, as each and every one of his friends had been quick to tell him.

They were right, of course. So if he had to, he would spend the rest of his life doing just that. Starting today.

"They are waiting for you in the west parlor, Your Grace." Jenner pursed his lips as if he was irritated. Robert couldn't blame him. He knew the attitude of the men in his parlor.

"Very good. There will be nothing else. Just be ready to call for their carriages." He glared down the hallway. "They will not be staying long."

The butler inclined his head and Robert headed away. He flexed his hands open and closed as the sound of the boisterous laughter of his guests filtered through the air from behind the closed door. He hesitated for a moment before he entered.

He was going to show his vulnerability. To vultures. And he would do it for Katherine.

He pushed the door open and the men in the room turned with wide grins. They were his...*friends* was one word for it. Men he had rabble roused and tom-catted around with. Men who fed his worst impulses.

Berronburg was chief amongst them, standing in the middle of a circle of four men. As Robert stepped inside, he began to clap and the others joined in. Robert's stomach turned as he shut the door behind him.

"Good show, old man," one of the others, the Earl of Middlemarch, called out.

It was Mr. Peter Ward who spoke next. "Yes, yes. Berronburg told us you have sealed the wager by bedding Lady Gainsworth. We all cannot wait to hear the details of your conquest."

"When you called us all here for the moment of your return, we knew there could be no other reason," said Sir Curtis Denton as he lifted a glass of Robert's finest scotch in salute. "Welcome home, conqueror."

Robert shook his head. He hated himself for what he'd been in the company of these men. He'd always told himself that he was careful, that he was harmless. That was so far from the truth.

"I did not call you here so I could crow," he said, keeping his voice soft somehow when he wanted to shout.

"You will have us tease the details out of you," Berronburg chortled. "You are a bastard. I saw the man at Abernathe's ball just a few days ago. You should have seen him with the countess. Stop being so coy. How delicious was she?"

Robert moved forward and caught Berronburg's collar, dragging him flush against him as he glared down into his friend...former friend's...face. "If you speak of the lady so cavalierly again, I will see you at dawn."

The jovial tone of the room dissipated in a moment and Berronburg swallowed hard. "I-I didn't mean to offend, Roseford."

Robert released him, pushing him away as he paced from the circle of scavengers waiting for tidbits. "You *do* offend. I did not call you here for some disgusting display. You are here because I want to make something very clear to each and every one of you."

Berronburg was still straightening his twisted clothing, and so it was Middlemarch who spoke next. "And what is that? Did you not win the wager? Is there still an open season on the countess?"

Robert speared the man with a look that drew all the blood from his cheeks and made the earl take a long step away. "The Countess of Gainsworth is off limits," he said. "She is not to be approached by any man in this room or any acquaintance outside our circle. She is not to be whispered about or sneered at in any way. Do I make myself clear?"

"He couldn't land her," Sir Curtis chuckled, clearly in his cups since he could not read the tone of the room. Berronburg reached out to grip his arm with a swift shake of his head.

Robert barely kept himself from marching across the room and breaking Denton's nose. "The lady," he said slowly, "will be my wife if I can ever convince her to forgive me for what a bastard I have been."

The collective mouths of his friends dropped open all at once and the stunned silence might have once made Robert laugh. Today he felt no joy in it, not when he relived what Katherine had said to him. What her crumpled face had looked like when she poured out her heartbreak, the devastation *he* had caused.

"You are going to...to marry her?" Berronburg stammered with a shake of his head.

"I am in love with the lady. And if you do not wish to risk my wrath, I would expect you will honor that," Robert growled.

It was funny. He had spent the ride back from Abernathe anticipating this moment. Worrying about what he would say, how his former friends would react. Declaring himself had been a point of great anxiety.

But now it felt easy. He didn't give a damn what these men thought of him. Only that Katherine would be protected from their sneers and whispers, whether she married him or not. If he could not have her, by God he would protect her.

"Raise a glass to the loss of the greatest libertine in London," Berronburg said solemnly as he swept up a tumbler from the sideboard and lifted it in Robert's direction. "And to the lady who finally tamed him. Wager or no."

Robert wrinkled his brow in surprise as each man lifted his glass in turn.

"Your lady has nothing to fear from us," Sir Curtis said with a sigh. "There will be no whispers from our set. Good Society is out of our control."

Robert pursed his lips. That was true. The duchesses were a help with that, of course. And if he could convince Katherine to hear him out, to listen to his pleas and be his wife, perhaps one day she would be accepted. Or at least have enough clout thanks to his name, his fortune, that she wouldn't have to care.

"So she knows of your wager, then?" Berronburg continued.

Robert nodded once. His friends had the good sense to look chagrined at that as they shifted and exchanged looks.

Berronburg shrugged. "Probably a bit piggish for us to make that wager in the first place."

"Very," Robert said. "And it is my last decree as the biggest...formerly biggest libertine in London...that it never happen again."

The men looked annoyed, but all of them nodded.

Robert scrubbed a hand through his hair. "I don't know if she'll forgive me."

At that, Middlemarch edged toward the door. "You know, Roseford, we are not the kind of men to ask for help on that score. I think your duke friends are more fashioned for advice of the heart. But we do wish you the best. And we'll make certain your wishes for Lady Gainsworth's privacy are circulated throughout our circles. Good day."

Robert nodded as the men filed away. When the room was empty, he let out a long sigh. That would probably be the last time he would spend with that group. These were not friends like his club, his brothers. They had always been fleeting, surface. And losing them meant nothing.

But losing Katherine still sat heavy on his mind. And now that he had taken care of his first matter of business, he was ready to move on to the next. Groveling. He could only pray that it would be enough.

Katherine let out a long sigh as she stepped into her parlor and looked around the room. Just a few weeks before, she had loved this little house. It represented her freedom, her ability to control her future. The quiet was wonderful then.

Now it was stifling. It reminded her of what was missing from her life, what she would never have again.

It had been five days since she last saw Robert. He had not come down to say farewell when she departed Emma and James's home the day after her argument with him. She'd told him to leave her alone and it seemed he would honor that request.

He had also not come to her door in London since her arrival the previous afternoon. He had not sent word, though her aunt had heard he was back in London, too. Bethany was cursing him at present, because Katherine hadn't been able to keep the truth from her aunt. And yet Bethany's comfort wasn't what she wanted.

It was his. Only his.

She sank into the settee and put her head in her hands.

"Little fool, you never meant a thing," she whispered. "You knew that from the start."

When she said those words out loud, they came out as a sob and she struggled to keep the tears at bay. Once they started, she feared they would never stop, and she couldn't face them.

"My lady?"

She glanced up to find her butler standing at her parlor door, shifting from foot to foot in discomfort. "Yes, Wilkes," she said, straightening. "What is it?"

"Your father has arrived," he said, and there was no mistaking the concern and disdain to his voice. "Demanding to see you. I know you said you wanted any callers to be told you were not in residence but—"

"It's fine," she lied, and got to her feet to pour her father tea. "I'm certain he will not be deterred. Send him in."

He bowed away and a moment later returned. She watched as her father pushed past him into the room. She nodded and Wilkes departed, leaving them alone.

"Do you know what I heard about you while you were gone?" Mr. Montague sputtered without preamble.

She sighed and motioned for him to sit. "Hello, Father. I am surprised to see you considering our last conversation, when I believe you cut me off forever. But thank you for the call regardless. My trip to the country was fine, thank you for asking. I heard there was rain while I was away. How is your rheumatism?"

He flopped into her seat and held a hand out for his tea. "I don't need your lip, missy."

"As I said, you dismissed me from your life the last time you called," she snapped as she handed it over, playing out a game they had participated in for years. "Why in the world would you come back to me now?"

"You're marrying the Duke of Roseford?" he said, lifting both brows. "One can only assume how a woman such as *you* could make a man like *him* commit to a lifetime shackled to you."

She stared at him in confusion. "I'm sorry, what?"

Her father shook his head and glared at her. "Don't play with me. It's all around Society gossip that you and Roseford will wed."

Her heart leapt at that thought. The one she had shoved aside the moment she knew of Robert's perfidy. The words that now warmed her heart and made her long for what she'd told herself she could never have with him.

"Well, the gossip is wrong," she said, hating that her voice shook. "Roseford and I did develop a—a friendship in Abernathe. But there is nothing more to it than that, I assure you. His Grace will not marry."

A smug smirk tilted his lips. "I *knew* it could not be true. Why would a man with such power lower himself so completely? A man of his reputation would only tup a woman like you, not pledge his life to hers. Whoever said he told them that must have misunderstood."

Katherine caught her breath as anger filled her. All her life, she had listened to him rail at her. Punish her for sins she had never committed. Paint her with a brush she had never deserved. He had abused her mind and her soul. She had always been the one to apologize for it.

And she thought of Robert, who had whispered to her that her "nature," as her father put it, was not something to be shunned or humiliated by. He had seen her true self. He had opened his arms to that and held her so gently in them.

Robert had accepted her. With a few days away from their argument, from her shock at what she'd overheard, she *knew* that the connection was real. The Duke of Roseford had seen her. And he had wanted her not despite who she was, but *because* of it.

"You hated my mother for her light," she said, her voice still shaking as she returned her attention to her father. "And you hated me for mine. You separated me from my family and you ripped me from my future, all while you pretended to be good. To be right. To be…godly. And now you have the gall to come here, into my home, and tell me what I am? Tell me who would love me when you have never known real love in your pathetic life?"

He stared up at her, mouth agape. "How *dare* you speak to me that way? I'm your father."

"No." She shook her head slowly as a calm came over her. Deep and unlike any she'd ever known. "You are no father. Not to me. I have never had a father. I had a keeper and an abuser and man who would destroy me. But *never* a father."

He stood, tea sloshing from his cup. "I tried to protect you from yourself."

"No, you didn't." She paced past him. "You tried to mold me into what you wanted, and nothing I ever did was good enough. And I *let* you. I let you do it because I thought you might love me if I did as you asked. Only what I've learned, quite recently, is that true love sees a person for what they are and accepts it. True love is understanding, not judgment."

"Fairytale notions. You must live in the real world," he spat.

"Yes," she agreed softly. "I must. But not your world." She stared at him, burning this image of him in her mind forever. Taking a moment to truly experience what she felt, what she knew in this moment of clarity that Robert had helped her find. Then she said, "You are not welcome in my home again. You are not welcome in my life at all. We are finished. Do you understand?"

"You dare to cut *me* out of your life?" he said, his tone dripping with shock and disdain as he set his cup down.

Only that pointed disapproval didn't hurt anymore. Not like it had all her life. She nodded. "I do dare," she said. "And unlike all the times you've threatened the same to me, I mean it. Your daughter is dead to you. Give your judgments to someone else. And get out of my house."

She pointed to the door and he stared first at it, then at her. His cheeks filled with high color and he huffed out a breath. "You'll be sorry when you're all alone."

He stormed out and she watched him go, heart heavy and

yet somehow free. As his carriage raced away from her drive she shook her head. "I would rather be alone than with someone who did not see my value."

She sat down. Now that her father was gone, now that she had taken charge of that part of her life, she could think again of what had brought him here. A rumor that she would marry Roseford? And Montague had seemed to think that it had come from the lips of the duke, himself.

She walked into the foyer and found Wilkes standing by. He gave her a kind smile.

"Wilkes, will you have my carriage brought around?" she asked.

He nodded. "Of course, my lady. Straight away."

He scuttled off to do it and she stepped through the front door to stand on her step and breathe the cool air. There was only one way to find out exactly what was going on. She had to go see Robert. And she needed to go right now.

CHAPTER TWENTY-FOUR

Robert sat at his desk, staring at the thick piece of vellum before him. He had been sitting there for half an hour and all he'd written was Katherine's name.

It wasn't that he didn't know what he had to say. It was that there was so much to say that he didn't know how to organize it. Did he apologize first? Beg to see her? Should he tell her he loved her? That seemed to be something he should say to her face, but it was possible she would not see him. Would not accept another letter after the first. So maybe it was best to say it in writing.

"Bollocks," he muttered, and threw the quill down.

"Your Grace?"

He glanced up to find Jenner standing at the door. "Yes?"

"I'm sorry to intrude, but—"

He didn't get to finish. Before he could, Katherine stepped around the butler and stood in his study, staring at him. His heart leapt into his throat and for a moment he couldn't breathe. She didn't wear a wrap despite the chill to the autumn air. Her hair was loose, like it had been done hastily.

And she was more beautiful than anything he'd ever seen his whole life.

"It's fine," he muttered, getting up. "I'm fine. Leave us."

Jenner gave Katherine an annoyed look, but left the room.

As he did, she reached back and shut the door behind him. Then she faced Robert again.

"You are here," he said, unable to find anything but that to say. "That sounds so foolish, but I am shocked. I hadn't even sent my letter."

She swallowed hard and stepped into the room. "You were—you were writing me a letter?"

He motioned to his desk and she came forward, tilting her head to read what he'd written. When she saw only her name, she arched a brow at him.

He shrugged. "I am not very good at writing letters."

She smiled, and some of the tension bled from her expression. "Somehow I doubt that, Robert. You are too witty not to be *very* good at writing letters."

He tried not to read too much into her use of his given name rather than his title and forced himself to remain calm. "This isn't a letter where my wit will serve me, though. It has to be something genuine, heartfelt, and I am not very experienced in being those things."

"More than you think," she said softly.

For a moment, her hand stirred, and he thought she might touch him. He ached for it, leaned toward it. Then she shook her head and backed away.

"My father called on me today," she said.

He flinched and all his need to reunite with her was pushed to the back of his mind. That could wait in the face of this news. "From our conversations in Abernathe, I thought he had cut you off."

"Our conversations in your bed," she said, her tone clipped. "In my bed. Where we shared all those things we had never said to anyone else."

"Yes."

She swallowed and seemed to gather herself. "Yes, well, it seems his disinheriting me before I left London didn't stick. It will now. When he started his usual abuse, I told him he was no longer welcome in my home. *I* cut him off this time. And I meant

230

it."

His lips parted. He knew how painful and complicated Katherine's relationship with her father had been over the years. How much he had stolen from her and how much she had longed for connection with him regardless.

"I so admire your strength," he said. "That must have been difficult."

"Impossible," she said, and her voice broke, revealing the pain she'd been caused. "And yet I did it. Do you want to know how?"

He nodded. "If I've earned any right to hear it."

"The strength came to me when I needed it." Her breath shook. "The form it took was *your* voice, telling me that I was worthy of so much more than he has ever given. Your words in my head, telling me that my nature is not something to be ashamed of."

Warmth rose up in him. "If something I said was in any way helpful to you, I am forever grateful for that. But your strength has been and always will be yours and yours alone, Katherine. It runs through you like a deep river. I wish I could be like you."

She held his gaze a long moment and he saw all those things he loved about her. And yet there was still hesitation, despite the good sign that she was here, talking to him. Bringing this painful experience she'd just had to him to share.

"Something brought him to me," she whispered. "A whisper on the wind. Someone told him that you said you would marry me."

He froze. When he'd confronted his friends the previous day, he had intended only to halt the gossip surrounding Katherine. And to protect her from advances she didn't want. But his admission that he loved her, that he intended to wed her, must have been even more shocking to them than he thought if the word was already spreading.

"Did you say that, Robert?" she asked.

He slowly walked toward her. "I have made a vow to myself that I will never lie to you again, Katherine. Yes, I did tell some of my friends that I intended to marry you."

Her lips parted. "You said that even after what happened between us in Abernathe?"

"My intention is one thing. Your answer is another. Perhaps you will never agree to be mine." He cleared his throat to push away the pain that thought brought him. "I would not blame you after what I did to you in the past few weeks, what I did to you long before that. But I still want to marry you, Katherine."

She staggered to a chair and sat down hard in it. "Why?"

He drew a few breaths. All he had wanted since their last meeting was a chance to talk to her. To tell her the truth, *all* the truth. And the chance was here and now he was gripped by terror that he would answer all wrong. That he would make things worse. That he would lose her.

He supposed that was why they said risk your heart. The risk was losing everything. The prize was winning it all.

"I have never let myself love," he said. "Not because it was inconvenient or foolish, though that was what I said to the world. I didn't let myself because it was terrifying."

Her gaze softened. "Your past does not make that a surprise."

"To love another, to open yourself to receiving their love, that is the ultimate power," he continued. "Another person's happiness at your fingertips. Your happiness at theirs. One wrong move, purposeful or accidental, and your life can be destroyed. I watched that with my mother. I saw the damage it could do. And yet…"

"Yet?" she asked, her tone suddenly breathless.

He reached out and took her hand. She let him, and it was the most beautiful and brilliant moment of his entire life.

"It is worth that risk, isn't it? Katherine, I love you."

She jerked and her hand began to tremble, but she didn't take it away. She just stared at him like he was speaking another language.

"I love you," he repeated. "I haven't properly shown it, I know that, because I feared it so deeply. But that didn't mean I could run from it. I love how you challenge me and match me. I love how you open me, how I trust you to do that in return. I love when you touch me, my body, of course, but my heart. My soul. You have made me see what I'm missing in my life and all of it is you."

Her breath came shallow now, short, and he kept going for fear she would stop him and turn away.

"I started out so badly with you. If I could go back in time and change everything I did, I would do it in a heartbeat. I would scream at my younger self to marry you. To keep you from ever enduring what you went through because of my cowardice. And I would tell that man I was just a few weeks ago that I was empty and awful when I made that stupid wager."

"But you can't go back," she said at last.

He bent his head. Her voice was shaking, and he was gripped with terror and pain. What he said likely didn't matter. If she had ever cared for him, he had destroyed those feelings.

"No," he said. "I can't. If you despise me, I understand. I will do as you wish, whatever that is."

"Look at me," she said. He looked up, meeting her eyes no matter how difficult it was. She reached out and then her fingers were touching his cheek, just as she'd done a hundred times. He leaned into her warmth, knowing it might be the last time he shared it. "It would be nice to be able to go back in time. To fix our mistakes. Only it is the mistakes, the pains, that sometimes take us to where we want to be, isn't it?"

He blinked. This was not an outright rejection. "Yes, I suppose it is."

"I could wish my marriage away, but perhaps I wouldn't be the person I am today without what I went through. We could wish you would have married me that night I came to you, but who is to say you wouldn't have hated me for trapping you? That you wouldn't have been ready, nor would I, for what we now share."

"What are you saying?" he asked, truly confused and yet hopeful.

She smiled. And he knew. He knew that she would forgive him even if he didn't deserve it. He knew that she would love him. He saw it, he felt it, he flew with it, and the world faded away, leaving only her.

"I-I love you," she whispered. "I didn't want to. I tried not to. Only you saw me, as no one else has ever done. And I see you, beneath the layers you wear as a cloak for the world, there is Robert. *My* Robert. Who I love and trust. I was so angry when I heard you talking to Berronburg. But if I walked away from you because of it, I would be tearing out my heart and throwing it away, too. I can't. I won't."

"So what do we do now?" he asked.

"You apparently told the world you would marry me. Will you?"

He laughed, joyful at the unexpected turn of events. "Isn't that what I am supposed to say?"

"Neither of us has ever stood on convention. But if you want to say it, I would love to hear it."

He dropped to his knee before her and stared up into her beautiful face. The one that reflected his future. The one that reflected the best version of himself.

"Katherine, I am far from perfect, but I love you so deeply. And I want nothing more than to join my life with yours forever, if you will have my hand. Will you please look past all my faults and marry me? As soon as possible."

Tears flowed down her cheeks and she reached forward to cup his cheeks. "Robert, *I* am far from perfect. And we will make ridiculous mistakes, I know. But the fact is that I am truly myself when I am with you. And to walk away from that, from you, would be like cutting away a piece of myself. I *will* marry you. Today, tomorrow, whenever you like. I love you so very much."

He lifted up on his knees and she leaned forward. They met in the middle, lips colliding, arms crushing around each other in a kiss he had been wanting for days and needing his whole life. And as he drowned in her, he knew that there was nothing else in the world that he would ever need but the woman in his arms.

For the first time, he looked forward to the future. And he couldn't wait to see what their lives would bring.

Kit motioned Sarah into a smaller parlor just down the hall from where his friends were gathered and watched her walk inside. She turned in the middle of the room to face him, her hands clenched in front of her.

She was trying to be strong. He could see that in the twitch of her cheek, the way her fingers fluttered against each other in their gripped position and how her gaze darted to him and away. Like a little bird flitting back and forth.

She was nervous. She was also very pretty. Her blonde hair was bound simply at the base of her neck, but there were a few honey strands that framed her face, highlighting the angles of her cheekbones. She had full lips that were a warm pink color.

He blinked as those facts rolled through his mind. None were surprising. He wasn't certain of the first time he'd noticed the young woman standing before him. Certainly they had shared many a ballroom or parlor in the years since she first came into Society. His attention had come fully to her that night of the ball when she'd spoken harshly to Meg, though.

After that, he'd watched her. Noticed when she entered rooms, felt when she left them. When her hairstyle changed. When she had a new gown.

"How is Phoebe?" he choked out, trying to clear his mind of the riot of thoughts clattering around in his head. Jumbled by grief, certainly.

Her eyes widened a fraction, like she was surprised by the question. She cleared her throat. "As well as can be expected, Your Grace." She hesitated a moment and then her expression shifted a fraction. Softened. "Despite her tender years, she is a very bright little girl. She seems to be a bit easier since you told her she would not be sent away."

He paled. "God's teeth, the very idea that she would be. Where would she get such a notion?"

Sarah shook her head. "I cannot imagine. A child's mind twists in its own way. Some offhand comment or something she saw in a story…who knows."

"Well, I'm glad that my words comforted her in some way." He shook his head. "I try to reach out to her, but…"

"It's difficult," she finished softly. "You've had a great deal to do since…well, since that day."

He drew a long breath. This was *not* why he'd asked her here to talk to her. This momentary connection where she comforted him with her gentle words, her soft tone. He took a long step away, putting his back toward her.

"Well," he said, sharpening his tone. "We will need to be very careful with her for a while."

"Of course," she said slowly. He turned to face her and found she had edged toward the door. "Will that be all?"

He arched a brow at the hopeful expression on her lovely face. The fact that she wanted to escape him was evident. It sparked a reaction in his belly that made him set his jaw.

"No," he said firmly. "My friends will be staying here a while. Is that going to be a problem?"

The color drained from her face slowly and she swallowed, the action making her throat flutter. Her slender, lovely throat.

"What do you mean, Your Grace?" she asked, her voice catching ever so slightly.

He stepped forward. "I saw you and Isabel talking and you were looking at Simon and Meg. I couldn't help but think of what I stumbled upon and if that will impact your ability to perform your duty."

For a moment she merely stared at him, eyes wide, hands trembling. Then she widened her stance a fraction, as if bracing herself for whatever would come next.

"I assume you are referring to the incident that occurred between myself and the now-Duchess of Crestwood years ago?" she asked, her voice surprisingly strong.

He arched a brow. "I am, indeed."

"I assure you, Your Grace, that we aren't going to have a problem," she said. "I know my place very well and what I am expected to do to keep it. Is that all?"

He nodded. "For now."

She blinked at his answer and a momentary terror entered her gaze. Then it was gone and she nodded. "Very good. If you need nothing else from me, I shall go collect your sister and see if she can be coaxed to try to sleep for an hour or so. She is overwrought, and I think it would do her good."

He nodded. "Very good."

She turned and moved to exit the room, but at the doorway, she stopped and faced him once more. "Y-Your Grace, I realize you have been overwhelmed by your duties these past few days. I wanted to tell you again how very sorry I am for your loss. I-I know what it is like to lose a much beloved parent. Good afternoon."

She walked away, leaving him to gape after her in surprise. Oh, of course he had been given condolences many times in the days since his father's death. Virtually everyone on his grieving staff had spoken to him and all his friends had done the same. He was certain he would hear many more words like hers in the days, weeks and even months to come, for his father had been much beloved in Society.

But no one had yet framed his loss in the light of their own. No one had expressed empathy of that kind until she had. He looked to the spot at the door where she had spoken to him and sighed.

He didn't want the woman here. She made him…uncomfortable in ways he could not express in words. But now that she had left him alone in the room, he also felt a little…empty. Like he had missed an opportunity he hadn't known existed.

He shook his head as he cleared away those odd thoughts. They meant nothing.

Other Books by Jess Michaels

THE 1797 CLUB

For information about the upcoming series, go to
www.1797club.com to join the club!

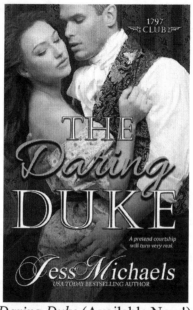

The Daring Duke (Available Now!)
Her Favorite Duke (Available Now!)
The Broken Duke (Available Now!)
The Silent Duke (Available Now!)
The Duke of Nothing (Available Now!)
The Undercover Duke (Available Now!)
The Duke Who Lied (Coming August 2018)
The Duke of Desire (Coming October 2018)
The Last Duke (Coming November 2018)

SEASONS

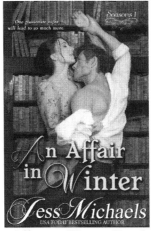

An Affair in Winter (Book 1)
A Spring Deception (Book 2)
One Summer of Surrender (Book 3)
Adored in Autumn (Book 4)

THE WICKED WOODLEYS

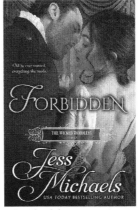

Forbidden (Book 1)
Deceived (Book 2)
Tempted (Book 3)
Ruined (Book 4)
Seduced (Book 5)

THE NOTORIOUS FLYNNS
The Other Duke (Book 1)
The Scoundrel's Lover (Book 2)
The Widow Wager (Book 3)
No Gentleman for Georgina (Book 4)
A Marquis for Mary (Book 5)

THE LADIES BOOK OF PLEASURES
A Matter of Sin
A Moment of Passion
A Measure of Deceit

THE PLEASURE WARS SERIES
Taken By the Duke
Pleasuring The Lady
Beauty and the Earl
Beautiful Distraction

About the Author

USA Today Bestselling author Jess Michaels likes geeky stuff, Vanilla Coke Zero, anything coconut, cheese, fluffy cats, smooth cats, any cats, many dogs and people who care about the welfare of their fellow humans. She watches too much daytime court shows, but just enough Star Wars. She is lucky enough to be married to her favorite person in the world and live in a beautiful home on a golf course lake in Northern Arizona.

When she's not obsessively checking her steps on Fitbit or trying out new flavors of Greek yogurt, she writes historical romances with smoking hot alpha males and sassy ladies who do anything but wait to get what they want. She has written for numerous publishers and is now fully indie and loving every moment of it (well, almost every moment).

Jess loves to hear from fans! So please feel free to contact her in any of the following ways (or carrier pigeon):

www.AuthorJessMichaels.com

Email: Jess@AuthorJessMichaels.com
Twitter www.twitter.com/JessMichaelsbks
Facebook: www.facebook.com/JessMichaelsBks

Jess Michaels raffles a gift certificate EVERY month to members of her newsletter, so sign up on her website: http://www.authorjessmichaels.com/

11373914R00148

Made in the USA
Lexington, KY
10 October 2018